I0693830

Also by the Author

The Erin O'Reilly Mysteries

Black Velvet
Irish Car Bomb
White Russian
Double Scotch
Manhattan
Black Magic
Death By Chocolate
Massacre
Flashback
First Love
High Stakes
Aquarium
The Devil You Know
Hair of the Dog
Punch Drunk

Bossa Nova
Blackout
Angel Face
Italian Stallion
White Lightning
Kamikaze
Jackhammer
Frostbite
Brain Damage
Celtic Twilight
Headshot
Vino Blanco
White Lady
Blackjack (coming soon)

Tequila Sunrise: A James Corcoran Story

Fathers
A Modern Christmas Story

The Clarion Chronicles
Ember of Dreams

White Lady

The Erin O'Reilly Mysteries
Book Twenty~Eight

Steven Henry

Clickworks Press • Baltimore, MD

First publication: Clickworks Press, 2025
Release: CWP-EOR28-INT-P.IS-1.0

Sign up for updates, deals, and exclusive sneak peeks at clickworkspress.com/join.

Ebook ISBN: 979-8-88900-032-7
Paperback ISBN: 979-8-88900-33-04
Hardcover ISBN: 979-8-88900-34-01

For the Reverend Will Healy who,
in addition to many other good works,
officiated at my wedding.

Special Preview

Keep reading after Blackjack to
enjoy a first look at the new series
coming soon from Clickworks Press

The Coventry Adams Mysteries
by Steven Henry

Want a reminder when the new series is out?

Join Steven's list at
clickworkspress.com/join/steven

White Lady

Combine 2 oz. gin, ½ oz. orange liqueur, ½ oz. lemon juice, and
1 egg white in a shaker. Shake vigorously without ice. Add ice and shake
again until chilled. Strain into a chilled cocktail glass and serve.

Chapter 1

"It has now been seventy-two hours since anyone saw Laurel Peterson. Hopes for her safe return are growing dim, but her family refuse to despair. Her mother, Andrea, has written the following heartfelt message for Laurel's captors."

Holly Gardner's face held just the right mix of sympathy and professionalism. The newswoman's makeup was flawless, emphasizing model-perfect cheekbones and bright blue eyes. Her hair was a lustrous golden blonde that must have come out of a bottle; no real hair had that sort of glow.

"For Christ's sake, turn that off," Vic Neshenko growled, throwing a crumpled napkin at the television. "I can't stand that bitch."

"You're the one who wanted to put a TV in the break room," Erin O'Reilly reminded him. But she picked up the remote and clicked the power button. The too-beautiful face of Holly Gardner, Channel Six News, disappeared mid-heartfelt plea.

"Yeah," Vic said. "So I could watch sports on my coffee break."

"You don't even drink coffee."

"And I don't watch the news," he said. "Can you believe that crap? It's all bullshit."

"You're saying Laurel Peterson hasn't been kidnapped?" Erin replied. "It's front-page news all over the country."

"That's what I mean," Vic said. "This is one lousy missing persons case. And nobody saw her get snatched, so maybe it isn't even a kidnapping. For all we know she's a runaway. Why is this getting so much play?"

"She hasn't been found yet," Erin said.

He waved a hand irritably. "Of course not. But why do people care so much about this one girl?"

She shrugged. "Sometimes a case goes viral. There's no rhyme or reason to it."

"That's where you're wrong," Vic said. "Let me put it this way. Suppose I got abducted. Would that be all over the country?"

"Who'd want to kidnap you?" Erin retorted. "No offense, but you're a surly, ugly Russian meathead."

"None taken," Vic said. "Whereas Laurel Peterson is what, exactly?"

Erin shrugged again. "A young, pretty woman."

"A young, pretty, *white* woman," Vic said. "You've seen her picture: the homecoming queen glamour shot. I know you know the one; it's staring at you off every goddamn newspaper on the East Coast and they show it all the time on TV. It's Missing White Woman Syndrome, that's what it is. If she was old, or ugly, or Black, or Hispanic, you can bet we'd have never even heard her name. But because she's this wholesome, all-American blonde beach babe, all of a sudden we gotta hear all about her. How many missing persons reports have we had since little Laurel dropped off the face of the Earth? Just in New York?"

"I have no idea," Erin said. "What's eating you, Vic? We didn't even catch the case. Missing Persons is handling it. And they've got the Feebies to run to if they get stumped. The Feds

are consulting and you know what they're like when you try to tell them anything."

"Yeah, I guess," Vic said. He pulled the tab on his can of Mountain Dew, waited for the fizz to subside, and took a sip. "It's not fair, though."

"Show me something that is," she said. Lieutenant Webb had brought donuts that morning. The box was almost empty, but Erin found her hand wandering toward it.

Rolf, standing at her hip, watched her hand closely. He loved his partner's hands. They gave food, caresses, and the best of all things, his rubber Kong ball. At the moment, there was a definite possibility the human hand might dispense a donut. If it did, the German Shepherd intended to be on the receiving end.

"You know why serial killers target young white women?" Vic asked.

"You know the Lieutenant doesn't like us calling them that," Erin said. "Not until there's no doubt. You want to talk about going viral? Tell a reporter we think there's a serial killer out there and we're talking media circus."

She took the second-to-last donut out of the box and raised it to her lips. Then she paused, broke off a piece, and dropped it. The fragment didn't get anywhere close to floor level. Rolf's head twitched in a movement too fast for the eye to follow and the morsel disappeared as completely as Laurel Peterson.

"You're right," Vic said. "But I'm speaking generally. I don't know if Laurel's been grabbed by the Long Island Slasher or whatever they'd call the bastard. That's not the point I'm trying to make. I'm talking about the guys who kill girls. Serial killers are sad little punks who can't get it up the normal way. I read a book about it."

"*You* read a *book?*"

"Shut up and listen. They kill out of displaced sexual inadequacy. And who do they target? The beautiful people. The

ones they can't have. The people the tabloids talk about. Gorgeous blondes. The media *creates* serial killers by taking these women and plastering their faces all over the place like goddamn celebrities. Then these punks get to feel famous by association. It makes them feel powerful. And that's sick."

"You might have a point," Erin said. "But none of that is going to help Laurel."

"You really think she's still alive? You know the odds. After three days missing, the only way most kidnapping victims come home is in a body bag. If Laurel's family's lucky, they may find the body. If they're really lucky, they won't have to ID it. The funeral's gonna be closed casket. I bet *those* pictures don't show up on the six o'clock news. They'd spoil peoples' appetites for dinner."

Vic took another morose sip of Dew. "This is a hell of a world to grow up in," he added. "Especially if you're a girl."

Understanding dawned on Erin. "You're thinking about Mina."

"You leave my kid out of this," Vic said.

She laid a hand on his arm. "You were talking about odds," she said. "What are the odds of being snagged by a serial killer? They're astronomical. Mina's going to be fine. Hell, she's only a couple months old anyway. You won't have to worry about her with ordinary boys for another fifteen years, let alone psychos."

"Twelve," he gloomily corrected her. "You wouldn't believe how fast kids grow up these days. Maybe if we're really lucky she'll take after me instead of Zofia. Then I won't have to worry so much. Zofia's a lot prettier than I am."

"Now that we can agree on," Erin said. "Come on, Vic. Break's over. Let's get back to work. And forget about Laurel. There isn't a damn thing you or I can do for her. Like you said, if she was taken, the poor girl's already dead. She's probably been dead for days."

"It's gonna be made into one of those goddamn True Crime stories," Vic predicted. "Wait and see. And that Gardner chick is gonna be the one doing the interviews. Somebody oughta shove that microphone right down her throat."

"You're probably right," Erin said. They left the TV off and returned to the Major Crimes office and their normal, everyday diet of murder and mayhem.

They tried to ignore Laurel Peterson, Holly Gardner, and the rest of the media nonsense. And they managed it pretty well for the next three days, until the corpse was found in Central Park.

*   *   *

"Are we sure it's her?" Erin asked.

"Pretty sure," Lieutenant Webb said. The Major Crimes squad was walking briskly along the paved path that wound through the park. Rolf and Erin, who went for regular jogs on this very path, and had run it only a few hours ago, were moving easily. Zofia Piekarski and Vic, who kept in shape, had no trouble keeping up. Webb, who smoked better than a pack a day and carried an extra forty pounds around his midsection, was breathing hard.

"I don't believe it," Piekarski said. "This girl gets snatched, the kidnapper holds her for six days, then he ditches her just like that?"

"I guess he got tired of her," Vic said.

"But no ransom demand," Piekarski said. "No communication with the family. Nothing!"

"He wasn't looking for money," Erin said grimly. "How much farther?"

"Over there," Webb wheezed, pointing to a white tent about thirty yards off the trail. A small crowd of New Yorkers clustered as close as they dared.

"That's one of ours," Vic said, recognizing the style of the tent. It was the kind used by the Crime Scene Unit to protect a scene from rain, wind, sun—and prying eyes.

"CSU's been here about an hour," Webb said. "A jogger saw the body and phoned it in around quarter to eight."

"Jesus," Erin murmured. "I was running on this path at six-thirty. I went right past the spot and didn't see a thing!"

"It's in the trees," Piekarski said as they veered off the trail and walked toward the site. "It probably wasn't obvious."

"I'm a cop!" Erin said. "I should've seen something! And you," she added, giving Rolf a stern look. "What's your excuse? Did you forget how to use your nose?"

Rolf cocked his head, not understanding the question. He was trained to seek out humans, both living and dead, but hadn't been on duty that morning. Erin had taught him to disregard interesting smells while running, as otherwise he tended to pull sideways and break her rhythm. Central Park was replete with the odors of dead and rotting things. It was amazing the humans didn't seem to notice. It was like dead squirrels didn't interest them.

"My understanding is she's pretty fresh," Webb said. "But we'll know more in a minute."

Several white-costumed CSU techs were walking to and fro, scanning the ground for evidence. A pair of uniformed officers stood guard outside the tent. Webb held up his gold shield.

"How about the rest of them?" one of the uniforms asked.

"They're my squad," Webb said.

"Copy that," the Patrolman said. "Can't be too careful. We've had press all over the place, trying to sneak in. Our Lieutenant made them move a ways off. They're over there."

He pointed to the clump of people which appeared to include several representatives of the media.

"Any Feds here?" Webb asked.

"I haven't seen any," the Patrolman said. "But the ME's inside. She arrived about fifteen minutes ago."

"We're late to the party," Vic said, lifting the tent flap.

Erin was braced for something awful. She was accustomed to the sights and smells of violent death. But there wasn't as much of a stench as she'd been expecting. The grass had been cut the day before, so the overpowering odor was of fresh-mown clippings; not a bad smell at all. She let out the breath she'd been holding and followed the other detectives to the body and the lab-coated woman kneeling next to it.

"Dr. Levine," Webb said to the Medical Examiner. "What've we got here?"

"Caucasian female," Sarah Levine said without looking up. "Late adolescence, approximately eighteen. Blonde hair, height one hundred sixty-seven centimeters, weight approximately fifty-six kilograms to judge from build."

"Five-foot six," Piekarski translated. "Weight around one twenty-five." She'd mastered metric to English conversions, something Erin had never quite been able to manage.

"Based on body temperature, time of death was approximately nine and one-half hours ago," Levine continued.

"Midnight," Vic said. "Spooky."

"Cause of death?" Webb asked.

"Preliminary COD is strangulation," Levine said. "Ligature marks indicate a scarf or other narrow strip of material. I speculate silk, but will need to examine the marks more closely to make a final determination."

"There's blood on her face," Vic observed.

Erin made herself look. "Jesus," she said. "She's cut to ribbons."

"The facial lacerations are superficial, but appear to have been inflicted by a bladed implement," Levine said. "Though some are deep enough to score the cheekbones, they would not be life-threatening."

"I don't see any defensive wounds," Erin said. She was looking at Laurel Peterson's hands, mostly so she didn't have to look at her face.

"Your observation is accurate," Levine said. "There appear to be no lacerations or contusions on the hands or forearms. Note the victim's fingernails, which are an impractical length and painted with blue lacquer. There is no unusual chipping or breakage of the nails."

"Were the cuts made while she was alive?" Webb asked quietly.

"Judging from blood flow, I believe they were inflicted postmortem," Levine said.

"Thank God for that," Piekarski said. "But it's a little weird, isn't it?"

"Define 'weird,'" Levine said.

"Don't bother," Vic said. "Some maniac grabbed a homecoming queen, held her almost a week, strangled her, carved up her face, and dumped her in the park. Nothing about this screams 'normal' to me. And you all know what we're thinking, but I'm not gonna say it."

Webb nodded. "True," he said. "This has all the marks of a sex crime. Do you see any signs of sexual assault?"

"The victim is fully clad," Levine said. "I won't be able to make that determination until the postmortem examination. But I see no bloodstains or other fluids on her pants."

"Other fluids?" Piekarski echoed. She looked suddenly ill.

"If you need to vomit, do it outside," Webb said automatically.

Piekarski turned and lurched out of the tent. Vic cursed under his breath and went after her.

"You all right, O'Reilly?" Webb asked.

"I'm fine, sir," Erin said. "I've seen plenty worse. Our girl's wearing pretty tight jeans."

"She is," Webb said.

"It seems unlikely the perp would go to the trouble of dressing her after killing her," Erin said. "I think she was wearing them when she died."

"Not necessarily," Webb said. "I've heard of cases where a rapist-murderer covers up his victim after he's done with her. It's usually a sign of shame or remorse."

"Sir," Erin said in a very low undertone. "This really looks like the start of..."

"Yes," he said unhappily. "It looks like it to me, too. And that's how it's going to look to everyone else. I can already see it. They're going to call him the Central Park Strangler."

"We'll get him, sir," she said.

"I don't doubt it," Webb said. "Eventually. Guys like this almost always get caught sooner or later. But how many more bodies are going to drop before we catch him? Because perps who do this never stop at one."

He took a deep breath. "That's why we call them serial killers," he added.

Chapter 2

Flashbulbs sparkled under the trees like muzzle flashes. For just a moment Erin remembered muzzle flashes under elevated train tracks and the echoing rattle of assault rifles. But it was only the reporters. At least they were hanging back a little, keeping up the appearance of basic decency.

"—will bring all the power of the Federal Government to bear until this heinous perpetrator is brought to justice," a man in a black suit was saying. Beside him stood another man in an identical suit, hands crossed in front of his belt buckle, eyes hidden behind mirrored sunglasses.

"And there's the Feebies," Vic said quietly into her ear. "Just follow the TV lights and look for the cheap suits and shades."

"You're one to talk about cheap suits," she replied. "That guy doing the talking has a pretty nice one."

"I don't *own* any suits," he shot back. "If I need a suit, I rent one. That way I never go out of style."

"It's hard to go *out* if you've never been *in*," she said.

The suit had finished his statement. A dozen microphones were pointed his direction. He raised a hand in a gesture of polite dismissal and turned away from the swarming press. He saw Webb and angled toward the detectives, flanked by his colleague.

"You'd be Lieutenant Webb, I presume," he said.

"That's right," Webb said, extending a hand. "Harry Webb, Major Crimes. These are Detectives O'Reilly, Neshenko, and Piekarski." One of the reasons he was a Lieutenant was that he knew how to play nice with the Feds.

The agent smiled. He had a surprisingly pleasant smile, like a good politician. He was younger than Erin had thought and good-looking in a square-jawed, clean-cut way. He took Webb's hand and gave it a good, firm shake.

"Mark Rockwell," he said. "Special Agent. This is Special Agent Dan Willard. Glad you could join us."

"I think maybe we need to clarify the chain of command," Webb said. He was still smiling. "It was my understanding that this is a homicide, which would place it under local jurisdiction. We're delighted to consult with the FBI, of course, and will be grateful for any assistance your office can provide, but we do need to be clear on who's calling the shots. Technically, you're joining us."

"Of course," Rockwell said with a friendly chuckle. "The last thing we want to do is step on any toes. It's your case, obviously, and you're in command of the incident. When I said 'join us,' I didn't mean to imply—"

"Of course not," Webb said smoothly. "And I appreciate you fielding the initial questions from the press. Did you have a prepared statement, or was it off the cuff?"

"Oh, I just threw them a couple of bones," Rockwell said. "Anything to keep the jackals off our backs, am I right? And this would be the famous Detective O'Reilly. It's a pleasure to meet you. A real pleasure. You're quite the celebrity."

"I wouldn't know, sir," Erin said, trying not to sound stiff. "I don't really follow the news. I'm just doing my job."

"And a fantastic job, from what I hear," Rockwell said. "You, too, Detective Neshenko. You're almost as famous as your partner here. And this would be your K-9. Ralph, isn't it?"

"Rolf," Erin corrected him.

Rockwell nodded. "Good, good. You never know when you'll need a good nose. Willard and I only just got here ourselves. I'm afraid neither of us has been in the Manhattan Field Office very long, so we haven't really got the lay of the land yet. But we're eager to help. This is a very high-profile case. There's going to be a lot of important eyes on everyone involved, so we're really going to need to bring our A game."

"We always bring our A game," Vic said, eyeing the FBI men with dislike. "That's how we get our good clearance numbers."

"Of course you do," Rockwell said, laughing again. It was a pleasant laugh, but Erin was starting to find it a little grating. "Now, we got a basic profile from Behavioral Analysis in Quantico, but it'll need to be updated with the new evidence based on the condition of the body. How soon do you think your doc will be done with the corpse?"

"Dr. Levine is extremely thorough, but she works fast," Webb said. "This will be her top priority. We'll have the results as soon as possible."

"Detective O'Reilly!"

Erin's head whipped around at the female voice shouting her name. She found herself looking at Holly Gardner.

"Great," Vic growled.

Erin didn't like reporters. She didn't like the way they fed off human misery, the way they were constantly thrusting their goddamn microphones into the faces of grieving families, demanding to know how the poor people felt. How did anyone *think* they felt? Cops regularly saw ordinary folks on the worst days of their lives; often the last days. You got used to it. You built up calluses. But cops knew better than to talk *feelings* with victims. You had to be a sadist, a masochist, or both to really enjoy that.

"Our viewers will be glad to know the *famous* Erin O'Reilly is on the case!" Holly said, flashing her megawatt prime-time smile. She was very pretty, Erin thought sourly, and would be gorgeous if she went a little easier on the makeup or bothered to let a genuine facial expression show through.

"That's nice," Erin said. It was the second time she'd been called famous in less than two minutes and she didn't like that either.

"What can you tell us about Miss Peterson's fate?" Holly asked.

"The NYPD doesn't comment on ongoing investigations." Her mouth spat out the words on autopilot.

Undeterred, Holly turned her attention toward Vic. "Detective Neshenko!" she exclaimed. "You have a daughter. A blonde, isn't she? How does this sort of case affect you now that—"

"Listen, lady," Vic growled. "You don't say one more word about my family, you got that? Or I swear to God you'll wish you'd kept those puffy lips shut."

Piekarski put a hand on Vic's shoulder. "Hey," she said. "Take it easy. You don't have to protect us from *her*."

"Yeah, I do," Vic said. "Because this bitch thinks my kid— *our* kid—is fair game for her friggin' ratings. Mina's three months old! I suppose I ought to be grateful Miss Ratings Bait here waited for her to pop her head out of the womb before angling for an interview. Don't you have any shame, Miss Gardner? One lousy little bit? If not for me, then maybe, just maybe, for the mother of Laurel friggin' Peterson?"

"Neshenko!"

Webb's voice cracked like a gunshot. Vic stopped mid-tirade, but only barely. The Russian's face was flushed. Erin, who'd been around a lot of dangerous, violent men, could see all the warning signs in Vic. He was about to explode.

Holly pouted prettily. "Vic," she said. "You don't need to be like that. After all we've been through together. I thought we liked one another."

"And just what do you mean by that?" Piekarski demanded, taking a step toward her and possessively screening Vic. It would have been comical, since Vic was almost twice her size, if not for the blonde detective's sudden scowl.

Webb got between them. "You'll have a statement from the Commissioner at the next press conference," he said. "In the meantime, I have to ask you to stop bothering my detectives. They have a difficult job to do, which requires all their attention and skills. That will be *all*."

"I could help, you know," Holly said. "We don't have to be enemies."

"Nobody said anything about enemies," Webb said. "Good day, Miss Gardner."

As the disappointed Channel Six reporter turned away, Erin caught a glimpse of another woman in the crowd. About four dozen bystanders were watching, but this one caught her eye. The face was remarkable.

The other woman's complexion was Mediterranean. Her hair was thick, black, and wavy. She had a prominent nose and extremely dark eyes. The eyes were amused, sardonic. Her face was striking and had the underlying bone structure to be truly beautiful. But what Erin saw was the scar. It ran from the woman's hairline down the inside curve of the nose, narrowly missing the eye, and carved its way through both lips on its way to her jawline. The flesh of the lips had drawn back as it had healed, leaving a mocking twist to what would otherwise be a well-shaped, attractive mouth. It looked like she was smiling, but the injury made it very hard to tell.

"Vic!" Erin barked, pointing. She couldn't explain her reaction, except that her instincts told her this was a woman who was *up to something.*

Vic picked up on her tone and reacted immediately. He blew past Piekarski, shouldered Holly out of his way without even pretending to be polite, and barged into the crowd. Erin and Rolf were right behind him.

Erin expected the woman to do what almost everybody did in that situation; run. When a guy like Vic came at you, it was time to either get ready for a fight or to run like hell.

The woman did neither. Instead, as Vic bore down on her, she hoisted a camera and snapped a shot of him.

Vic pulled up short, momentarily confused. *Damn,* Erin thought. It had been a false positive. This wasn't some psycho killer returning to the scene of the crime. It was just another goddamn reporter.

"Okay, lady," Vic said. "What're you doing here?"

"I'm doing my job, Detective Neshenko," the woman said coolly. Her voice was a throaty contralto, a little husky.

"What is your job, ma'am?" Erin asked, coming alongside Vic.

"I'm a writer," the woman replied. "Here are my press credentials. I have at least as much right to be here as you do, Detective O'Reilly. It's a public park."

Erin looked at the documents in the other woman's hands. They looked genuine enough, though Erin figured they'd be easy to fake. The name under the photograph on the press card read ANDROMEDA CARVER.

"That's an unusual name," Erin commented.

"It's *Greek,*" the reporter said. "Andromeda was a princess whose father sacrificed her to a sea monster. She was chained to a rock, classic submissive female, and was rescued by a hero. She married him, of course. I usually go by Andy."

"Andy Carver," Erin repeated. The name rang a bell. "Wait a second. I've heard of you."

"I'm flattered," Andy replied. "Not all of us have your same degree of celebrity or, shall we say, *exposure*."

"You write for that tabloid," Erin said. "The one that ran that story on me around Christmas."

Piekarski had joined them. "*NYPD in Bed with Irish Mob*," she recited from memory. "*Hero Detective 'Goes to the Mattresses.*'"

Andy was definitely smiling now. "Yes," she said. "That was a good headline."

"You're a scum-sucking bottom-feeder," Erin snarled, astonished at the anger she felt surging up in herself. "I've got nothing to say to you."

"You came to me," Andy said, unperturbed. "Besides, I'm not your problem. Shouldn't you be looking for the evil bastard who killed poor Laurel Peterson? You'd better look hard and fast, Detective, because unless I'm mistaken, he'll be looking for another girlfriend before long. That won't look good on your hero resume. Pretty blonde bodies do attract so much attention."

"I think that's enough fraternization with the press," Webb said. It had taken him a little while to catch up with the others, but now he was here. "Unfortunately, Manhattan detectives aren't in the habit of giving impromptu interviews, so I'm going to ask you to please excuse us."

"Lieutenant Webb," Andy said. "What were your feelings when you discovered your lover, porn star Marie Lewis, alias Maureen Sinclair, had seduced you into murdering Terence Volkman in Los Angeles?"

Holly Gardner had also pursued the cluster of detectives. "Murder?" she echoed, eyes sparkling. "Porn star?"

Webb gave the reporters a bland, generic smile. "I'd encourage you to double-check your facts before publishing anything that might expose you to legal liability, ma'am," he said. "Good day."

*   *   *

"I expected better from you, O'Reilly," Webb said once they were safely back in the privacy of Erin's unmarked Charger, with only Rolf for an audience.

"Oh, really?" Erin said, cranking the gearshift savagely and stepping on the accelerator much harder than necessary. "I didn't pick that fight. Vic—"

"You know him as well as I do," Webb interrupted. "Nobody expects better from him. Though I'll definitely be having a talk with him. You represent the New York Police Department. When you're wearing your shield, you're the face of the Department. You have professional responsibilities and an appearance to maintain. Squabbling with members of the gutter press doesn't help anyone, least of all our victim."

"You're right, sir," she said, but she was still fuming and couldn't help herself. "But do you know who that was?"

"The tabloid journalist who penned that story about you and Morton Carlyle," Webb said. "What about it?"

"She called me a slut in front of the whole damn city!" Erin snapped. "Was I supposed to play nice with her?"

"You were supposed to ignore her," Webb retorted. "For Pete's sake, O'Reilly! Didn't you ever run into a playground bully when you were a kid? As long as they're teasing you, the best thing to do is ignore them. You've been called plenty of worse things by perps. Are you angry that she called you names, or that she dug up the truth?"

"I'm not some whore with a shield!" Erin insisted.

"Of course not," Webb said. "I'm talking about the way Ms. Carver unearthed your relationship with Carlyle. That woman is competent, smart, and ruthless, on top of which she's a writer with a readership in the tens of thousands. Is that the sort of person you want to make into an enemy? Why did you go charging after her?"

"I didn't know who she was," Erin said, a little sulkily. "I didn't like her eyes. I thought maybe she was involved in the Peterson case. Sometimes perps revisit the scene of the crime."

"I see," Webb said, more gently. "Well, that's understandable. But Agent Rockwell is right. This is an extremely high-profile case. We can't go flying off the handle or behaving recklessly. We only just managed to shrug off Internal Affairs after the last kerfuffle."

"Sir," Erin said. "You just said 'kerfuffle' and 'for Pete's sake.' Are you feeling okay?"

"I'm coasting on the residue of my best behavior," Webb sighed. "It was all I could do to keep from swearing my head off at those parasites. So I understand where you're coming from. I really do. But we're not private citizens. We can't react to personal insults. The moment the Job becomes personal, it's time to step away from it."

"Copy that, sir," she said. Then, unable to help herself, "Who was Terence Volkman?"

Webb didn't answer right away. He stared out the Charger's window at the Manhattan streets, his face suddenly very old and thoughtful.

"Sorry," she said after about half a minute of silence. "I didn't mean to pry."

"It's a fair question," he said, not looking at her. "Terry Volkman was a struggling actor. A beautiful woman manipulated him and me into a situation. He thought it was an acting gig. I thought it was something else. He pulled a gun full of blanks on me and I put two rounds in his chest. He died at the scene."

"Oh," Erin said. "Shit." Suicide by cop was the worst nightmare of plenty of Patrol officers. To gun down a man who wasn't a threat, but who forced you into it, would haunt you for years. Maybe forever.

"I was a little drunk and a lot stupid," Webb said. "Oh, it was a clean shooting, there wasn't a bit of doubt about that. But I didn't have to do it. And Ms. Carver has almost all the facts. I wonder how she managed to dig them up and have them on hand. She must have had her eye on our squad for some time. This is old news, from the end of my time with the LAPD."

"Was it why you left Los Angeles?" Erin asked.

"Part of the reason," Webb said. He shrugged. "My divorce was about to be finalized. That's my second divorce, you understand. You remember Cathy Simmons."

"Yeah," she said. "I remember that time she came to New York and got tangled up with that dead guy."

"Right," he said. "I needed a change. It was like I had cancer of Southern California. LA was killing me by inches. I thought New York might put some life back in me."

"Wait a second," Erin said. "You lived in Los Angeles and thought coming to *New York* would perk you up?!"

He smiled. "It was different," he said. "If you'd lived in LA, you might understand."

They drove on in silence for a few minutes, until they were getting close to the Precinct 8 station.

"What did Andy Carver get wrong?" Erin asked, just before pulling into the garage.

"Maureen wasn't my lover," Webb said quietly. "We never slept together. I'm not bragging. If she'd let me, before I knew just what she was, I would've gone for it. Instead I threw her in jail."

"Oh," Erin said again.

"Watch out for Carver," he said. "That woman could hurt

you. What is it you always say? Forget about it? That's my advice."

"I'll try. Anyway, we have a killer to catch."

"That we do," Webb said. "Hopefully Levine's autopsy will get us something we can use. In the meantime, let's see what the brain boys at Quantico have dreamed up. Have you ever seen a profile from Behavioral Analysis?"

"No," Erin said. "The only serial killers I've gone after were the Heartbreaker Killer and that psycho kid during that power outage. We nailed both of them without any of that psychobabble bullshit."

"It can be pretty wild," Webb said. "I wouldn't be surprised if they tell us our killer's height, weight, eye color, and favorite food. It's like visiting a carnival fortune teller."

"Will it be accurate?" Erin asked, sliding the Charger into its place.

"We'll know once we catch him," Webb said.

Chapter 3

"Every serial killer kills to fulfill a deep need," Agent Rockwell said.

"Oh brother," Vic whispered to Erin and Zofia. "School's in session."

Rockwell and Willard were standing in front of the whiteboard in Major Crimes. Rockwell was holding an honest-to-God wooden pointer in one hand. Erin wondered where he'd gotten it. Willard had a whole handful of dry-erase markers in various colors.

"This isn't a need for sex," Rockwell continued. "His sexual desires have been displaced, usually on the basis of serious childhood trauma, into the need for three things: manipulation, domination, and control."

Willard, taking his cue, wrote the three words on the board in red marker. Webb and Piekarski were listening politely and seemed to be paying attention. Piekarski was actually taking notes. Vic wasn't even pretending. Erin was waiting for the FBI guys to say something she didn't already know.

"This doesn't tell us much about our particular killer," Rockwell said. "Every unsub has a specific MO and signature."

"Aren't those the same?" Piekarski asked.

"Good question," Rockwell said, smiling at her. "The MO is his methodology. The signature is the need he seeks to fulfill by killing. An unsub can, and often will, change his MO. But he'll never change his signature, because that's the reason he's killing in the first place."

While waiting for Rockwell to tell her something she didn't already know, Erin was trying to figure out why she didn't like him. He was a little too friendly, a little too smooth. It made him seem artificial. And the way he was lecturing came across as condescending. They weren't schoolkids. They were experienced detectives. She could tell he was just waiting for someone to ask him what an "unsub" was, but Erin wouldn't give him the pleasure. It was standard FBI jargon. All it stood for was "unknown subject."

"Behavioral Analysis has been working on this unsub since two days after our victim was kidnapped," Rockwell went on. "We didn't have a lot to go on. It looks like we've all got the same case file."

Everyone nodded. Webb, being old-school, had a physical printout. The others had the file up on their computer screens. Willard began sticking photographs to the board.

"Laurel Peterson, age nineteen, was a sophomore at Columbia," Rockwell said. "She was described by her friends and family as friendly, outgoing, and attractive. 'Vivacious' is a term from her Sociology professor. She was studying to be a social worker. She had no criminal record; not even a speeding ticket. She had a boyfriend."

"We always check out the boyfriend," Vic said.

"Absolutely," Rockwell agreed. "Unfortunately, in this case the boyfriend was in Moorhead when Ms. Peterson was taken. Where is that exactly, Dan?"

"Northwestern Minnesota," Willard said without hesitation. "A little over fourteen hundred miles away. Twenty-two hours by car. Five hours by plane, if flying out of the nearest major airport in Fargo."

"Our girl's Minnesotan?" Erin asked.

"Born and bred," Rockwell said. "Only daughter of Stanley and Rebecca Peterson. Graduated Moorhead High School with honors. Letters in Cheerleading, Academics, Knowledge Bowl, Tennis, and Band. She played the flute."

"Did anyone confirm the boyfriend's whereabouts?" Vic asked, not willing to let go of it just yet.

"Moorhead PD talked to him the day she was taken," Webb said, flipping through the file. "The kid's name is Timothy Collins. Looks like he goes to the University of Minnesota, Moorhead campus. His alibi's airtight. Ten people confirmed his presence in Minnesota."

"Damn," Vic said. "Doesn't she have a local guy here in New York?"

"Not according to what we have here," Rockwell said. "She didn't go to parties, didn't run around with guys. It appears she wasn't sexually active."

"Bullshit," Vic said, earning him dirty looks from both Erin and Piekarski.

"Explain," Webb said.

"This girl was gorgeous," Vic said. "She was a cheerleader. She's away from home for the first time, in the big city. Her high-school sweetheart's four states away, and you're telling me she wasn't getting it on with somebody? I don't believe it. Or if it's true, we need to find some creep who tried to hit on her and got shot down."

"That isn't our profile," Rockwell said with an apologetic smile. "If I can continue summarizing how we got here?"

"By all means," Webb said. "Neshenko, give it a rest."

"Last Sunday afternoon, Ms. Peterson was scheduled to meet with her academic advisor," Rockwell said. "She left her dorm room at 2:16 for a 2:30 meeting. Her roommate, Mei-Ying Wong, was the last person to see her. Ms. Wong didn't recall anything out of the ordinary. Ms. Peterson was dressed in a blue T-shirt and jeans, wearing a brown leather backpack.

"The backpack was turned in to the campus lost and found a few minutes after four o'clock the same afternoon. It was found at the bus stop at West 116th and Broadway. The pack contained three academic textbooks, a spiral notebook, two pencils, a ballpoint pen, and Ms. Peterson's cell phone and wallet. The wallet held a few dollars—"

"Twelve dollars," Willard interjected. "Seven singles and a five."

"—her student ID, driver's license, a credit card, and assorted pocket litter," Rockwell finished. "The presence of the money and credit card suggest the contents of the backpack had not been rifled. After campus security spoke with Ms. Peterson's roommate, they contacted the NYPD and reported her missing."

"Patrol units interviewed everyone they could find from the area around the bus stop," Webb said. "They didn't turn up any leads. Traffic cameras don't have coverage of the specific area, and the City hasn't gotten around to installing cameras at all the bus stops yet."

"That's coming soon," Piekarski said. "In the next few years. Not that it does Laurel any good."

"A citywide BOLO was issued," Webb said. "It generated several dozen sighting reports, none of which were confirmed. And that was the last anyone heard of our victim until this morning."

"I'm afraid so," Rockwell said. "Here's what Behavioral Analysis came up with. Our unsub is white, male, between twenty-five and forty years of age. He has a working-class background and a blue-collar income level. He holds a job that allows him to observe students on a daily basis, but his social standing doesn't permit close association with them. He's most likely a janitor, a groundskeeper, something of the sort. He is meticulous and fastidious in his personal habits, possibly obsessive-compulsive. He is polite and unthreatening in appearance. He lives alone, probably in a basement or ground-level apartment. He comes from a home in which his parents were divorced or separated."

Rockwell finished talking. He smiled expectantly, as if he expected a round of applause.

"Why?" Vic asked.

"I beg your pardon?"

"Where did all these predictions come from?" Vic leaned forward. "Okay, I get the bit about him watching students and being meticulous. This was a carefully planned kidnapping, not some spur-of-the-moment snatch. He had to know our girl's schedule and movements, and if he targeted her, he would've been watching her for a while. But the rest of this sounds like hocus-pocus bullshit to me."

"Living alone would be necessary," Webb said. "Unless he kept his victim off-site, he wouldn't want to chance a roommate or spouse finding out about her."

"Unless they're in on it," Vic countered.

"Most serial killers work alone," Rockwell said.

"But not all," Vic replied.

"This is a numbers game," Rockwell said. "It's based on probabilities. Our unsub wouldn't want to keep her at a separate location. His need for control requires him to be in close proximity. He wouldn't want to risk her escaping or being found by someone else."

"What about his race and age?" Erin asked.

Rockwell shrugged. "That's the numbers again," he said. "Most serial killers target members of their own ethnic group. Our unsub would need to be young and strong enough to overpower our victim. She wasn't particularly large, but she was athletic. Cheerleaders have a surprising amount of leg and core strength, and she was a varsity tennis player. She could have put up a considerable fight."

"You think he's polite and unassuming because he was able to get close without alarming her," Erin guessed. "Otherwise she would have raised the alarm."

"Right," Rockwell said.

"Do you think you might be looking for another student instead of an employee?" Webb asked.

"I doubt it," Rockwell said. "Students living on campus wouldn't have the necessary privacy to hold a young woman captive and incommunicado for almost a week. That requires isolation you can't get in a dorm or campus house. When we find our unsub, he'll probably have some sort of dungeon."

"A *dungeon?*" Piekarski repeated, looking ill. "Like, with whips and chains and metal bars? Jesus."

"It's possible," Vic said. "Did you ever hear of H.H. Holmes?"

"I've heard of Sherlock Holmes," Piekarski said.

"No relation," Vic said. "H.H. Holmes was a serial killer in Chicago during the World's Fair back in eighteen something-or-other."

"1893," Willard said. "I'm familiar with the case."

"Yeah. He ran a hotel and he'd turned it into a murder house. Secret doors, passageways, a friggin' torture chamber in the basement."

"You're making this up," Piekarski said.

"Unfortunately not," Willard said. "The house is well documented. However, it was damaged by arson shortly after Holmes was apprehended. Holmes himself was hanged in 1896."

"So we're looking for a neat freak with a torture basement," Vic said. "That's friggin' creepy."

"That's the best information we have at this time," Rockwell said. "Of course, our Profiling people didn't have much to go on. The autopsy should provide a wealth of new details. I'll forward it to Quantico as soon as your ME is finished. Everything tells us something. The method of killing, the weapon, the postmortem mutilation; all of it. Finding the body is a real windfall for us."

Erin cringed inwardly at Rockwell's casual callousness. But her face gave nothing away.

"We have Patrol units scouring the park," Webb said. "If we get lucky, we might be able to get someone who saw our killer lugging the body into the park."

"Yeah, that's unusual," Vic said. "Even by Central Park standards."

"I wouldn't bet on it," Erin said. "If they dumped the body in the dark, there aren't a lot of people around at that time of night. Even if we get some street person who spotted it, all they'll have seen is a dark shape carrying another dark shape."

"You're probably right," Webb said. "But we pull on all the threads. We only need one to be the right one. And on that subject, let's get moving."

"Where to?" Vic asked.

"College," Webb said.

* * *

"Are you sure this is a good idea, sir?" Erin asked.

"It's good procedure," Webb said.

"I know that," she said. "But these campus cops aren't exactly my biggest fans."

"You're just saying that because they tried to get you kicked off the Force," Vic said.

"Yeah, that's exactly why I'm saying it," Erin said.

"Would you rather go back to the office and get chummy with the FBI?" Webb asked.

"I'm good, sir."

"Then quit bellyaching. There won't be much to do at the Eightball until Levine finishes the autopsy, and that'll be a few hours yet. In the meantime, I want to go over the ground. Maybe we'll find something that got missed by the other detectives."

But Erin still wasn't convinced. She half expected the head of security to jump out and yell at her.

"Remember the last time you snuck on campus?" Vic asked. "You tased a date-rapist in the nuts. It was awesome."

"You weren't there," she said, giving him a sour expression.

"But you told me all about it," he said. "And I've got a real vivid imagination. When I think about it, I can practically smell his balls frying. I wish I'd seen it, though."

"There'll be none of that today," Webb said.

"Nope," Vic agreed. "On account of us leaving our Tasers behind. If we run into any scumbags, I'll have to use good, old-fashioned muscle torque."

He made an expressive grabbing and twisting gesture that, if Erin had been male, would have made her cross her legs.

"No," Webb said. "On account of my having called campus security and cleared our visit. There's the chief now."

"We've met," Erin said. She tried to drift nonchalantly behind Vic and make herself less obvious.

"Chief Oglesby," Webb said, offering his hand. "Thank you for accommodating us."

Oglesby had heavy jowls that reminded Erin of a bulldog. He was overweight and red-faced and looked very unhappy. But he shook hands with Webb readily enough.

"Anything we can do to help," he said. "This is a little over our heads, I have to admit. We're still trying to believe it. This is a safe campus. People feel secure here. Or they did."

"And we'll do everything in our power to make it safe again," Webb said. "You know most of my squad, I think, but you won't have met Detective Piekarski."

"Pleasure," Piekarski said.

"And here's Neshenko and O'Reilly," Webb added.

Oglesby's eyebrows lowered, making him look even more bulldog-like. "Yeah," he growled. "I remember."

"Sir, this isn't about me," Erin said, stepping out from behind Vic. "This is about finding out what happened to Laurel. I'm sorry for our past history, and I apologize. There'll be no trouble from me, you have my word."

"Sure," Oglesby grunted. "So what is it you need?"

"Let's start with a list of all campus employees," Webb said. "I don't mean faculty. I'm talking maintenance personnel, custodians, et cetera. We're especially interested in anyone who works in Ms. Peterson's dormitory, or would have spent time around her."

Oglesby nodded. "I can get that for you," he said. "She's really dead, then?"

"It looks that way," Webb said. "We're not a hundred percent on the ID yet, so if you could avoid spreading it around, we'd appreciate it."

"Are you kidding?" Oglesby said with profound disgust. "You think I want those damn reporters any thicker than they have been? I've had to boot ten of them off campus so far today. It's not just disrespectful, it's disgraceful. Classes are getting disrupted and we keep getting calls about creepy strangers that turn out to be more reporters. I'm not giving them a goddamn thing. Nobody in my office is talking to them, and anyone who tries will be filing for unemployment by the end of the day."

"Excellent," Webb said. "We'd also like to take a look at Ms. Peterson's room, if that would be acceptable."

"Follow me," Oglesby said, talking while he walked. "Can the dog do anything useful?"

"Not right now," Erin said. "We don't have any proof her attacker was in her room. I could take him to the bus stop, but hundreds of people have passed through since Laurel was there."

"We turned over her pack and everything in it to the Missing Persons detectives working the case," Oglesby said. "Their names were Hancock and Fleder... Fleder something."

"Fledermaus," Webb said. "They're with the Missing Persons squad. I talked to them when Major Crimes took over."

"I don't understand why Major Crimes didn't handle it from the beginning," Oglesby grumbled.

"We had no definite proof she'd been abducted," Webb said. "She might have run away, or had an accident, or just dropped off grid for a while. Do you know if she was having any personal problems?"

"I didn't know her," Oglesby said. "I hadn't even heard her name before this happened. We have over thirty thousand students enrolled. You think I know them all? That's as many students as the NYPD has officers, and with a lot more turnover."

Webb held up a hand. "No offense, sir," he said. "I was just asking."

"Here we are," Oglesby said. "Broadway Hall. It's mostly Juniors, but some Sophomores live in doubles. Let me key in."

He scanned his badge and opened the door, leading the detectives to the stairs. They climbed to the second floor and followed him to the third door on the right. A sign on the door proclaimed WONG and PETERSON. Someone had decorated it with colored pencil artwork of a pair of anime-style cartoon characters; one blonde, one dark-haired.

Oglesby knocked. After a moment, the door opened a crack. A young woman peered out at them.

"Miss, I'm Chief of Security Oglesby," he said. "Are you Mei-Ying?"

"Do I look like Mei-Ying?" the girl retorted. Her skin was the color of coffee grounds and her accent was pure Bronx. "I'm Shae Garner. No wonder you jerks couldn't find her. Jesus."

Oglesby's face went even redder. "Sorry," he muttered. "Listen, I've got the NYPD here. They need to take a look at the room. Who all is in there?"

"Jane Backlund, Mei-Ying, and me," Shae said. "We're here, because we're her friends and she asked us to be. You got a problem with that?"

"Shae, it's okay," another voice said from further in the room. "They're trying to help. Let them in."

That voice was quieter and milder than Shae's, with a rough edge that suggested the speaker was in a difficult emotional spot. Shae frowned but stepped back, letting the detectives in.

The dorm room was neat and tidy compared to most Erin had seen. One side of the room was clearly Laurel's, the other Mei-Ying's. Laurel's tennis racquet leaned against her desk. Her flute case sat next to a laptop computer whose screen was closed.

Mei-Ying was sitting on her bed next to another girl. They were holding hands. A box of tissues lay nearby. Mei-Ying held one in her other hand. She was a round-faced, dark-eyed girl of Chinese extraction. Her eyes were puffy and bloodshot. Her companion, was very tall. Erin pegged her for some sort of athlete; she was long-limbed and muscular, wearing her hair in a ponytail.

"It's a little crowded in here," Oglesby said. "I'll just wait in the hallway."

"I'm Lieutenant Webb," Webb said. "I understand this is a difficult time, but we need to ask you a few things. We're trying to figure out exactly what happened. It would be best if we could do this privately."

Mei-Ying nodded. "I'll be okay," she told her friends.

"If you need us, we'll be right outside," Jane said, squeezing her hand and standing up.

"Remember, you don't have to tell them anything you don't want to," Shae said, glowering at the cops. Vic glowered back, but kept his mouth shut.

"Don't mind her," Mei-Ying said once the door had closed behind her friends. "She doesn't like police officers."

"Nobody likes us very much," Vic said. "We're used to it."

"I'd like to help," the girl said. "But I already told those other detectives everything I know. Did they tell you about our conversation?"

"I'd prefer to hear it directly from you," Webb said. "They might have left something out by mistake. Were you close with Laurel?"

"She is... was my friend," Mei-Ying said. Her eyes filled, but she didn't break down. She dabbed at her face with her tissue. "We met Freshman year. We were on the same floor. I didn't know anybody. I'm from the West Coast. I'd never been so far from home. She was so friendly and kind. I can't imagine why anybody would want to do... to do that to her."

"Did you or she get any unusual phone calls?" Webb asked. "E-mails? Any sort of unsolicited communications?"

"Not that I know of. Our room has a landline, but nobody uses it. We joked that whenever it rang, it was a telemarketer. We just let it roll to voicemail."

"Did Laurel say anything about anyone following her around or trying to engage her in conversation?"

"No, but she wouldn't."

"She wouldn't talk to a stranger?" Webb asked.

"That's not what I meant," Mei-Ying said. "She'd talk to everyone. She just wouldn't think it was worth mentioning. Laurel wanted to hear everybody's story. She'd talk to homeless people on street corners, or elderly folks on buses, or anybody who looked lonely or sad. She always wanted to help people. I thought it was dangerous, but how could I tell her that? Maybe... maybe if I had, she wouldn't have... have..."

"No," Erin said firmly. "This wasn't your fault. Don't say that. Don't even think it."

"So if she was approached by someone unusual, she might have talked to them?" Webb asked. "Or maybe followed them somewhere?"

"Laurel's from the Midwest," Mei-Ying said. "I live in San Francisco, so I'm used to big cities. Moorhead is tiny compared to a place like New York. Laurel didn't know how dangerous this place could be. She wasn't stupid. She didn't go to wild parties, she didn't get drunk, she didn't sleep around. But she was trusting."

"No substance use?" Webb asked. "I'm not just talking about alcohol."

"None," Mei-Ying said flatly. "I never saw her take a single drink. She is... she was a Methodist. She wouldn't touch alcohol. And she was scared of hard drugs."

"Was she seeing someone?" Vic asked.

"Tim," Mei-Ying said. "She'd known him since they were kids. She was on the phone with him almost every night."

"I meant locally," Vic said.

"You mean cheating on him?"

"Yeah. That's exactly what I mean."

"She'd never do a thing like that! She loved him!"

The outrage in the girl's voice was so genuine that Vic actually looked ashamed of his question.

"Okay," he muttered. "Sorry. We gotta ask these questions."

"Is anything missing?" Webb asked, gesturing to Laurel's belongings.

"I don't think so," Mei-Ying said. "Well, the other detectives took her computer drive, so they could examine it. They wanted to check her e-mails and internet history. Everything else looks like it's where it ought to be. But I don't know for sure. I didn't do an inventory."

"Can you think of anything else?" Erin asked. "Anything unusual?"

"No," Mei-Ying said. "I'm sorry. I wish I could tell you something. I've been asking myself the same question. If there was something I could have noticed, or should have. I was hoping maybe it was all a mistake, that she'd gotten lost or something silly like that. But then, the news this morning... is it really her?"

"We think so," Webb said gently. "The girl we found was wearing what Laurel was wearing when she vanished. We're doing a DNA match, but it's mostly a formality."

"DNA?" The girl was confused. "Couldn't you tell from her face?"

Webb didn't answer.

"Oh, no," Mei-Ying said quietly. "What did they do to her?"

Her shoulders began to shake and she buried her head in her hands. Erin took a step toward her, then paused and looked inquiringly at her commanding officer.

"I think we're done here," Webb said. "Thank you for your time, Ms. Wong. We'll stop bothering you now. I'm very sorry."

*   *   *

"This is so much easier when the victim's an asshole," Vic said after they'd left the dormitory.

"I know what you mean," Webb said. "But an innocent victim should fire you up with righteous resolve."

"Oh, it pisses me off," Vic said. "But I feel like puking, too."

"So do I," Piekarski said. "Jesus. I've scooped up some bodies working the Street Narcotics unit, but they were all drug dealers and gang members. Sure, they'd all had bad shit happen to them when they were kids, but they'd all done bad shit themselves. They were victims but they were perps too. You don't feel so bad about them."

"And they don't get plastered all over the news," Erin added.

"I'm just wondering why her?" Piekarski said. "She sounds like the nicest girl in the world."

"Maybe that's why," Erin said.

"Too good for this sinful Earth?" Webb suggested with a wry twist of his mouth.

"No," Erin said. "I'm thinking that was what our killer was looking for. He wanted to kill a good girl."

Chapter 4

"The problem with this kind of case is there isn't a motive," Webb said.

"Sir?" Erin wasn't sure she'd heard him correctly.

"Of course there's a motive," Vic said. "This whackjob gets off on killing girls."

"I meant there isn't a *personal* motive," Webb said.

"It doesn't get much more personal than sex," Vic disagreed.

But Erin understood what her commanding officer was getting at. "There's probably no relationship between the victim and the killer," she explained. "Our guy may have been looking for a pretty, blonde, blue-eyed cheerleader, but he didn't care whether it was Laurel or some other girl."

"Exactly," Webb said. "We'd better hope we get someone off the staff at Columbia, because otherwise we're shooting in the dark. The boyfriend isn't even in the same state. Our girl didn't have enemies. I think O'Reilly's right. This girl wasn't targeted because she was promiscuous or a sex worker or an ex-girlfriend. She was targeted because she was none of those things."

"The girl next door," Vic said.

"Unfortunately we don't have a creepy next-door neighbor as a suspect," Webb said dryly. "And her dorm room doesn't have good sightlines for a peeping Tom."

"I think the killer knew her," Erin said. "At least by sight."

"I've asked the Missing Persons detectives to drop by the Eightball," Webb said. "They've been combing her computer and phone. If you're right, maybe our guy left a communication trail. It's a long shot, though. If anything had turned up there, we'd know it by now. Is there any point in taking Rolf around?"

Erin shook her head. "Like I said, the trail's gone cold. We'll want some article of Laurel's clothing handy, for when we do nail down a suspect. Rolf will be able to tell if she was in a house."

"We'll have what she was wearing when she was found," Webb said. "Let's head back to the Eightball and regroup."

"What should my people do?" Oglesby asked. He'd been hanging back, watching and listening.

"You can decide how much you want to communicate to the student body," Webb said. "But if it was up to me, I'd recommend your female students use the buddy system whenever possible. Students should report anybody acting suspicious, even if they turn out to be reporters, and your personnel should ID anyone loitering. Get pictures of suspicious characters."

"We'll do that," Oglesby said. "And I'll get that list of staff to you ASAP."

"Thank you, Chief," Webb said, shaking hands with him.

"Detective O'Reilly?" Oglesby said.

"Sir?" Erin replied warily.

"No hard feelings about the other thing," he said. "We're all on the same team here."

"Absolutely," she said, giving him a smile. He even sounded like he meant it. He must be really scared.

*　　*　　*

The number of suit-wearing men in the Eightball's Major Crimes office had doubled while the squad was out. Rockwell and Willard were updating the whiteboard while another pair of guys studied it. Their suits were cheaper and older than those worn by the FBI agents, but the gold shields on their belts marked them as NYPD. As always seemed to be the case, there was a tall thin one and a short fat one.

The tall detective approached them. He looked to be a few years older than Webb, his mustache completely gray. "Lieutenant?" he guessed.

"Harry Webb," Webb said. "You'd be Detective Hancock?"

"Guilty as charged," Hancock said. "This is Joey Fledermaus. In our house we all call him Batman."

"Huh?" Vic said. Fledermaus was short, pudgy, and balding. He wore thick eyeglasses. The only way he'd look less like a superhero was if he'd been missing a limb.

Erin, with her smattering of German, was the one who got it. "His name," she said. "Fledermaus is German for 'bat.'"

"Or 'flying mouse,'" Fledermaus said, smiling. "There's worse nicknames."

"Depends," Vic said. "Which Batman are we talking about? West, Clooney, Keaton, or Bale? Or that new one with Affleck?"

"Take your pick," Fledermaus said. "I'm partial to Christian Bale. The Nolan Batman is the best Batman."

"Detective O'Reilly?" Hancock said to Erin.

"Good to meet you," she said, taking the hand he offered.

"I knew your dad," he said. "I was down in the One-Sixteen for a while, back in the day. You have his eyes. I bet he's proud of you."

"I hope so," she said.

"He never made Detective, did he?"

"He liked working Patrol," she said, swallowing a sharp retort and reminding herself to be on her best behavior.

"Coffee's in the break room," Webb said. "Make yourselves at home here, gentlemen. What can you tell us?"

"Not much," Hancock admitted. "The girl's hard drive is clean."

"Not even any porn," Fledermaus said.

"You sound disappointed," Vic said.

"She was active on social media sites," Fledermaus said. "But we didn't find any improper or suspicious communication with anyone online. This girl was... wholesome."

"Her web history is all stuff pertaining to her schoolwork," Hancock said. "Or social causes. She was an activist. Big into helping people in inner-city areas. A real Mother Teresa type. She put up a bunch of stuff about New York's homeless and transient population. Her phone's clean, too. The only call history is family and friends. Texts are the same. We had a couple unknown callers, but we traced those back to spam bots overseas."

"We dealt with some Russian human traffickers a while back," Vic said. "You think there's a connection?"

"No good," Hancock said, shaking his head. "The spammers aren't connected to white slavers or drugs or serious organized crime. They're just your garden-variety scammers."

"No malware on her phone or computer," Fledermaus added. "I swear, these are the cleanest electronic devices I've seen on anyone older than age twelve."

"How much attention did you guys give to this case when it first dropped?" Erin asked.

"What are you suggesting, Detective?" Hancock demanded. Erin could practically see the hackles on his neck coming up.

"She's suggesting that you have a large backlog of missing persons," Webb said smoothly. "And you can't be expected to devote the full resources of the Department to every one. She's wondering what level of priority Ms. Peterson occupied on your list."

"Number one," Hancock said immediately.

"How come?" Vic asked.

"It was a weird one," Hancock said. "She didn't fit any profile for a runaway or a trafficking target. All that crap about sweet, innocent girls getting kidnapped by slavers? That Liam Neeson shit doesn't really happen very often. We had this one pegged as a potential series from the start."

"And yet Major Crimes only got pulled in after she got killed," Vic observed.

Hancock shrugged. "Bureaucracy," he said. "What can you do? It wasn't our call. But I was pretty sure we wouldn't find her alive."

"She was alive," Erin said. "Right up until last night."

"That's unusual," Agent Rockwell interjected. "If an abductor keeps his victim alive for a prolonged period, he's usually either torturing her or holding her for ransom. This one did neither. It was not only uncommon, it was risky. Peterson might have escaped or found a way to make herself heard. I'd like to know whether she was harmed in any way before death."

"So would I," Webb said. "O'Reilly, why don't you and I take a trip down to the morgue and see how the autopsy is coming?"

Just what I'd love to do, Erin thought. *Have a nice chat over the cut-up corpse of a murdered coed.* "Sure thing, sir," she said.

* * *

Sarah Levine's calm, clinical detachment made the morgue easier to bear. It was sort of like being in a high school science lab with a slightly weird teacher. Levine had no problem dealing with the dead; she preferred it to talking to the living.

When Webb and Erin walked in, Levine was bent over a microscope, oblivious to all else. The mortal remains of the victim lay on the stainless-steel table a short distance away. The air smelled of chemical solutions and bodily fluids.

"I was hoping we could bother you for a moment, Doctor," Webb said.

"You succeeded," Levine said. She didn't take her eyes off the specimen on her slide.

Erin smiled. Once you got used to Levine it was hard not to like her a little.

"How's the examination coming?" Webb asked.

Levine considered this question for a moment. "I estimate I am sixty-seven percent complete," she decided. "Plus or minus three percent."

"What can you tell us?" Erin asked.

"None of my findings are classified or uncertain," Levine said, continuing to stare into the scope. "No special permissions will be required."

"Summarize your findings thus far, please," Webb said, finally opting for a more direct request.

Levine straightened up and turned to face them. "I have positively identified Laurel Peterson," she said. "In spite of postmortem damage to soft tissue, facial recognition is a ninety-seven percent positive match, and fingerprints are also a match. As previously noted, she was killed at approximately midnight last night. Cause of death was strangulation with a rolled piece of silk fabric, red in color."

"Fibers?" Erin guessed.

"Correct," Levine said. "I have retrieved six red silk fibers from the victim's neck."

"Any other premortem wounds?" Webb asked.

"No," Levine said. "However, I discovered faint ligature marks on her wrists, indicating her hands were bound with another piece of red silk fabric, or possibly the same one."

"Was she tied up at time of death?" Erin asked.

"That is impossible to determine," Levine said. "But it is a valid hypothesis and would explain the lack of defensive wounds on the victim's hands and arms. Her health was otherwise good. I find no sign of malnutrition. Her stomach contained a partially digested meal of chicken, rice, and salad."

"Home cooking," Webb murmured. "That's unusual."

"She shows no signs of molestation or sexual abuse," Levine continued. "In fact, I discovered an intact hymen."

"She was a virgin?" Erin said, startled in spite of herself.

"That is a term with a variety of cultural and physiological interpretations," Levine said. "If you are using it to mean she had not participated in full sexual intercourse, you are probably correct. However, there are a variety of definitions."

"I remember the Clinton administration," Webb said dryly. "We don't need to go into that."

"I am currently examining some spores I extracted from lung tissue," Levine continued.

"Spores?" Webb said. "Mushrooms?"

"Mold," Levine said.

"Mold," Webb repeated. "What kind?"

"*Chaetomium*," Levine said as if the word was an answer anybody would understand.

"Is that bread mold?" Erin guessed.

"No."

Erin considered guessing again and gave up. "What kind of mold is it?"

"It is a genus of fungi found in the *Chaetomiaceae* family," Levine said. "The name *Chaetomium* is Latin for 'the plume of the helmet,' referring to the distinctive shape of the spore. While less well-known than *Stachybotrys*, it is likewise a hazardous contaminant."

"Less well-known than which?" Erin asked. She hadn't gotten above high-school biology class, which had taught her that mold was a type of fungus.

"*Stachybotrys* is more commonly known as black mold," Levine said.

"Copy that," Erin said. "So this... other mold is toxic, too?"

"It is an allergen," Levine said. "It can cause fatal deep infection in immunocompromised individuals. However, this victim does not show signs of dangerous infection or serious allergic reaction."

"Was it introduced deliberately?" Webb asked.

"A more likely hypothesis is environmental contamination," Levine said. "She could have unintentionally inhaled the spores from being in close proximity over a prolonged period."

"In other words, she was probably being kept in a place which had a mold colony," Erin suggested.

"That is a reasonable conclusion, supported by the available data," Levine said.

"Where would you find this mold?" Webb asked.

"In her lungs, as I have just explained," Levine said with visible irritation. "I also found traces of it under her fingernails, together with what appear to be samples of fairly well-aged concrete and cement."

Webb took a deep breath, which he immediately regretted when he drew in the morgue's unique bouquet. "I'm sorry," he said. "I was unclear. My mistake. In what location or locations in the greater New York area would I be likely to find colonies of this mold?"

"Subterranean locations are the most likely," Levine replied. "The places to seek it would be dark and damp."

Webb and Erin looked at one another. "Basement," they said in unison.

"The victim's clothing has some dirt," Levine added. "I will compare soil samples from the region of Central Park where the body was recovered."

"Her clothes looked pretty clean to me," Erin said.

"You are correct," Levine said. "I am not an expert, but I believe the clothing was laundered sometime within the past twenty-four hours."

"That doesn't make sense," Webb said. "Laurel was missing for six days."

"I guess she wasn't wearing her clothes the whole time," Erin said with a grimace.

"What about the facial injuries?" Webb asked.

"All cuts appear to have been made by the same implement," Levine said. "A very sharp blade with a slightly convex edge. Based on kerf marks on the cheekbones, I believe it was most likely a butcher's knife."

"Is our killer a cook?" Erin wondered aloud.

"That is a logical leap," Levine said. "Those blades are readily obtainable and are found in most kitchens. The facial mutilations indicate no special anatomical knowledge or surgical prowess."

"Do you have anything else to report?" Webb asked.

"Obviously," Levine said. "I am summarizing. Would you like a more detailed description?"

"You can put it in your report," Webb said hastily. "Thank you for your time, Doctor."

Levine turned away and returned to her microscope. Webb and Erin began to retreat from the morgue. They'd reached the door when Levine spoke again.

"Thank you, Lieutenant Webb," she said abruptly.

"Um, you're welcome," Webb said. "What exactly were you thanking me for?"

"Jasper Ackermann believes you saved my life when you arrested that man in the hospital supply closet some time ago," she said. "You might not remember it. He thinks I should thank you in person, so that is why I said it."

"I remember it," Webb said. "And I'm glad I got there in time. Have a pleasant day, Dr. Levine."

"I anticipate no serious hardship or difficulty," Levine replied.

Chapter 5

"This is getting weird, sir," Erin said as they rode the elevator back up to Major Crimes. "And I'm not talking about Levine's lack of social skills. I'm glad you told me about that thing in the hospital morgue when it happened, or I would've been really confused."

"We're dealing with abnormal psychology," Webb said. "If it wasn't weird, we'd be on the wrong track. And when I mention abnormal psychology, I'm not talking about Dr. Levine either."

Rolf had been waiting beside Erin's desk. She didn't like taking him into the morgue, on account of the chemicals. The Shepherd disagreed with the decision, but was too well-trained to argue. When she came in, he sat up and began vigorously wagging his tail.

"Did Levine work her magic?" Vic asked.

"Maybe," Webb said. "We have some new information."

"Excellent," Rockwell said. "Anything we can give the profiling boys will be a help."

"Our killer took care of her," Webb said. "She was well fed. Home-cooked food, not cheap takeout or TV dinners."

"A real bleeding heart," Vic said. "Right up until he strangled her and slashed up her face. Speaking of which, did you guys get a load of that tabloid bitch's scars?"

"Andy Carver?" Erin replied. "It was kind of hard to miss them."

He snickered. "It's ironic, isn't it?"

"What is?" Webb asked, poker-faced.

"A lady named Carver gets a knife dragged across her face."

"It isn't funny," Piekarski said, glaring at Vic.

"If it'd happened to a nice girl, I'd agree with you," he said. "But you saw what that skank wrote about Erin. Am I supposed to feel sorry for her?"

"Depends," Piekarski said. "What happened to her?"

"I have no idea," Vic said. "But whatever it was, it doesn't give her an excuse to drag a good cop's name through the mud."

"If we could please get back to the subject at hand?" Webb asked with exaggerated politeness.

"I thought she was relevant," Vic said. "Our killer cut up our victim's face, too. It's an interesting coincidence."

"That scar on Ms. Carver's face was old," Webb said. "It had been healed for a long time; years, I'd guess. The chances of it having been done by the same attacker are basically zero. Besides, the MO is totally different. That was one diagonal cut, delivered to a living woman. Our perp killed his girl and then went absolutely nuts with his knife. We're talking about two completely different crimes committed by different perps."

"Carver is probably interested in this case because of her own injury," Erin guessed.

"That's a good point," Rockwell said. "She might be looking for a little closure for her own past trauma. Maybe we should talk to her."

"She's a reporter, not a witness," Webb said. "And we really don't want to talk to reporters right now."

"If she knows anything, we'll find out soon enough," Vic said. "All we have to do is buy her scandal rag at the checkout counter. Hell, Zofia reads that trash anyway. Can't get enough of that worthless gossip. She can tell us."

"You really aren't planning on getting laid ever again, are you," Piekarski said.

"What?" Vic said, spreading his hands with an air of wounded innocence. "What'd I say?"

"Our victim was kept somewhere dark and damp," Webb said loudly. "She inhaled a particular type of mold spores, suggesting she may have been kept in a basement. She had bits of old concrete under her nails."

"That's a hot lead," Rockwell said.

"Yeah," Vic said. "We just need to find out which old buildings in New York have basements in them and we're home free."

"Not every basement has a mold infestation," Erin said. "That suggests water damage. Maybe the basement in question was flooded at some point."

"Good thing we're not on an island," Vic said, dripping sarcasm. "Or that wouldn't be helpful at all."

"Hurricane Sandy," Erin said, snapping her fingers. "It flooded a bunch of buildings back in 2012, especially in Brooklyn."

"Yeah," Vic said. "Brighton Beach got hit hard. You think that's where our girl was kept?"

"It's a possibility," Webb said. "But that isn't the only neighborhood with flooding problems. It might've been something more local, even a simple thing like a burst pipe. I don't think that narrows it down very much."

"Every little bit helps," Rockwell said. Willard was busily scribbling the update onto the whiteboard.

"How soon will the boys at Quantico update that fancy profile of theirs?" Vic asked.

"I'll get them what we've gathered immediately," Rockwell said. "We have our best psych guys on it. Don't worry. Organized serial killers don't go straight from one victim to the next. There's usually a cyclic aspect to their hunting. Sometimes it's tied to moon cycles. Some people think that's where the idea of werewolves came from: psychopaths hunting at the full moon and mutilating their victims. Peasants thought it must be some sort of beast-man."

"Werewolves," Vic repeated flatly, giving the FBI agent a look.

"I didn't say they *were* werewolves," Rockwell said. "I said that may be where the legends originated. Don't you have any interest in history or mythology?"

"I'm a little more interested in the murderer running around present-day New York," Vic said. "I don't really give a crap what Medieval peasants would have thought. Those guys believed you could keep the plague away by burning incense or some shit. They didn't know a damn thing."

"They understood the timing element," Rockwell said, undeterred. "My point is that we have a window before the next victim is taken. You know the word 'lunatic' refers to the moon. People have believed the cycles of the moon have an effect on abnormal psychology for a very long time. It'll probably be at least two or three weeks, maybe a month or more, before we have another victim. We'll have plenty of time to collate our data."

"That's comforting," Piekarski said. "But wouldn't it be nice to catch this guy before he snatches another girl?"

"He kidnaps her," Webb said thoughtfully, staring at the whiteboard. "He holds her several days, but doesn't abuse or torture her, at least not in any way that leaves a mark. He feeds her. He washes her clothes. Then he strangles her, hacks her up, and dumps her in the park. This doesn't make sense. What need is he fulfilling?"

"Dominance," Rockwell said. "Dominance and control, like I said. It probably gets him off having complete control over his victim. He may not even need to touch her. Just knowing he could if he wanted to, that's intoxicating to a certain type of personality. I've been reading up on the Heartbreaker Killer."

"We know about him," Erin said dryly.

Rockwell grinned. "I know you do. That was excellent work, catching him the way you did. You'll recall he didn't assault his victims, didn't even touch them more than he had to. He posed them and photographed them. The really unusual thing about him was that he used poison. Our typical subjects are much more likely to use blades or strangulation, like our current unsub."

"The personal touch," Vic said.

"Precisely," Rockwell said. "If I had to guess, I'd say our unsub is a seriously repressed personality. He kept his victim as long as he could stand it, just watching her, psyching himself up. Then he finally touched her. Maybe he didn't even intended to kill her, but once he started he got carried away. He choked her to death, and once he realized she was dead, he went completely berserk. We don't see any signs of anger until after she was dead. Then we see the rage coming out."

"Maybe he felt bad about it afterward," Piekarski said. "That might make him stop. Maybe he won't do it again."

Erin, Webb, and Rockwell were all shaking their heads.

"That won't matter," Rockwell said. "A lot of these guys know what they're doing is wrong. They feel guilty, but the rush is what matters. It'll overwhelm everything else. Our guy will tell himself next time will be different, better. He'll watch another girl and convince himself she'll be the one, not the girl he just killed. He may already be stalking her."

"You said he wouldn't do anything for weeks!" Piekarski said.

"I said he wouldn't kill for weeks," Rockwell said. "The cycle's already started again. But this guy is patient. He'll need time to stake out a new victim, learn her patterns, figure out how to take her. I'm telling you, we have some time."

"I guess you guys know what you're talking about," Vic said doubtfully.

"We have decades of experience dealing with this sort of unsub," Rockwell said with a confident smile.

Later that night, sitting at the counter at the Barley Corner, Erin remembered that smile when the TV news update popped up saying Valerie Richards, sixteen, had vanished from a bowling alley in Brooklyn.

* * *

"I'm thinking copycat," Vic said as they hurried across the parking lot. "Or maybe people are panicking and calling in stuff they shouldn't."

Erin shook her head and didn't say anything. She'd been looking forward to a quiet night with her fiancé. Instead she'd seen the breaking news in the middle of a European soccer game on the Barley Corner's TV. She'd already been halfway to her car when Webb had called.

The bowling alley was thronged with squad cars, harried Patrol officers, and New Yorkers. The sun hadn't quite gone down and the blue and red flashers blazed luridly against the sunset. The TV reporters had their spotlights in place and were talking to their cameras with serious expressions stamped on their faces.

The overlapping chatter of dozens of voices added to the confusion. Rolf stuck close to Erin's leg, panting. The K-9 was no stranger to chaos, but he didn't love bright lights and loud noises. He figured he'd keep a close eye on his partner. She always seemed to know what to do.

Erin flashed her gold shield to the ranking Sergeant, who waved them through the cordon of blue uniforms into the building. Like every bowling alley she'd ever been in, it was dimly lit and smelled funky from sweaty feet, spilled beer, and old cigarette smoke from the days when smoking had been allowed.

They found Webb already on scene, which wasn't surprising. He lived in Brooklyn, only a couple of miles away. The Lieutenant was talking to a group of teenage girls. They kept interrupting one another, which was hard to understand at the best of times, and all of them were crying, which only made it worse.

"One at a time, please," Webb said wearily. "Ashley, you were the last one to see Valerie?"

The girl on the left nodded. Her mascara was running down her cheeks. "Val went to the bathroom," she said. "She didn't come out, but we didn't notice right away. It was because of the boys."

"Which boys?" Vic asked, stepping into the conversation beside his commander.

"Those boys," another girl said, pointing to a cluster of adolescent males who were standing awkwardly to one side. "Kayla was flirting with them."

"I was not!" Girl Number Three said indignantly. "Well, maybe I was, a little, but so were you!"

"No, I wasn't!" Girl Number Two retorted. "I just didn't want you to embarrass yourself!"

"Ladies, please," Webb said. "So Valerie went to the restroom. When was this?"

"I don't know," Kayla said.

Neither did any of the others. After a brief discussion, they agreed it had been about seven o'clock.

Erin and Vic exchanged looks. It was now after eight. An hour was a very long time in a situation like this.

"She could be in friggin' Jersey by now," Vic muttered under his breath.

"We thought she was, maybe, throwing up or something," Ashley said.

"You thought that," Courtney said. "I thought it was her, you know... that time."

"I went to check on her," Girl Number Four said quietly. "But she wasn't there."

"You checked the entire ladies' room?" Webb asked. "And she wasn't anywhere inside? What was your name again? Jill?"

Jill nodded unhappily. "It was empty," she said.

"And you're sure that was where she went?" Webb asked.

"I saw her go," Ashley said.

"You saw her go into the restroom?" Webb pressed. "You need to be sure."

Ashley hesitated. "She went into the hallway," she said. "You can't see the ladies' room from where we were. She didn't come back this way."

Webb nodded to Erin. "Check it out," he said.

"Do any of you girls have anything of Valerie's?" Erin asked. "Clothing, lipstick, anything like that?"

"They've got her shoes at the counter," Jill suggested.

"Perfect!" Erin said. She walked quickly to the counter where the bowling alley attendant was only too eager to help. In a moment she and Rolf were on their way to the restroom hallway, armed with one of Valerie's sneakers.

There weren't many options. Two restrooms, one for men and one for women; a locked maintenance closet; and an emergency exit. Erin knelt next to Rolf and held the shoe in front of his snout.

"*Such!*" she said, letting him get a good long sniff.

Rolf's nostrils twitched. He inhaled, filling his olfactory receptors with Valerie's scent. His ears perked up and his tail started wagging. The girl's trail was fresh and ran straight in front of him. It was almost insultingly easy, but Rolf wasn't about to complain. He trotted forward without hesitation, snuffling happily.

He angled to the restroom. Erin paused long enough to pull on a pair of disposable gloves. "NYPD!" she called. Then she pushed the door open.

Another female officer was inside, standing watch. It made sense. They'd have to treat the restroom as an active crime scene, and it was important to prevent contamination by ignorant civilians. Rolf paid no attention to the Patrolwoman, making his way to the first stall. He sniffed the floor for a moment, angling his ears forward intently. Then he spun on his paws and went straight back out again. This time he turned the other way, toward the exit.

The door had a metal bar across it with a sign that said an alarm would sound if the door was opened. But Rolf shoved his nose against the crack at the bottom of the door and snuffled loudly a couple of times. Then he scratched at the door with his claws and barked, just in case his partner hadn't gotten the message.

"Find anything?" Vic asked, coming down the hallway after them.

"Rolf says she went this way," Erin said.

"Those girls didn't say anything about an alarm," he said. "Maybe the door was wedged open?"

"Someone probably would've noticed," she said. "Maybe the alarm was disabled."

"Only one way to find out," he said.

Before Erin could tell him what a bad idea it was, he reached out and shoved the crossbar. At least he was wearing gloves too. She cringed, expecting the strident blare of the alarm. But there was only a metallic click as the latch disengaged. The door swung open, revealing an empty alley.

Rolf plunged through the doorway eagerly. He started to the left. Then he froze, one paw raised, testing the air. He circled, sniffing more urgently. He whined softly and looked over his shoulder at Erin.

"Damn it," Erin said, disappointed but not surprised. "She got in a car."

Vic was on one knee, examining the door. "Someone monkeyed with this," he said. "Someone with electrician skills. Looks like a bypass got soldered onto the wires. Then they cut the originals."

"I didn't know you knew wiring," Erin said, peering over his shoulder. She took Rolf's rubber Kong ball out of her pocket and tossed it to him to soothe the pain of losing the trail. The Shepherd cheered up immediately and settled into his routine of happy gnawing.

"A little," Vic said. "This isn't Jason Bourne-level shit. But you gotta know what you're doing or you'll set off the alarm."

"How long would it take?" she asked.

He shrugged. "Not too long. Half an hour, maybe, or an hour."

"But you couldn't do that while the alley was open," she said. "Somebody would notice."

"Absolutely," he said. "We'd better check with the guys who work here. But I'm betting this was done last night at the latest. What're you thinking?"

"You don't want to know."

Vic rolled his eyes. "You're right. I don't want to know. That's why I asked, because I didn't want an answer."

Erin laid out the points on her fingers. "This wasn't a random thing; it was set up in advance. That means it's an abduction, not a runaway or a misunderstanding. This was definitely deliberate. And if it's our same attacker, and he did it at least a day ago…"

"Then he did it while Laurel Peterson was still alive," Vic said. "Holy shit, he was already setting up his next snatch before he'd even finished with the last one. That's not good."

Erin held up her fourth finger. "And that means either we're dealing with a methodical monster who works like murder is a damn assembly line, which means either the FBI guys are totally wrong about his cycle, or we've got two of these bastards on the loose."

Chapter 6

Victim notifications were one of the worst jobs a cop could have. To have to be the one to tell a wife, a husband, a parent, or a child that they'd never see a loved one again was absolutely awful. Erin could remember every face she'd ever seen in those moments, the look in every eye as the light went out of it.

But this was worse, because it was ambiguous. Anguish and grief were bad; when you coupled that pain with faint, desperate hope, it was almost unbearable.

It had to be done, for reasons that had as much to do with good policing as with human decency. Erin and Webb were the ones visiting the Richards house. Vic and Piekarski had stayed at the bowling alley to coordinate with the CSU techs, continue talking to witnesses, and hopefully dig up a useful lead.

Bob and Carol Richards lived in a brick townhouse on 71st Street. It was exactly the sort of working-class dwelling Erin had grown up in. Mr. Richards was a contractor who specialized in water damage. His wife was an aide at a preschool. They struck Erin as ordinary, decent, hardworking folks. Now they were sitting together on their couch, huddled against one another, holding hands. Carol's eyes were puffy. Bob looked stunned, like he'd just been hit in the face with a wrench.

"We'll have a counselor coming to help you through this," Webb said. "We'll be monitoring your telephone lines, in case anyone contacts you. I would strongly advise you not to talk to anyone in the media about this, or to anyone outside your family. We don't yet know what's going on, and anyone you don't know may not have your family's best interests at heart."

"But she's been taken," Carol said. "That's what they said on the news. By the... by that awful person who... who took the Peterson girl. The... the Central Park Strangler. Oh, God."

"It's way too early to say that, ma'am," Webb said. "We don't even know for sure if Valerie's been abducted. We're doing our very best to find her. I need you to tell me exactly what happened this evening."

"Val went bowling," Bob said quietly. His voice was flat, almost emotionless. He was staring straight ahead, not even looking at Erin or Webb. "It's Ashley Rehnquist's birthday. Ashley and Val have been friends since kindergarten. They've gone to that alley dozens of times. It's a safe neighborhood. She wasn't alone. This shouldn't have happened."

"Ashley told me they met at the alley at six," Webb said. "Valerie drove there in your car. That's a blue Hyundai Elantra, correct?"

"Yes," Bob said. "She borrowed the car. She's an excellent driver. Never had a ticket."

"Who knew she was going to be at the alley tonight?" Erin asked.

"All the girls," Carol said. "Ashley and Courtney and Kayla and... and..."

"Jill," Bob added.

"Yes, Jill," Carol said. "But they probably told other people at school. And maybe online."

"Does your daughter have her own computer?" Erin asked. "Or does she use yours?"

"She has her phone," Bob said. "We have a home computer we share. It's in my study."

"Could we see it, please?" Erin asked.

"Of course." Bob stood up, mechanically disentangling his fingers from his wife's.

"Would you like some coffee?" Carol suddenly asked.

"We don't need anything, ma'am," Webb said. "But I can get you something if you'd like."

Carol also got up. "It's my kitchen," she said. "You don't know your way around. It'll be quicker if I do it."

"You don't have to—" Webb began.

"Let me do this!" Carol snapped with sudden ferocity. "Let me do this one damn thing so I don't have to sit here like a lump! My daughter's in trouble and... and... she might be... be..."

Her anger dissolved into tears. Bob and Erin both stepped toward her, but Mrs. Richards fled into the kitchen, sobbing.

"I'll show you the computer," Bob said dully.

Bob powered up the computer, while Erin and Webb looked over his shoulder. Rolf lurked next to Erin. The Shepherd didn't understand technology and didn't want to. At Erin's direction, Bob opened the web browser and brought up the site history.

"Do you know what websites Valerie visits?" she asked.

"No," he said. "We trust her. I've never even checked on her before."

Erin exchanged glances with Webb and said nothing. In the twenty-first century, parents were well advised to keep tabs on the online activities of their children, but this wasn't a good time to say so. It would sound like victim-blaming.

"There," Erin said, pointing. "Looks like she's on social media. Let's see if she stays logged in."

Apparently familial trust went both ways, because Valerie's account was set up to stay active. They didn't need a password. The site opened, showing a flurry of posts and messages between Valerie and dozens of classmates and friends.

"What are you looking for?" Bob asked.

"Anybody who might have been talking to her," Webb said. "Do you recognize these people?"

"Which ones?" Bob replied, obviously bewildered. "There's got to be hundreds of folks here. I recognize some of the names, I guess, but Val's probably never met half of them herself. I don't really pay attention to that sort of thing. I'm not good with computers."

"May I?" Webb asked, stepping forward.

"Help yourself." Bob pushed his chair back from the desk.

Webb leaned over the keyboard and began scanning Valerie's recent activities. Erin looked at Bob. He was clearly lost.

"Why don't you go into the kitchen and check on your wife?" she suggested. "The best thing you can do right now is take care of her. Your family needs you, Mr. Richards. I know it's hard, but you have to stay strong. They're counting on you."

He nodded and swallowed. "That's my little girl out there," he said in a hoarse whisper. "Can you find her?"

"We're going to do everything we can," Erin promised. It was a weak offer, but the only one she could make. You never promised results, only effort. That was one of the first things you learned on the street. For all she knew, Valerie was already dead and it wouldn't matter what they did.

After Bob had left, Webb took his chair and continued his scrutiny of Valerie's online activities. Erin watched for a few minutes.

"Anything?" she asked.

"I don't know," Webb sighed. "It'll take time to tease any leads out of this. Jesus, look. There's already fifteen messages from people asking if she's okay in the last ten minutes alone. That'll be because of the news. It'll be a hundred by morning. Anything useful is going to get lost in the background noise. We'll need one of our computer guys to go through this. But I don't think they'll find anything."

"They didn't get anything off Laurel's electronic devices," Erin said. "But maybe they can find a common thread between the girls."

"I hope so," Webb said. "Because we're on a clock."

"We should have several days," Erin said softly. "If this is the same guy, he'll probably work within his pattern."

"We can't count on it," he replied. "Guys like him tend to escalate. And who knows what may happen. Nobody expected him to move this fast with a second victim."

"Something's wrong here," Erin said.

"You're stating the painfully obvious," Webb said.

"No, I mean with the way this guy operates," Erin said. "A pattern killer who starts on a second victim before he's done with his first? That doesn't happen. And this was premeditated. It's too smooth, too organized."

"What's your theory?" Webb asked.

She shook her head. "I don't have one. I don't know these guys' psychology. I've only met a couple of them and I don't understand them. But I think... maybe killing isn't the point for this guy."

"You think it's the captivity?" Webb asked. "Holding them helpless?"

"Maybe," Erin said. "God, I hate this. I feel so damn helpless."

He turned away from the computer to look directly at her. "You're not," he said. "You're a Detective First Grade with the

New York Police Department. You have the best training the city can provide and a dozen years of street experience. You carry two guns, a gold shield, and one end of a leash. At the other end is the best K-9 I've ever seen. You have over thirty thousand officers at your back and the immense power of the Department ready to be wielded. Don't you *ever* tell me there's nothing you can do, because it's not true. Do you get me, Detective?"

"Copy that, sir," Erin said, startled and embarrassed.

"Good," Webb said more gently. "Because this guy wants us to feel helpless. He gets off on being in control. You, Neshenko, Piekarski, and I are going to show him he isn't. We're going to take control back and watch him fall on his face. And we're going to do it in time to save Valerie Richards."

"We can't promise that," she said.

"I'm not telling the family," he said grimly. "I'm telling you."

*   *   *

"Nobody saw nothin'," Vic said, rolling his eyes. "No creepy men. No men by themselves, except a couple alley regulars, and the owner swears they're harmless old dudes. And forget about her phone. We tried pinging it, no answer. It's turned off or broken."

Erin, Webb, and Rolf had returned to the bowling alley. It was full dark now, but that hardly mattered between the police flashers and the TV spotlights. A CSU team was swarming all over the building. Cops and newspeople were everywhere. The detectives had retreated inside and were meeting in the arcade. The electronic explosions and blinking lights provided the closest thing to privacy they could get.

"Security cameras?" Webb asked.

Piekarski shook her head. "They only turn them on after hours," she said. "And the owner swears nobody was messing with the emergency exit over the past week."

"Check the footage yourself," Webb said.

"I'll look," Piekarski said. "But they erase it after three days if they haven't had an incident."

"Check the past three days, then," Webb insisted. "I'm not taking some random civilian's word on this. Go."

"Copy that, sir." Piekarski headed toward the manager's office.

"She won't find anything," Erin predicted. "Just like CSU won't."

"You seem awfully sure of yourself," Webb said. "Why?"

"Can't you feel it?" she replied. "This guy's careful. I don't think he leaves evidence."

"Everybody leaves evidence," Webb said. "You're familiar with the principle of transference. It's the first law of—"

"First law of forensics," Erin finished for him. "Yes, sir. I know. But remember the Peterson kidnapping? No eyewitnesses saw anything out of the ordinary and that was on a Manhattan sidewalk in the middle of the afternoon! CSU went over her backpack with a damn microscope and they didn't find a thing."

"We got fibers off the victim's throat," Webb reminded her. "We know the murder weapon."

"Okay, great," she said. "Once we get a suspect, maybe we'll find a red silk scarf and match the fibers. Then we can burn his ass. But that doesn't do us much good if we can't find him. The clock's ticking. We have six days, maximum, before Valerie's dead."

"I'm well aware," Webb said. "I'm also thinking about how our killer chooses his victims. Let's assume, for the moment, that this abduction and the Peterson killing were done by the same perp. What do they have in common?"

"They're good-looking blondes," Vic said. He pointed to the TV screens that hung above the bowling lanes. Every one of them had Valerie Richards's photo staring back at them. The girl was long-haired, blue-eyed, and strikingly attractive.

"Thanks for stating the obvious," Erin said. "But Valerie's still in high school. Laurel was a college student. One was snatched off Columbia campus, the other down here in Brooklyn. We retrieved Laurel's phone, but Valerie's is missing. One kidnapping happened in broad daylight, the other in the evening. Laurel was alone, Valerie was out with friends."

"Yes, she was," Webb said. "She shouldn't have been vulnerable."

"I dunno," Vic said. "I wouldn't be scared of four sixteen-year-old girls."

"Then you're an idiot," Erin said. "Teenage girls can be vicious."

"Our perp waited until she was by herself," Webb said. "Taking a bathroom break. Then he nipped inside and grabbed her."

"I thought he was waiting in the bathroom," Vic said.

"No," Erin said. "Even if he looks harmless, a guy can't loiter in the ladies' room."

"Of course not," Vic said. "But then how did he know she was going to take a piss?"

"He had to have eyes inside the alley," Erin said. "Or he was here the whole time."

"Nobody was here," Vic said. "I talked to every single customer and employee. Nobody left except by the front door. And I told you, there weren't any creepy dudes."

"Vic, not all kidnappers look like drooling lunatics," Erin said. "Some of them look like ordinary people."

"I know that," he said, glaring at her. "I specifically asked him about guys hanging around solo or watching the girls.

That's what I meant by creepy. Let's face it, our boy isn't going out bowling with his local league. Guys like this are loners."

"He's right," Webb said. "But I think you're right too, O'Reilly. He may have had some sort of surveillance device inside the alley. If so, CSU will find it."

"Maybe," Erin said doubtfully.

"This guy's a friggin' ghost," Vic said. "How do you grab a girl off a New York street with nobody noticing? I know New Yorkers don't give a crap about random happening, but once the cops start asking questions, somebody should've seen *something*."

"O'Reilly, take a walk outside," Webb said. "Take your K-9. Canvass the area."

"We already tried," Erin said. "Our girl got in a car out back. There's no trail."

"But that wasn't the first time our perp was here," Webb said. "You were tracking our victim last time. Try looking for the kidnapper."

"We'll give it a go," she said. "If I can explain to Rolf what we're looking for."

*   *   *

It was hopeless. Erin knew it. Rolf knew it. Webb probably did, too. But when you didn't have good options, you went with the bad ones. They needed a break. Maybe the chances of getting it were one in a thousand, but as long as they weren't zero, you might as well try.

Rolf snuffled his way around the back of the bowling alley. Erin saw only old brick, scraggly bits of grass and weeds, and litter. To Rolf's nose the place was much more interesting; fascinating, even. A cigarette butt wasn't just a discarded scrap of charred paper to him. He could smell the ashes, the leftover nicotine, and most interesting of all, the human lips that had sucked on the cancer stick. To a dog, a back alley was a wonderland. He could have happily spent hours there on an olfactory odyssey.

But he had a job to do, so he did his best. All sorts of people had been here. His partner wanted him to track a particular one. But he couldn't tell which. The human scents were all mixed up. Men, women, children. He tried to tease out the most excited or upset smells. Humans gave off a different scent when they were keyed up, and he'd learned those were usually the people he was supposed to follow. He worked his way to one end of the alley, turned, and started back the way he'd come. His tail wagged hopefully. Rolf wasn't a quitter.

When Erin saw the other woman leaning casually against the wall, she nearly jumped out of her shoes. The media circus was out front, along with the light show, so the alley was illuminated only by a single yellow streetlamp and the dull crimson of the EXIT light. All she saw was a female silhouette, less than fifteen feet away.

Erin didn't waste time or breath swearing. She sprang to one side on instinct, in case the other woman was aiming a weapon, and grabbed her own pistol. The Glock came out and up. Rolf, his attention pulled away from his nose, froze in an alert posture, anticipating his "bite" command.

The woman straightened and clapped her hands slowly; three soft, sardonic claps. "Good reflexes," she said. "You want to put that toy away before you hurt someone?"

"Keep your hands where I can see them," Erin said, keeping the gun level, sighting on her target's center of mass. "Identify yourself."

"You're pretty jumpy, Detective O'Reilly," the woman went on. "Not what I'd expect from someone with nerves of steel. That's what the article in *Time* said about you. I'm sure you read it. *Respectable* people read *Time*, after all. I bet even Mom and Dad have a copy. Did you send them one?"

"I'm not playing games," Erin said through gritted teeth. "Don't jerk me around. How'd you get through the police perimeter?"

"Those jokers?" The woman took a step toward her. "They couldn't keep out a drunken hobo."

"That's close enough," Erin said. "I'm going to ask you again to ID yourself."

"You don't know me? I'm hurt. I know you. We met recently. But then, you're a lot more famous than I am. You've had your picture in the paper. I guess, to be fair, your pic's a lot nicer to look at than mine."

"Andy Carver." The name came out as a growl.

"There!" Andy laughed. "That wasn't so hard, was it? Of course, you're a detective, so I shouldn't be surprised."

"What are you doing here?"

"I heard another sweet young thing had gone missing," Andy said. "I'm following the story, just like my colleagues out front. I saw you nip around back and thought, where Erin O'Reilly is, that's where the story's going to be. So here I am. How's the investigation going?"

"You know damn well I'm not going to tell you that," Erin said. She slowly lowered the Glock and returned it to its holster.

"You can't blame a girl for asking." Andy was close enough now that the red light shone on her face. The terrible scar showed as a black gash. Her eyes were sunken in shadow, but there was an eager gleam in them. "I could help, you know."

"If you have information about either disappearance, you can contact the NYPD," Erin said. "We have a hotline. Any assistance you can provide will be gratefully received."

"Does a case like this hit you harder?" Andy asked. "Being female? Do killers who target women have a particular meaning for you? Like the Heartbreaker Killer?"

"Are you doing another hit piece on me?" Erin retorted.

"You're still mad about 'Going to the Mattresses,' I see," Andy said.

Erin said nothing.

"Sex sells," Andy said. "And you have to admit, it was as much your fault as mine."

"Yeah," Erin said. Sarcasm dripped from her tongue. "I held you down and forced you to write that bullshit."

"Was it bullshit?" Andy replied. "What did I say that wasn't true? If you can provide information debunking anything I wrote, I'll be happy to type a retraction."

"That isn't the point," Erin said angrily. "That wasn't news. Half of what was going on was an undercover police operation. The other half was my personal life. You had no right to write any of it!"

"The right to write," Andy said, chuckling softly. "I like that. You have a way with words. Did you ever think about writing some of this down? People would pay for your memoirs. I could put you in touch with a publisher."

"No thanks. Nobody would want to read it anyway."

"That's where you're wrong." Andy smiled. "People want to see their heroes being human. They want to know what's under your skin, the skeletons in your closet."

"Tough," Erin said. "The whole point of skeletons is that they stay hidden. That's why we have skin."

"We also have X-rays," Andy replied. "You're a public servant. You're empowered to arrest citizens, even to kill them. That's a lot of power. You're held to a higher standard. People should know the truth about you."

"Is that what you care about?" Erin shot back. "The truth? You're an entertainer, not a historian."

"Of course I am," Andy said. "What do you think the news is? It's all entertainment. You think people give a damn about the truth? These days they've got their pick of news channels and papers, so they pick the ones that'll tell them what they want to hear. It doesn't matter if it's *true* or not. Who cares? Of course we sex up our stories. Otherwise, nobody would read them. These days you have to work pretty hard to shock people. And that's the way the men in charge want it, so why fight it?"

"You're almost cynical enough to be a cop," Erin said. "What's your stake in this?"

"I told you. I'm chasing the story."

"So I'm supposed to believe it's just a coincidence?" Erin replied. "Our first victim's face and the scar on yours? And the way you assumed this had some personal significance for me? This is personal, all right, but it's personal for you, not me."

Andy's hand came up, her fingertips tracing the terrible gash that bisected her face. "It's funny," she said. "Hardly anyone asks me about it, or even mentions it. Everyone critiques a woman's appearance, but sport one of these and, all of a sudden, you're invisible. Not only don't they talk about it, they don't see you at all. They look *around* you. Take away a woman's looks and you take away the woman."

"Do you think that's what Laurel Peterson's killer was trying to do?" Erin asked. "Make her invisible? Wipe away the guilt of what he'd done to her?"

"That's an interesting theory," Andy said. "Don't worry, I won't write it. I don't traffic in speculation. But I'd love to know what the FBI profilers have to say. They'll probably figure it's fulfilling some dark, twisted, deep-rooted sexual fantasy. It's always about sex with those guys. They're all a bunch of Freudians."

"And here I thought it was the tabloids that were all about sex," Erin said with a thin smile. She was surprised how much she was enjoying this conversation now. She had to remind herself this woman was the enemy.

Andy laughed. It was a natural, pleasant laugh, in spite of her mocking smile. Erin realized the scar was what made her look like she was sneering. It was almost impossible to read a genuine expression on her face.

"That's a fair point," the reporter said. "The pot's calling the kettle black. But the kettle *is* black, isn't it?"

"How did you get your scar?" Erin asked abruptly. "When did it happen?"

"You think it was done by the same guy who did the Peterson girl? It wasn't."

"But it was done by a guy," Erin guessed.

"You could say that." Andy wasn't laughing anymore.

"Tell me about it," Erin said. She knew she didn't really have time for this, that she ought to be concentrating on Valerie Richards, but part of what made her a detective was the urge to pull on loose threads. Even if they were from the wrong piece of fabric altogether.

"Have you ever been raped?" Andy asked.

"What? No!"

"Don't sound so shocked. According to RAINN, that's the Rape, Abuse, and Incest National Network, one in six American women are victims of attempted or actual rape. Roll a die. If it comes up one, it's your turn. Believe it or not, I do look at actual data. Assumptions are the mother of all fuckups."

"Well, I haven't been," Erin said. "Lucky me."

"There's still time," Andy said coldly. "But you're a cop, so you've met plenty of women who haven't been so lucky. Now you've met another."

"Did we get him?" Erin asked. "The guy who attacked you?"

Andy shook her head. "No, and you won't. It was too long ago."

"The statute of limitations is twenty years," Erin said. "Longer if you were a minor when it happened. We could still go after him."

"Wow. You really are an idealist. How could I possibly prove it? There's no medical evidence. No DNA samples. No pictures. No eyewitnesses. Just he said, she said. Reasonable doubt."

"He cut your face," Erin said. "Don't you at least want to try—"

"I never said that," Andy said sharply. "I was a pretty girl. Beautiful, even, if you can believe it. Once upon a time."

Erin could. Under the scar, Andy had the bone structure of a model. Her eyes were remarkable in their intensity. The woman could still smolder if she set her mind to it.

Andy shrugged. "Lots of girls want to be beautiful. They like the attention. Until they learn what it means. I managed okay until senior year of high school. Then a guy on the football team noticed me. He caught me outside the locker room after practice. I said no, but he didn't listen. He said I was asking for it, wearing that makeup and that skirt."

Erin was aware of her hand curling into a fist. Rolf glanced up at her, wondering who he ought to bite. He was definitely getting a biting vibe off his partner, but didn't have a target.

"He was right," Andy went on. "That was the real hell of it. I had been asking for it."

"That's not true," Erin said. "You can't blame yourself. It was his fault."

Andy's mouth twisted into its sardonic smile. "Really? Then why was I hanging around outside the boys' locker room, wearing too little skirt and too much eyeshadow? I knew what could happen. I just didn't believe it would happen to me."

"You were just a kid," Erin said.

"That's true," Andy said. "I was a kid when he dragged me into that bathroom. I came out a woman. I was crying. He just laughed and said I wasn't half bad and maybe we'd do it again sometime. So I went home, threw up in the toilet, washed my face, got my dad's folding razor, and made sure he'd never want to come after me again. Nobody would."

Erin stared at her. "Jesus," she murmured. "You did that to *yourself*?"

"It didn't hurt as much as I expected," Andy said calmly. "I guess I was in shock. There, Detective O'Reilly. Now you know a skeleton in my closet. You can even see the bone if you look close enough. I bet your fling with that mob boss seems like kind of small potatoes by comparison."

"It's not a fling," Erin said absently.

"Oh, of course," Andy said. "My mistake. You're getting married. Congratulations. Is he good to you?"

"He's a perfect gentleman," Erin said.

"What would he do if you ever said no to him?"

"He'd accept it."

"You really believe that?"

Erin looked her in the eye. "I do," she said. "Not every man is like that jock douchebag."

"That's where you're wrong," Andy said, matching her stare. "Haven't you been paying attention? Look at Laurel Peterson. Look at Valerie Richards. Look what happens to nice girls who try to say no."

"What are you saying?" Erin countered. "Laurel's dead because she should've said yes?"

"I'm saying the world gets us all, one way or another," Andy replied. "Good, bad, everyone gets dragged down in the end."

"That's a pretty hopeless philosophy."

"This from a street cop," Andy said. "Do you really find a lot of optimism out there, among the bodies?"

Erin was spared having to answer that by the buzz of her phone. She stepped back from the reporter and fished it out, seeing Webb's name on the screen.

"O'Reilly," she said.

"Are you in the middle of something?" Webb asked.

Erin glanced at Andy. "Nothing I'd be sorry to set aside."

"Meet us out front. We have a lead."

Erin felt a thrill at the words, and more at the tone in her commander's voice. He really believed they had something.

"On my way, sir," she said, hanging up the phone and dropping it back into her pocket.

"Duty calls?" Andy asked with her sardonic smile.

"No comment," Erin said over her shoulder. She was already moving. The reporter could wait until later, or preferably never.

Chapter 7

"I just heard from the FBI," Webb said as Erin drove out of the bowling alley's parking lot. He was riding with her. Vic and Piekarski were sharing Vic's Taurus.

"Where are we going?" Erin asked.

"Not far. Our guy's right here in Brooklyn. I'll bring up the address."

The apartment Webb directed her to was less than a mile away. It would only take a couple of minutes to get there. Webb spent the brief ride talking to Dispatch, bringing ESU into the loop.

"Fifteen minutes?" Webb said in answer to Dispatch's time estimate. He sighed. "Yeah, I know. That's pretty good response time. Send them."

"Do we really need a tactical team?" Erin asked as he hung up.

"He could have a teenage girl in there with him," Webb replied. "This could turn into a hostage situation. We don't want to take more chances than we have to. You're coming up on it now. Don't park in front. Go on past and stop around the corner."

Erin obeyed. She concentrated on driving while Webb eyeballed the building. Vic and Piekarski followed suit, parking behind the Charger. The detectives congregated out of sight of the target building.

"Who is this punk?" Vic asked.

"Ethan Warburton," Webb said. "He's a facilities worker at Columbia, commutes across the river."

"So he'd be in close proximity to both our victims," Erin said.

"He lives alone," Webb went on. "No pets, even. He has three complaints filed against him by female students."

"Jesus Christ," Vic said. "How does this guy still have a job?"

"None of the complaints involved physical contact," Webb explained. "Not even conversation. They just said he gave them the creeps, hanging around and staring. The university couldn't prove anything and..."

"Let me guess, sir," Piekarski said. "They were worried about getting sued for wrongful termination."

"Precisely."

"They're gonna be looking at a big goddamn lawsuit if this jerk turns out to be our guy," Vic said.

"That's not enough for a warrant," Erin said. "What else do we have?"

"He's a perfect match for the FBI profile," Webb said. "He comes from a broken home and grew up in foster care, where he may have been abused. He has a job that puts him in close proximity to young women. He's blue-collar. He's polite when he talks, but very shy and withdrawn. He's a little OCD. He has a basement apartment."

"Isn't that all circumstantial?" Erin asked. "I mean, I want him to be our guy too, but this is a little thin."

Webb smiled wryly at his favorite descriptive phrase being turned around on him. "There's one more thing," he said. "Agent

Rockwell told me this in confidence, but it's enough for a sealed warrant. The Feds are engaged in an online child-pornography sting, nationwide. They don't want to make any noise about it until they're ready to drop the hammer on everyone at once, but he tipped me off."

"Our suspect likes looking at pics of underage girls?" Erin guessed.

"He's on their list," Webb said.

Vic ground his teeth so hard that Erin heard it from five feet away. The big Russian abruptly turned away and popped the trunk of the Taurus. He took out his body armor and strapped it on with quick, savage motions. Then he picked up his M4 assault rifle and began giving it a once-over.

"That son of a bitch," Piekarski said quietly. She joined Vic and donned her own Kevlar vest.

"You'd better suit up, too," Webb said to Erin. "And your dog."

"So should you, sir," she said. "Remember those Russians who ambushed you that one time?"

"I'm unlikely to forget," Webb said. "That buckshot cost me a good trench coat."

"Bullshit, sir," Vic said. "We all saw that coat. It wasn't good to begin with."

"It had sentimental value," Webb said.

"We could go in now," Vic said. "Hit him fast and hard. The asshole won't know what's coming. I say we don't even knock. Just take the door. I could have him down and in cuffs fifteen seconds after we breach. And if I don't, Erin's dog will."

"No," Webb said firmly. "We wait for ESU."

"This guy's a friggin' janitor!" Vic argued. "He's not some special-forces Green Beret Rambo wannabe. He probably doesn't even have a gun!"

"That'd play great at your Departmental funeral," Webb said. "We'll put it on your tombstone. Last words: 'The killer probably doesn't even have a gun.'"

"I've taken down worse guys than this two at a time," Vic grumbled.

"We wait," Webb repeated.

*　　*　　*

It was really only a few minutes until Lieutenant Lewis and his ESU squad arrived, but it felt longer. They rolled up in their Lenco Bearcat, the most fearsome vehicle in the NYPD motor pool.

"Nice and subtle," Vic commented as the hulking armored behemoth came to a stop at the street corner. "Low-key."

Officers in heavy armor and helmets piled out of the Bearcat. One of the smaller men jogged across the street and disappeared into the shadows, lugging a long-barreled rifle. The rest of the ESU guys formed up around the Major Crimes squad.

"Lieutenant," Webb said to Lewis, shaking hands with him. "Glad to have you with us."

"Do we have confirmation whether the girl's inside?" Lewis asked, skipping the preliminaries.

"That's a negative," Webb said. "We don't know if the suspect's home either. But we need to move on this."

"Agreed," Lewis said. "We checked the blueprints on the way over. Our target's in the basement?"

"That's right," Webb said. "He has windows that open onto the sidewalk, but I don't think they're big enough to squeeze through."

Lewis nodded. "Close quarters," he said. "We'll be working in a confined space. It could get messy. But it'll be easy to secure the perimeter. Carnes, you and Twig cover the exit. Parker, you'll make entry. The rest of us will stack up on you. We need this to go fast and smooth. Our boy can kill his prisoner if we give him seconds to react. If you see him make a move, you put him down. But remember there may be a civilian in there with him, so for God's sake watch your background and don't just start spraying."

"Piekarski, you're outside with Carnes," Webb said.

"Sir!" Piekarski protested.

Webb held up a hand. "This isn't a debate," he said. "I want a Major Crimes cop on the door."

"But—"

"And it's not because you're a woman, and it's not because you've got a baby. We may need O'Reilly's dog and Vic's gun downstairs. That leaves you on perimeter duty."

"Yes, sir," Piekarski said sulkily.

"Here's our suspect," Webb said, holding up his phone. On the screen was Ethan Warburton's campus ID photo.

"What a monster," Parker said, drawing snickers from a couple of other ESU officers. Even Erin, despite the seriousness of the situation, smiled. Warburton was a small, bespectacled man in his mid-forties. His hairline had receded to the point where his combover was no longer effective. He had watery light-blue eyes that had a cringing, pleading look in them, as if he was about to beg the photographer not to hurt him.

"According to his driver's license, he's five-foot eight and weighs a hundred thirty," Webb said.

"Watch out for the little guys," Lewis reminded his team. "They fight harder than the big ones."

"And they fight dirty," Vic added. "Everybody up to date on their rabies and tetanus shots?"

"Enough bullshitting," Lewis said. He touched his earpiece. "Twig, are you in position?"

Erin was close enough to hear the squad sniper's answer. "Setting up now, Boss. I'm on the roof across the way. Got a good field of fire on the front of the building."

"Let's do this," Lewis said. "Remember, gentlemen: slow is smooth—"

"—and smooth is fast," Erin said in unison with the others. It wasn't the first time they'd heard Lewis say it.

Parker studied the exterior door for a moment. Then he produced a short-handled crowbar from his belt, shoved it into the doorjamb, and levered the door open with a brief squeal of protesting metal. Erin winced at the sound, but Parker was already in, waving the others forward.

The ESU team moved through the building like heavily-armed ghosts. The lobby was dark, but the moon was nearly full, lending enough ambient light so flashlights were unnecessary. That was good. The problem with a flashlight was that while it might light up your target, it would definitely show your target exactly where you were. Lewis and his squad were equipped with night-vision goggles, but those weren't issued to Major Crimes. Vic was wearing his personal pair of NVGs, bought from an ad in *Soldier of Fortune*. Erin and Webb were shit out of luck. Rolf, who had better night vision than a human and relied on his nose more than his eyes, didn't care.

One of the tactical guys paused in the lobby long enough to call the elevator, which he locked in place. Now the only way up or down was the stairs. The line of officers moved swiftly into the stairwell. Parker was still in the lead. Then came Officer Hopper. Erin and Rolf were third in line, followed by Officer Madsen, Lieutenant Lewis, Vic, and Webb. Officer Diaz brought up the rear.

The concrete stairwell smelled of cheap tobacco and cleaning solvent. It was lit by a flickering, buzzing fluorescent bulb. The ESU guys flipped their NVGs up on their foreheads as they moved. All Erin could see was Hopper's back and the backside of his helmet. She gripped Rolf's leash with one hand and her Glock with the other.

They filed into the basement hallway and stacked up along the wall. The overhead bulb here had burned out and it was nearly pitch black. Parker flicked on his flashlight and examined the door. Then he put it away.

Erin couldn't see a damn thing. She waited, mouth dry, palms sweating. She could feel her adrenaline spiking. Her pulse was so loud she could actually hear it in her own ears, almost drowning out the soft rustle of fabric as the team shifted position, getting ready.

"Three," Lewis whispered. The sound of his voice made Erin jump.

"Two."

She tried to think tactically. Move fast, clear the doorway. If they took fire, look for the muzzle flash. Watch the background. Don't shoot the hostage. Send Rolf, but not into a crossfire.

"One."

Erin had time for a very quick, truncated internal prayer. *Please, God. Let this be the right door. Let the girl be alive. Hail Mary, full of—*

"Execute!" Lewis hissed.

Some ESU doorkickers favored handheld battering rams. Parker had decided to go old-school for this operation, opting for a sledgehammer. The hammer slammed into the door just above the knob and deadbolt. The door practically exploded from the impact.

"NYPD!" Parker bellowed, plunging through the doorway before the splinters had time to hit the floor. "Hands up! Show me your hands!"

Everything was darkness, chaos, and motion. Erin was jostled from behind. She stumbled forward and bounced off someone else, probably Hopper. Rolf, close beside her, was panting eagerly. She felt more than saw the doorframe and managed to get through it.

Everyone was shouting. The whole point of a dynamic entry was to disorient and confuse the suspect, to make him freeze or panic. The ESU team flooded the apartment, guns ready. Their NVGs would be showing the scene in green and black. All Erin had was black. She saw vague shapes of her fellow officers and sidestepped out of their way. She felt Rolf's eagerness. He knew exactly what was going on and wanted a piece of the action, but she had no target to send him after.

"Living room clear!" Lewis announced. "Give me two, bedroom!"

"Bathroom clear!" Hopper called.

"Kitchen clear!" Madsen and Vic said in near-unison. They'd peeled off and gone the other direction upon entry.

A door swung open and slammed against the wall. Then Hopper shouted, "Bedroom clear!"

"All clear," Lewis said, and just like that the energy went out of the room. There were about three seconds of silence.

"Nobody's home," Vic said.

"Lights," Diaz said, warning the others to turn off their goggles. Then the apartment was bathed with soft golden light, revealing the black-clad ESU team.

"Shit," Vic said, emerging from the kitchen. "It's a washout."

"O'Reilly?" Lewis said, nodding toward her dog.

"Rolf! *Such!*" Erin ordered, unsnapping his leash.

It was exactly what the Shepherd had been waiting for. He began eagerly searching the apartment, snuffling industriously. Erin tailed him, watching and listening for him to indicate he'd found something. Lewis's instructions made sense. A kidnapper very well might have a secret door or hidey-hole. If he did, Rolf would find it.

The K-9 was thorough. He inspected every room. Erin paid attention to her own pathetically short, hapless nose. She smelled bleach and soap and unidentifiable chemical odors. But neither she nor her dog found a hidden dungeon.

They finished their circuit and returned to the living room, where Webb and Lewis were directing their officers to look for evidence. Erin hadn't attended to the furnishings. She'd been too focused on the search for hidden human beings. Now she took in her surroundings.

Warburton's apartment was pristine. There was no other word for it. The ESU squad had knocked a few things around on their way through, but otherwise everything was perfectly squared away. The books on the bookshelves were lined up exactly at the front edge of every shelf. The carpet showed lines of having been vacuumed very recently, probably within the past twenty-four hours. The bootprints of the police, and Rolf's pawprints, were clearly visible depressions in the pile.

"This guy's a neat freak," Vic reported after looking in the bathroom. "He's got something like a dozen kinds of soap in there, not counting the hand sanitizer. And he has about a million rolls of paper towels under the sink."

"He's some kind of freak," Parker said, emerging from the bedroom. "You guys are gonna want to take a look at this."

Vic, Webb, and Erin trooped in. Lewis stayed outside, talking on the radio with Twig and Carnes, warning them that their target hadn't been present.

Parker pointed to the dresser next to the bed, which was neatly made. The top drawer of the dresser was open.

"Hospital corners," Webb said, looking at the bed.

"The sheets were just laundered," Erin said. "Can you smell the fabric softener?"

"I was checking the drawers," Parker said. "And I found... well, just look."

Vic was the first one over. He peered into the drawer. He stared for a second. Then he blinked and something happened to his face. His eyes went stony and his jaw tightened. A muscle under his left eye twitched.

"What is it?" Webb asked.

Vic said nothing.

Erin and Webb got there and looked. Erin wasn't sure what to expect. She had visions of jars full of dismembered body parts, or maybe jewelry made of human bones. What she saw was so ordinary it took her a moment to process it. She was looking at three stacks of neatly folded panties, all colors and styles. There were about a dozen pairs in a variety of sizes. Some of them were patterned with cheery cartoon characters and were very small.

Then she understood and felt sick to her stomach.

"Sweet Jesus," Webb murmured.

"Where is this bastard?" Vic demanded.

"He's not here," Webb said.

"Rolf can track him," Vic said, turning to Erin. "Right?"

"Maybe," she said. "But only as far as his parking space or the subway station."

"Twelve," Webb said softly. "Twelve girls."

"These sick sons of bitches do that," Vic said. "They take trophies. From the people they... that sick *fuck!*"

"Shut up, everybody," Parker said, putting a hand to his ear. He was getting something on his squad's radio. The others paused, listening.

Lewis appeared in the doorway. "Lieutenant?" he said to Webb. "We have a problem."

"What now?" Webb asked. He appeared slightly dazed.

"Carnes says a couple FBI guys just showed up out front. And they've got a news crew with them."

Chapter 8

"How the hell did the press get here so fast?" Erin wondered aloud.

"How do you think?" Vic retorted. "The goddamn Feebies tipped them off."

"Police radio scanner, more likely," Lewis said. "How do you want to play this, Lieutenant?"

"It doesn't matter how they know," Webb said. "We can't keep it quiet. The Bearcat out front makes that pretty much impossible."

Lewis bristled. "If you're suggesting my team had anything to do with this—" he began.

"Nobody's blaming you," Webb said. "I'm just stating facts. Talk to your guy at the door. Don't let any reporters down here."

"The windows are blacked out," Vic reported. "Kinda weird, if you ask me. He painted over them. So the news punks can't see in."

"Small mercies," Webb said. "I'd better get out there. O'Reilly, you're with me. Neshenko, stay here. Keep looking for evidence, but don't touch anything if you don't have to. Call

CSU and get them onsite forthwith. We're looking for physical evidence to tie our suspect to either disappearance."

"What do you call that?" Vic asked, pointing to the dresser.

"A weird but harmless fetish, until proven otherwise," Webb replied. "Unless and until we get DNA or fibers that connect the underwear to missing persons. Do you understand your job?"

"Yes, sir," Vic said.

"Good." Webb waved Erin to follow him and walked quickly out of the apartment.

"I don't understand, sir," Erin said, catching up to him.

"What don't you understand?" Webb asked without breaking stride.

"You're the ranking detective, so you're the one to talk to the Feds and the media," she said. "But I'm your second in command. Shouldn't I be securing the scene and Vic coming with you?"

"Think about it," Webb said. He started puffing his way up the stairs.

"Vic's hopped up on adrenaline," Erin said. "He's pissed because we washed out, even more pissed because he thinks this guy goes after underage girls. You don't want to put him anywhere near a reporter or a camera."

Webb nodded approvingly. "Keep thinking like that," he said. "Maybe they'll give you my job when I retire."

"God spare me," she said.

They stepped into the lobby and the blinding glare of a portable spotlight. The lobby was already populated by Agents Rockwell and Willard, Holly Gardner, Holly's cameraman, and a pair of tense cops. Carnes was being careful to keep his assault rifle pointed at the floor, but he looked angry. Piekarski was glaring at Holly, who was talking into a microphone. Rockwell and Willard were standing next to the reporter. Both agents were wearing good suits, their hair neatly combed. Rockwell was smiling.

"Here with me is Special Agent Mark Rockwell of the FBI," Holly said, favoring Rockwell with a dazzling smile and a good look at her cleavage. "Agent Rockwell, what can you tell us about tonight's operation?"

"Ms. Gardner, this raid is the result of close cooperation between the Federal government and the NYPD," Rockwell said. "It is the culmination of a weeklong effort to construct an accurate psychological and behavioral profile of the perpetrator of these heinous crimes. I would like to congratulate the NYPD on their prompt and effective action in response to information provided by the FBI."

"I see why you didn't want Vic here," Erin murmured into Webb's ear. "Punching a Fed on national TV wouldn't be a great look for the Department."

"I'll handle this," Webb said. He walked up to Rockwell and Holly, plastering a false smile across his weary face.

"And here's the hero of the hour," Rockwell said, grinning good-naturedly. "Lieutenant Harold Webb, a seasoned veteran of both the NYPD and the LAPD. Did you bag our bad guy, Lieutenant?"

Jesus Christ, Erin thought. *Does he really expect to get an after-action debriefing in front of live TV cameras?!*

"The NYPD, unfortunately, can't comment regarding an ongoing investigation," Webb said. "We are very grateful for any and all assistance provided to our investigation by the FBI. However, I'm going to have to borrow Agent Rockwell for a few minutes, if it's no trouble."

"Absolutely, Lieutenant," Rockwell said. He was still grinning, but Erin caught the hint of uncertainty behind his good humor.

"This is an active crime scene," Webb added. "So I'm going to insist all non-law enforcement personnel step outside."

Carnes and Piekarski took their cue and advanced on the news team, shepherding them out onto the sidewalk.

"There was no call for that, Lieutenant," Rockwell said through his ever-present smile.

"I understand the FBI operates differently," Webb said. He was smiling too, which Erin found so unusual and alarming that she actually took a step back. "So I'd like to take this chance to educate you how we do things here. We give press conferences *with* the prior knowledge of sister agencies, *after* we've closed the case."

"You mean you let him get away?" Rockwell asked.

"That would have been difficult," Webb said. "Mr. Warburton would have needed to be on the premises in order to escape them."

"But it's late," Rockwell said. "Our profile says he keeps regular hours. He should have been home!"

"The world doesn't run on 'should,' sir," Erin said, providing one of Carlyle's nuggets of wisdom.

"We didn't have surveillance on him," Webb said. "We might have gotten lucky and snapped him up, but that's all it would have been; luck."

"Where is he now?" Rockwell demanded.

"That's an open question," Webb said. "Did you really call a reporter on the assumption we'd collar the guy and the additional assumption he'd be the guy we want?"

"Isn't he?" The smile ducked away from Rockwell's lips. "You found the girl, didn't you?"

"No," Webb said grimly. "We didn't find anybody. The apartment is empty."

"You need to put out a citywide alert!" the FBI agent exclaimed. "Now!"

"No!" Erin snapped.

Rockwell turned on her. "You're not in command, Detective O'Reilly," he said.

"Neither are you, Agent Rockwell," she said, not giving an inch. "This is an NYPD case. And I'm not giving orders. I'm giving advice to my Lieutenant, who *is* in command here."

"Which I will be glad to hear," Webb said. "Please, O'Reilly, share your thoughts."

"Let's suppose this is our guy," she said. "And he's got Valerie Richards somewhere else. I don't know where; maybe a storage unit or something. If so, that's probably where he is right now. If we plaster his face all over the news, there's a good chance he'll know we're looking for him before we can find him. Then he'll kill Valerie."

"That's an excellent point," Webb said. "I would strongly suggest, Agent Rockwell, that you or your partner request Ms. Gardner keep the name of our suspect a secret. We'll issue a BOLO within the Department, but we don't want to go public yet. O'Reilly's absolutely right. If we spook our perp, Ms. Richards is dead."

"I can't go out there and tell Holly... Ms. Gardner that," Rockwell spluttered. He'd completely lost his composure, which Erin was enjoying more than she ought.

"It's probably easier than explaining to your boss in Quantico why Valerie Richards died," Erin pointed out.

Rockwell, red in the face, spun on his heel and left the building, angling toward Holly. Willard followed, but as he went, he gave Erin a furtive smile and a wink.

"Was that guy flirting with me?" Erin wondered after Willard had left.

"I don't think so," Webb said. "I suspect he was glad to find a kindred spirit. Can you imagine what it must be like, working with a partner like Rockwell?"

Piekarski drifted over to them, leaving Carnes minding the door. "What's the word?" she asked.

"Warburton's a creep," Erin said. "And he's in the wind. No sign of Valerie either. CSU should be on their way."

"It'll take them hours to pick over the apartment," Piekarski said. "We can't waste that kind of time."

"What would you suggest we do?" Webb countered.

"I don't know," she said. "But we have to do *something*. We're on a tight clock."

"We'll put a couple of plainclothes officers outside on stakeout," Webb said. "If Warburton comes home, they can nab him. I'm going to put out that BOLO I was just talking about."

"I can't believe Rockwell tipped off the press," Erin said.

"He doesn't understand something fundamental about fame," Webb said. "If we succeed, there'll be plenty of time then for curtain calls. If we don't, all the PR spin in the world won't help. This isn't the private sector. On the street, you'd better put up or shut up."

"Image matters," Erin said.

"Results matter more," Webb countered.

"That's not what Carlyle says. He says perception is what matters."

"Carlyle's lucky he's not cooling his heels in prison with the rest of his old gang," Webb shot back.

Erin stared at her commanding officer. "You don't mean that. We'd never have taken down the O'Malleys without him. He's one of the good guys, like it or not."

He sighed. "I'm sorry. I shouldn't have said that. Chalk it up to stress and fatigue. Now I need to make some calls to Dispatch and Captain Holliday. He'll brief the PC."

"The Commissioner?" Piekarski said. "What's he got to do with this?"

"Welcome to your first really high-profile Major Crimes case as a detective," Erin said. "The PC looking over your shoulder is the least of your worries. You're in for all kinds of fun."

"I've had fun before," Piekarski said. "It didn't feel like this."

*   *   *

They waited for a Patrol unit to set up inside Warburton's apartment and a pair of plainclothes cops to take position outside. This only took a few minutes, but Erin was terribly conscious of the way time was slipping away from them.

The FBI agents left after a short conversation with Channel Six News. Holly and her cameraman also departed. Piekarski wondered where they were headed. Vic's opinion was that their destination was a place the sun didn't shine, and good riddance.

The detectives circled up at their cars. The others took off their vests. Vic kept wearing his. The Russian paced restlessly on the sidewalk, clenching and unclenching his big, meaty fists. Rolf kept a wary eye on him, the way he would have watched a reactive dog at the park.

"The worst part is, Rockwell isn't wrong," Webb said. "It's after ten o'clock on a work night. Warburton should have been home and asleep. You saw the apartment. That's the home of a creature of habit."

"He scrubbed it down," Erin said. "He'd just vacuumed and you could smell cleaning products all over the place."

"Do you think he had the girl there?" Piekarski asked. "Maybe he was trying to get rid of trace evidence."

"Then where is she now?" Webb asked.

"In the trunk of his car," Vic said darkly.

"I don't think he kept any prisoners in the apartment," Erin said. "It isn't soundproofed, for one thing. And it's *too* clean. I think he just cleans every day."

"OCD," Webb said, nodding. "That's what they say about him. I didn't see any stains on the underwear, either."

"Eww," Piekarski said, making a face.

"He's talking about bloodstains," Erin said.

"That's not any better."

"Yes and no," Webb said. "Body fluids would be useful, as long as they belong to someone other than Warburton."

"Eww," Piekarski said again, with more feeling.

"He wasn't packed," Webb said. "There were clothes hanging in his closet and folded in his dresser. And he had his trophies, of course. He expects to come back home, and I still think that's our best chance of nailing him."

"Maybe we should stay here and greet him," Vic said. He cracked his knuckles.

"As you pointed out, this isn't some sort of commando we're dealing with," Webb said. "We have four cops watching this spot. If he shows, they'll get him. We need to be more proactive. Piekarski, I want you back at the Eightball."

"Why me?" Piekarski asked, then caught herself. "I mean yes, sir. What do you need me to do?"

He nodded approvingly. "You're good with financial records. We have a warrant for everything in Warburton's name. Find out if his name is on any other properties. Check his bank records and credit cards for storage unit rentals, vehicle rentals, boat rentals, anywhere he could stash a person, living or dead."

"Copy that, sir."

"Neshenko, you know Brooklyn as well as any of us," Webb continued. "Pound pavement around the bowling alley. Get some uniforms to help. Work a four-block radius. Find out if anyone saw anything strange, particularly a scrawny man dragging or carrying a girl. Show Warburton's picture. Get make and model of the car he was using."

"Will do," Vic said.

"O'Reilly?"

"Sir?" Erin said.

"Get to Columbia campus and talk to Security. Find out everything you can about our suspect's habits."

"Sir, it's pretty late and I think Chief Oglesby works daylight hours."

"Even better. You ought to get along better with whoever else is on duty."

"Copy that," Erin said. "Where will you be, sir?"

"At the Eightball, talking to Dr. Levine. I expect I'll find her in the basement. She might have something we can use. Neshenko, Piekarski and I are borrowing your car."

"What am I supposed to do?" Vic demanded. "Stick out my thumb and hitchhike?"

"Talk to the Seven-Oh and get one of their Patrol unit," Webb said. "Do I have to do all the thinking for this squad?"

"I copy, sir. Who's driving?"

"Piekarski," Webb said.

"Zofia? Remember to move the seat back when you're done with it."

"I think I'll leave it pulled forward," Piekarski said with a grin. "It's funny watching you fold up like an accordion."

"I'm glad I amuse you," Vic said.

"Constantly," Piekarski said. She blew him a kiss.

Chapter 9

It was close to eleven when Erin and Rolf walked into the security office at Columbia. A pudgy young man with a good-natured face was sitting with his feet propped up on his desk, watching TV. He had a bottle of Coke and a box of Little Debbie snack cakes to keep him company.

Erin knocked on the open door. "NYPD," she said. "Major Crimes. Got a minute?"

The man jumped up. His heel caught the box of Little Debbies and sent it tumbling to the floor. A cheap chocolate cake bounced and rolled in front of Rolf, who gave it a casual sniff, decided it wasn't food, and ignored it.

"Yeah, of course," the man said. To Erin's amusement, he actually saluted. "Grizz... I mean, Chief Oglesby said to give you guys whatever you need."

"Thanks," she said. On the TV was a photo of Valerie Richards. She had a dazzling smile, wavy blonde hair, and sparkling eyes. She looked absolutely gorgeous. Erin felt something twist in her gut and looked away.

"I'm Castle. That is, Archie... I mean, Archibald Castelnuovo. Officer Castelnuovo, I guess. People call me Castle. My friends, that is. But you can call me whatever you want."

"Okay, Archie," Erin said. "Take it easy. I'm not going to breathe fire at you and Rolf won't eat you. At least not unless I tell him to."

"Sure, sure," Castelnuovo said with a nervous smile. His round face made him look like he was about sixteen. Just standing there talking to him made Erin feel old.

"I have some questions about one of your staff," she said. "Ethan Warburton."

"Is he a security guard?"

"No. He's a custodian."

"You'd really do better talking to Facilities about that," the kid said.

"Is anyone going to be in their office this late?"

"I guess not."

"Then I'd better talk to you, don't you think?"

He looked down. "Yeah, that makes sense. Geez, I don't want to screw anything up. This is about that girl who got killed, isn't it? Laurel?"

"Right now let's focus on Warburton," Erin said. "Can you access employees' schedules?"

"Yeah, sure. On my computer." He rolled his chair over in front of his monitor and woke up the machine. The monitor flickered to life, showing a half-finished game of solitaire. Castelnuovo turned pink and quickly shut down the game.

"Sorry," he muttered. "There isn't a lot going on right now, and someone's got to be in the office all the time, and—"

"Forget about it, kiddo," Erin said, trying to put him at ease. Nervous people made mistakes and she didn't have time for mistakes. "You don't report to me and I'm not going to tell your chief. Why do you call him Grizz?"

"Oh, that? It's just a nickname. It's short for Grizzly Bear, on account of him being kind of hairy and bad-tempered. Could you maybe not tell him I said that, either?"

"He won't hear it from me. Can you bring up the schedule, please?"

"Here it is." Castelnuovo displayed it on screen. "Looks like he got off at four-thirty, so he's long gone if you're looking for him. That was, geez, more than six hours ago. He's probably home and asleep. Do you need his address?"

"We've got it, thanks," Erin said absently, studying the schedule. Four-thirty left Warburton plenty of time to get home from work, change clothes, change vehicles if he wanted to, and set up on the bowling alley. He'd been alone, so probably wouldn't have an alibi, even if he was innocent.

"He works a lot of overtime," Castelnuovo went on. "But not tonight, I guess. Leastways he's not on the schedule."

"Where does he work?" she asked, squinting at the screen.

"Mostly at the gym. He cleans the locker rooms. Does a good job, too."

"I'll bet he does." Erin was thinking of freshly-vacuumed carpet. "I assume he has keys to all of the buildings?"

"Of course. All the cleaning and maintenance guys do."

"And Security?"

"Yeah, so do we."

"I need you to take me to the gym."

"It'll be locked."

"Which is why I need you and your keys," she said patiently.

"But why are we going there?"

"I'm playing a hunch."

"But the Chief says someone needs to be in the office at all times."

"What happens if someone calls Security?" she asked.

"It goes to that phone there." He pointed to the phone on his desk.

"And what if nobody answers it?"

"Then it rolls to the top guy's cell."

"Automatically?"

"Yeah."

"So what you're telling me is, you don't need to physically answer that phone?"

"I guess not."

"So you don't actually need to be sitting here eating Ding-Dongs and watching TV?"

He looked at his feet. "No. But the Chief—"

"If you get in trouble for this, tell the Chief to call Erin O'Reilly. Got that?"

"Erin O'Reilly," he repeated. Then he blinked. "Hey, aren't you that lady cop who busted up that gang at Christmas?"

"That's me," Erin sighed.

"Wow! You're famous! Could I, like, get your autograph?"

"Tell you what," she said. "After we take a look around the gym, I'll sign something for you. But I'm not signing any body parts, you got that?"

*   *   *

Levien Gymnasium was at the corner of West 120th and Broadway. The building was mostly dark and silent, but a few lights glowed.

Castelnuovo keyed them in. He wasn't done being thrilled about meeting the famous New York Detective. He'd been talking the entire way from the security office.

"Wait'll I tell my mom about this!" he said. "She's, like, your number one fan!"

"That's nice," Erin said. "Where are the locker rooms?"

"This way, then down the stairs. When you give me your autograph, could you sign it to Carmelita Castelnuovo? She'll be so jealous I got to meet you in person. Is it true you got thrown a hundred feet by a car bomb?"

"No." Erin started down the stairs. Like the basement outside Warburton's apartment, the corridor was dim enough that she wanted a flashlight, but decided not to use the one she carried in her pocket.

"Oh." Castelnuovo was momentarily crestfallen, but he recovered fast. "But you shot a bunch of guys, right?"

"A few," Erin said.

"They don't let us carry guns," he said.

"I wonder why."

Castelnuovo wasn't wearing body armor, but his skull was apparently impervious to sarcasm. "I don't know," he said. "All I have is this bottle of pepper spray. How do you decide when to do it? To shoot a guy, I mean."

"You do it when you don't have a choice," she said. "When a bad guy's going to kill you or a civilian and it's the only way to stop him. Or when you're in a sensitive situation with a guy who doesn't know when to shut up."

"Good one!" He laughed nervously.

Erin didn't.

"I mean, that was a joke, right?"

"Where's the women's locker room?" Erin asked.

"That way. You wouldn't really shoot me, would you?"

"Not in the head."

"Oh." Castelnuovo considered some of the other possibilities. That kept him blessedly quiet for a few moments. They reached the locker room. He knocked loudly on the door.

"Campus security!" he called. "Anyone in there?"

"Jesus!" Erin hissed. "Keep it down!"

"I have to say it's me," he said. "What if there's a student in there and she's… you know, not wearing anything?"

Erin sighed. He had a point. But if, by some outside chance, Warburton had been there, he'd probably been alerted.

Nobody answered the security guy's call. He shrugged and opened the door.

Locker rooms had a particular smell, impossible to mistake. Erin could have walked in with her eyes closed and still known where she was. Rolf's nostrils flared as he inhaled the mingled scents of old sweat, deodorant, and cleaning products. Every third light was lit, probably in an effort by the college to save energy. Rows of lockers stood cold and quiet.

Erin wasn't sure exactly what she was looking for. Her instincts had told her this was Warburton's hunting ground, but it didn't make sense to look for him here. He already had a victim. You didn't expect a lion that had just brought down a zebra to be out stalking the herd. But this killer was unusual. He'd picked a second victim before the first had stopped breathing. Damn it all, where *was* he?

A metallic clang sounded somewhere further into the room, around the third aisle or so. It sounded like a locker door.

"Who's there?" Castelnuovo called.

Footsteps flapped on the concrete, heading away from them at a run.

"Oh no," Castelnuovo said. "I scared a student."

Erin wasn't listening to him. When someone ran from a cop, you chased them. That was something she and Rolf understood on a gut level. Whoever this person was, they were up to no good, and that was plenty of reason for pursuit. She started running. So did Rolf. They left the rotund security guard far behind.

As she raced past row after row of lockers, she saw one door hanging open. She ignored it. There'd be time to check it later.

For now, she was letting her ears guide her. She came to the door at the far end of the locker room and yanked it open, revealing a concrete hallway. It was brightly lit, but only for a moment. Then there was a click and Erin was plunged into darkness.

That decided her. Someone running away and turning out the lights on her was absolutely a bad guy. She could still see a little from the EXIT sign behind her, at least enough not to plow into walls. She ran.

Rolf loped beside her, easily matching her pace. He was panting, but that was mostly excitement. He could go much faster and longer than this. He wished his partner was quicker on her feet, but he knew she did the best she could. It wasn't her fault she didn't have enough legs.

A concrete stairway loomed suddenly at the end of the hall. Erin tried to take it at a run, missed a step in the dark, and pitched forward. A wedge of pain spiked into her shin. She caught herself with her left hand, which sent shooting pains up her arm and took some skin off her palm. Rolf scrambled past her up the stairs, turned, and panted at her from the top, as if to say their quarry was getting away, and what was she doing lying down in the middle of a chase?

She levered herself upright, hissing at the feel of cool air across freshly abraded flesh. She didn't think she'd broken or sprained anything. Her hand found a railing and she used it for support to climb the rest of the way up.

A pair of metal doors met her. She fumbled for a handle, found it, and pulled the left-hand door open. She hurried through, clearing the kill-zone bottleneck in the doorway.

She and Rolf were on the basketball court, in a passage between banks of bleachers. Erin paused a moment, listening. She heard the distinctive squeak of shoe rubber on polished wood, ahead and to her right. She ran onto the court and angled that way.

The arena was eerily dark and quiet. Moonlight slanted in from windows high up on the walls. In that cold radiance Erin saw a figure in a white shirt running toward the nearest exit. It looked like a small man. The moonlight reflected off a shiny bald spot on top of his head.

"Warburton!" she shouted, making a guess.

He stopped and looked over his shoulder, eyeglasses flashing momentarily white in the moonlight. He had something in his right hand, but it didn't look like a weapon. It was a limp, floppy object. He stared at her. About thirty yards separated them.

"NYPD!" she called. "Keep your hands where I can see them! Stay right there! I have a K-9!"

Warburton turned on his heel and thrust his arms at the door. It didn't open; it was locked. Erin jogged toward him.

"Damn it, I said don't move!" she shouted. "You're under arrest!"

Warburton gave a frightened little yelp and darted to one side, clambering up the bleachers in a frantic scramble.

Where the hell did he think he was going? All he was doing was cornering himself. Even if he made it all the way to the top of the bleachers, he'd end up face first against the stadium wall. But that was panic for you; fear made you stupid.

"Stop running!" she said, more exasperated than anything else. "I'll send my dog and he will bite you! Give it up! There's nowhere to run!"

He ignored her, clawing his way higher. He'd dropped the thing he'd been holding. His shoes slipped and slid on the bleachers. He was making a frightened whimpering sound that disgusted her.

"Okay, you asked for it," she said, not bothering to draw her gun. "Rolf! *Fass!*"

That was what the Shepherd had been waiting to hear. As Rolf felt the click of his leash being unsnapped, he exploded into motion. He crossed the room in a few easy strides. He leaped up the bleachers, making it look effortless, and closed the distance in a matter of about three seconds.

Warburton saw the dog coming out of the corner of his eye. He lurched left, trying to dodge, just as Rolf sprang. The K-9 hit the man at an angle, moving at nearly thirty miles an hour. The resulting collision spun Warburton halfway around even as his own center of gravity was shifting.

Warburton was a small man and Rolf was a big dog. Physics was not in the human's favor. He made an awkward half-somersault, the Shepherd's jaws already snapping shut on his arm. His foot caught on the underside of a riser. The leg twisted sharply. Warburton started to cry out in shock and pain, but then his head hit the angle of the nearest set of stairs and he cut off mid-scream.

The flat crack of the impact when his head hit the bleachers was remarkably loud. The man bounced, but that was just residual momentum. He slid limply down a couple of steps and lay perfectly still.

Rolf, obedient to his training, kept his grip on Warburton's arm. He wagged his tail and growled joyfully.

"Holy shit," Erin murmured.

Seconds lengthened. Warburton still wasn't moving or making a sound. He really had hit his head awfully hard.

"Shit," she said again and went for her phone. She called 911.

"*911, what is your emergency?*" Dispatch said.

"This is Detective O'Reilly," Erin said. "Shield four-six-four-oh. I have a TBI at Levien Stadium, Columbia University. We're on the basketball court. I need Patrol units and a bus forthwith!"

Chapter 10

Erin was worried but not crazy. She snapped her handcuffs around Warburton's wrists before doing anything else. Blood was streaming from his scalp. He appeared totally nonresponsive. But he was also a suspected kidnapper and murderer, smart enough to snatch two young women without anyone seeing it happen. He might be playing possum.

Rolf sank back on his haunches, grinning hugely. His tongue lolled over his teeth. His ears stood at full attention. He'd caught the bad guy and gotten his teeth into him. That was the second-best thing in his life; even better than suppertime. Now he was waiting for the best.

Erin took his rubber Kong ball out of her pocket and flicked it toward him. His head hardly seemed to move, but suddenly the ball was between his teeth.

"*Sei brav*, kiddo," she told him absently. "Good boy."

The praise was the cherry on top, but the ball was the main course. Rolf was already happily chomping away.

Erin wasn't so happy. She took Warburton's pulse. It was there, but didn't feel strong. He was breathing shallowly. She hauled out her pocket flashlight and turned it on, aiming it directly at the man's pupil. The center of the eye remained wide and black, without a hint of contraction.

"God damn it," she muttered.

Heavy footfalls and wheezing breath heralded the arrival of an overweight security guard. Castelnuovo came puffing onto the basketball court.

"Campus... security," he gasped out. Then he doubled over and put his hands on his knees.

"Castle!" Erin snapped. "Get your shit together. I need your help."

"Okay," he said weakly, waving an arm in her general direction. "Just a sec."

"We don't have a sec," she said. "There's an ambulance on the way. I need you to go out to the street and meet the EMTs. Bring them straight here. This man's hurt pretty bad and he needs immediate medical attention. You got that?"

"Sorry," he murmured. "Feel like I'm gonna... throw up."

"That's the Ding-Dongs talking," she said. "You need to dig deep, buddy. Find more. Keep going. This is your job. Here and now. Time to earn that uniform you're wearing. Two lives are counting on you. Go!"

"Two?" Castelnuovo echoed. He obviously had no idea what she meant. But her words had some effect, because he jogged slowly off to the nearest exit, which was the door Warburton had tried to open. It was locked, as Warburton had found out the hard way, but Castelnuovo's keys opened it and the guard disappeared.

"Now what the hell am I supposed to do with you?" Erin wondered aloud, looking down at her comatose prisoner. There wasn't a thing she could do for him. He wouldn't bleed to death from the scalp laceration; head wounds always bled a lot, but there weren't any arteries up there. And serious concussions weren't something you could treat with a first-aid kit or a Band-

Aid. She didn't even dare move him, for fear he might have suffered a spinal injury. He needed to go to the hospital and get an MRI. He might wake up any moment and be more or less fine, or he might be dying of a brain bleed, or anything in between. She wasn't qualified to make that determination.

"You'd better wake up," she told him. Because if he didn't, they had no idea where Valerie Richards might be.

*   *   *

First to arrive were a pair of Patrolmen, who didn't have much to do but stand around. The paramedics showed up ten minutes later, escorted by Castelnuovo. They gave Warburton a quick examination and came to the same conclusion as Erin. They fitted him with a C-collar and backboard, then got him on a stretcher and wheeled him out to the ambulance.

"Be careful with that guy," Erin said as they were loading him into the back of the vehicle. "He's a major felony suspect."

"He's down for the count," the EMT replied. "Don't worry, he's not going anywhere."

"I'm serious," she insisted. "Watch him. Keep him restrained."

"Sure thing, lady," he said. "Do you want to ride along?"

"I have to stay here and collect evidence," she said. "I'm sending one of these officers with you. Where are you taking him?"

"Bellevue. They've got the best neuro team. Do you know his name?"

"List him as John Doe."

The EMT rolled his eyes. "Whatever. Not my problem. I just deliver them."

He climbed in and pulled the doors shut behind him. The ambulance rolled out, taking the wounded suspect and a Patrol officer with it. Erin watched it drive around the corner. Then she went back inside.

Castelnuovo followed her. He'd gotten his breath back. "What happened in there?" he asked. "Did you punch him out? Was there a fight? I saw blood on his face. What move did you use to take him down? I've been taking karate. I'm going to be a white belt pretty soon. What martial art do you study?"

Erin turned on him. She was four inches shorter and ninety pounds lighter than the guard, but he stepped back from the look on her face. She was tired, frustrated, and worried, and she'd had about enough of him.

"Listen," she growled. "This isn't a goddamn action movie, okay? This is the street. People fight dirty when they fight. We don't do fancy martial-arts bullshit. If a guy comes at you swinging, you put him on the ground quick and hard, any way you can. If you try some stupid Chuck Norris roundhouse kick on a street thug, he'll just break your leg with a pipe and then cave in your skull. But that isn't what happened here. You want the truth? He ran away like a little bitch, I sicced my K-9 on him, he panicked and slipped, and he hit his damn head. Does that answer all your questions?"

"Thanks," he said, eyes shining. She saw she wasn't getting through to him at all. She'd meant to shut him up, but all she'd succeeded in doing was looking cool in his hero-worshiping eyes. She'd just convinced him she was a badass bitch not to be trifled with, nothing more.

"Forget about it," she muttered, giving up. "You want to help?"

"Absolutely! What do I do?"

"You can help this officer secure the scene. Lock the doors to the locker room and don't let anybody in. You got that? *Anybody.* Not until the Crime Scene Unit arrives. Then come back to the basketball court and watch the door."

"Watch the door," he repeated. "Got it. Should I wake up the Chief?"

"That's up to you," she said. "He'll find out in the morning one way or another. You choose which'll make him madder: getting woken up now, or learning about a major event on campus from the news over his morning coffee."

She left him working through that one while she figured out the lights in the basketball arena. Soon the place was bathed in bright light. Rolf was still where she'd left him, one paw wrapped around his ball, snuffling and chewing. His tail was wagging. The only other thing out of place, besides the splash of blood on the bleachers, was the small crumpled object Warburton had dropped. It was lying near the base of the bleachers.

She walked over to it and knelt, not touching it. The best thing was to leave it right there for CSU. It was, she saw with no surprise, a pair of women's underwear.

Erin rocked back on her heels and tried to think. But there really wasn't anything to decide. Her next action had already been determined by departmental procedure. She took out her phone and made a call.

"Webb," the Lieutenant said.

"I found him, sir," she said.

"Warburton?" Webb had sounded worn out and depressed. He was suddenly energized.

"Yes, sir."

"Is he in custody?"

"Yes, sir."

There was a brief pause. Webb was a smart guy, and experienced enough in dealing with Erin to recognize her patterns. When she stuck to rote repetitions of "Yes, sir," it usually meant trouble. The next time he spoke, some of his energy had been replaced by caution.

"What did you do to him?"

"I didn't touch him," she said, which was technically true. "I caught him in the women's locker room at the stadium at Columbia. He ran, so I sent Rolf after him."

"That stupid, stupid man," Webb said. "How bad did your dog bite him?"

"The bite wasn't bad, but he hit his head when Rolf dragged him down. He got knocked out cold. He was still out when the bus picked him up."

"How long?"

"Maybe fifteen minutes total."

"That's a long time to be unconscious. That's a serious TBI."

"I know, sir."

"Did they take him to Bellevue?"

"Yes, sir."

"Where are you?"

"Still at the stadium. I need to stay here until CSU arrives."

"Okay. Get them on site. I don't suppose you have our missing girl's location."

Erin closed her eyes. "No, sir."

"Do you think she could be somewhere nearby?"

"I don't see how. This is a busy campus. But I guess it's possible."

"Look around. I'm sending Neshenko to help."

"Do we have Valerie's sneakers in Evidence?"

"They should be there by now. You want one for Rolf?"

"That'd be great, sir."

"I'll ask Neshenko to bring it. How about you? Are you hurt?"

"No, sir."

"Glad to hear it. I'll get to Bellevue and see if I can do anything with what's left of our suspect."

"Copy that, sir."

*   *   *

The first new arrivals were two more Patrol units; a pair of veteran officers and a field training officer riding herd on a rookie. Erin set them on perimeter duty. They taped off the locker room and the basketball court. Then CSU showed up and began going over the scenes with their usual care. Finally, Vic hurried in with an evidence bag in his hand.

"Whoa there," Castelnuovo said, stepping in front of him. "This is a crime scene. No civilians allowed."

"Then what're you doing here?" Vic retorted.

"I'm a campus security officer!" Castelnuovo said, holding up his badge.

"Where'd you find that?" Vic asked, unimpressed. "A cereal box? Now this, around my neck, is an NYPD gold shield. Take a good close look. This is what real cops wear."

"Sorry," the security man said sheepishly. "I'm just trying to do my job."

Vic clapped him on the shoulder so hard it nearly knocked him over. "Forget about it. I'm just busting your balls. A guy walks in looking like me, you'd better stop him. Where's O'Reilly?"

"Over here, Vic," Erin said. She'd been watching CSU collect blood samples from the bleachers, which struck her as a complete waste of time. It was Warburton's blood. That wasn't up for debate. But they were meticulous. A plastic yellow number marked the bloodstain. Another sat next to the discarded pair of panties.

"Wow," Vic said, glancing at the underwear. "And I thought my college days were wild. Looks like I missed one hell of a party."

"It's not funny," she said. "Rolf put our guy in the hospital."

"Yeah, I heard," Vic said. "Good job, Furball."

Rolf didn't even look at him. He didn't answer to that name.

"There's nothing good about it," Erin said. "Warburton might not pull through."

"And what a tragic loss to humanity that would be," Vic said. "Stop it, you'll make me misty."

"Think!" she snapped. "He might be the only guy who knows where Valerie Richards is! What if nobody finds her? If she's tied up, she won't be able to get food or water."

"Shit," Vic said, sobering up. "You're right. That must be why Webb told me to get my ass up here in a hurry. You think our perp stashed her somewhere nearby?"

"I don't see how," she said. "Or why. Valerie was snatched in Brooklyn. Why bring her all the way up here? And how could he do it without someone seeing?"

"Beats the hell out of me. What was he doing when you found him?"

"Robbing a girl's locker." Erin pointed to the underwear.

"Jesus. You beat the shit out of him for *that?* You and Rolf are hardcore."

"We didn't do it on purpose," she said, irritated. "And he's still our number-one suspect."

"Our only suspect, you mean," he replied. "The FBI guys seem pretty sure of him. But I'm just as sure Rockwell's an idiot glory hound, so there we are."

"Hey, Ms. O'Reilly?" Castelnuovo said, sidling into the conversation.

"Yeah?"

"I'm going to go call Chief Oglesby, if that's okay with you."

"You don't need my permission, kiddo."

"I mean, if you don't need me for anything else..."

"I think we've got this covered," Erin said. "Thanks for your help."

"You're welcome, ma'am," he said. Then he hesitated. "Um, if I could have that autograph...?"

"Sweet Jesus," Vic said.

"Got a pen?" Erin asked, ignoring Vic.

Castelnuovo produced a pen and a pocket notebook. Erin scrawled a quick signature, making it out to Carmelita. The kid went on his way, visibly swelling with pride.

"I can't believe it," Vic said in dreamy tones, clasping his hands together and fluttering his eyelids. "Erin O'Reilly! In the flesh!"

"Knock it off, Vic."

"It's like a dream come true! Please, Detective O'Reilly, may I sweep the floor in front of your feet?"

"I said knock it off."

"Can I name my next kid after you? Male or female, it doesn't matter. Erin or Aaron, it's all the same."

She glared at him. It was as effective as usual.

"I didn't know we were giving out autographs," he went on. "I notice he didn't ask for mine. I guess he's not trying for the complete set. It's funny, people never seem to want my signature. Maybe it's because it was usually on traffic tickets when I was working Patrol."

"Speaking of which," Erin said. "Can we do some police work, or do you have any more bullshit to get out of your system?"

"My bullshit is a renewable resource," he said. "I'll never run out. The more I spew out, the more I've got. But I'm good for now. I've got our girl's shoe here. Want to give the mutt a refresher sniff?"

"Rolf!"

The K-9 sprang to attention. He was ready for more work, especially if it meant more time with his ball. This was shaping up to be a fantastic night.

Erin opened the evidence bag, which contained Valerie's sneakers. She held it in front of her dog.

"*Such!*"

Rolf immediately recognized the scent. The Shepherd never forgot a human smell. He had a big chunk of his brain devoted to them. He didn't attach names to them. He didn't consciously think about them at all. But he always knew when he smelled them again.

One sniff was plenty to bring Valerie Richards to mind. Rolf was glad. He hadn't found her the last time he'd looked. Her scent had vanished. Human smells had a nasty habit of doing that. It had something to do with doors, and with cars. Rolf liked cars when he got to ride in them, but not when they took his target away. He was pretty sure it was cheating when humans did that. Humans, in his experience, cheated a lot.

He circled, testing the air. His tail wagged expectantly. Any hint of Valerie would be enough to get him on the right track. He spun around once, twice, three times. The motion of his tail slowed.

"Is he okay?" Vic asked.

"He's fine," Erin said sharply. Then, to Rolf, "Go on, kiddo. You've got this."

But Rolf didn't. He tried again. Plenty of humans had been here, some of them quite recently. Basketball players sweated a lot. They left extremely vivid scent trails. Excited fans in an overheated gymnasium produced a cornucopia of musky smells. Rolf wasn't good at math. He was good up to five or six, but after that he got lost. There'd been a lot more than six humans here, but not one of them matched the scent from the sneaker.

He stopped circling and looked at Erin. He flattened his ears back against his skull. His head drooped below shoulder level, so he was staring up under his eyebrows. His tail swished in a low, apologetic motion. He whined quietly.

"It's okay," she told him, ruffling the fur at the base of his ears. "I know you tried."

Rolf kept wagging, but he whined again. It didn't look like he'd be getting more time with his ball. It wasn't fair. The humans had cheated him again.

"What does that mean?" Vic demanded.

"It means she's not here," Erin said.

"Somewhere else in the stadium, maybe?" Vic suggested.

She shook her head. "If Warburton was in contact with her, he ought to have her scent on him. I suppose we might as well try the locker room, too, but I don't have high hopes."

As Erin feared, the locker room was a bust. Rolf gave it his best shot, but soon got disheartened. Failure wasn't good for search dogs. To perk him up, Erin had him take a sniff at Vic and sent the Russian to hide behind the bleachers. Rolf easily tracked him down and was rewarded with a little more ball time. He cheered up immediately. Vic wasn't a bad guy, so Rolf didn't get to bite him, but the K-9 had been trained for search-and-rescue work, too, so teeth weren't always the endgame.

"Now what?" Vic asked after Erin had returned the slobbery rubber sphere to her pocket.

"I guess we go to the hospital," she said. "CSU won't be done for a while. We can check in with Webb. Maybe Warburton's woken up."

Leaving the CSU Lieutenant and the Patrol FTO to finish processing the scene, the detectives headed out of the stadium. The squad cars out front had attracted a fair number of late-night rubberneckers. Erin, Vic, and Rolf skirted them and made for their own vehicles.

"I'm parked at the corner," Vic said, pointing.

"I'm further south," Erin said. "I walked here from the security office."

"I'll give you a lift to your car," he offered.

They were just about to climb into Vic's Taurus when the blonde woman popped up, as if she'd sprung out of a storm drain right next to them. Vic cursed and tensed, hand dropping to his gun, then relaxed when he saw who it was.

Erin's heart had jumped into her mouth. Unlike Vic, she didn't relax; not because she didn't know who'd shown up, but because she did.

"Have you got a moment?" Holly Gardner asked. "Off the record?"

Chapter 11

"You mean that?" Vic said. "We're off the record?"

"Do you see any camera?" Holly replied. "I mean it. No recording, no notes."

"Oh, good," Vic said. "In that case, here's my comment. Sit on this."

With great emphasis, he put up his fist and deployed the middle finger.

"Would you like me to?" Holly asked with a saccharine smile. "You should at least buy me dinner first."

"Sheesh, lady, take a hint," he said. "Get lost, why don't you? I'm not interested. I'll never be interested."

Holly's smile twisted into something wry and cynical that would be more at home on a cop's face than her own. "You really think you're that attractive?" she asked. "Or that I'm that easy?"

"I know I don't look so good," Vic said. "So I guess that leaves us with the alternative."

"Jesus Christ," the reporter said. "You think I'm some sort of slut."

"If you're not, you're doing a great job pretending."

"And here I thought detectives were smart," Holly said. "I'm in the entertainment business, Viktor."

"Only my mom calls me that," Vic said. "And only when I've been misbehaving. We're not on a first-name basis, *Ms. Gardner.* And what the hell do you mean, entertainment? I thought you were interested in the news."

"Nobody's interested in the news," Holly said contemptuously. "These days people tune in to their favorite web sites and TV channels to hear people tell them what they already want to believe. It's all one big echo chamber, a nationwide circle-jerk. If I want more viewers, I need to get their interest. Sexiness sells. Haven't you ever seen a perfume ad? Wait, I forgot who I was talking to. Haven't you ever seen a halftime beer ad? Or watched the cheerleaders on the sidelines? It's all legs and tits and pretty faces. But if you believe all those girls are putting out instead of putting you on, you're dumber than you look, and if you're that dumb, you'd forget to breathe."

Vic snorted a laugh.

"She just insulted you, Vic," Erin said.

"I know," he said. "I didn't think she had it in her. I'm impressed. And I think she just told me the truth for the first time since I met her."

"I told you," Holly said. "We're off the record. We can speak plainly."

"Then what are you doing here?" Erin asked. "Come to think of it, how did you know to come here at all? We're a long way from Brooklyn. Are you monitoring police frequencies?"

"I've been known to," Holly admitted with that same wry smile. Erin found the other woman's face more pleasant with that half-sneer than with its trademark brilliant grin. It was more genuine. "But not this time. I've been doing a little sleuthing of my own."

Vic snorted again.

"Laugh it up, meathead," Holly said. "But I do have a four-year degree, which is two more years than you have under your belt. Yes, I know your credentials. I've even seen your transcript. You really could've done better than a C-minus in Sociology, even if you are a misanthrope."

"What's a misanthrope?" Vic asked. "Is it some kind of animal that lives in Africa?"

"You're thinking of antelope," Erin said.

"A misanthrope is a person who hates other people," Holly said.

"Oh, right," Vic said with a dismissive wave of his hand. "Everybody knows that about me."

"That's why I don't take it personally," Holly said and winked.

"You should," he said. "Because I mean it personally."

"I'm glad we're all getting along so well," Erin said. "What do you mean, sleuthing? How did you track us up here?"

"I got Ethan Warburton's name from Special Agent Rockwell," Holly said. "Now *there's* a man with his brain in his dick."

"We've finally found common ground," Erin said.

"How'd you get Warburton's name out of him?" Vic demanded. "Pillow talk?"

"Agent Rockwell wants publicity for the Bureau," Holly said. "And for himself. The thought of seeing his own face on the evening news turns him on more than my boobs ever would, even if I was wearing my special bra."

"Back up a second," Vic said. "Your special..."

"Wouldn't you love to know," Holly said. "But I don't think you'll be seeing it. What, you thought it was *my* idea showing up to Warburton's apartment at the same time as the FBI? Agent Rockwell wanted his photo op. He was so sure you guys would be marching Warburton out in handcuffs. The look on his face when you came up empty was priceless."

"But now you're here," Erin said.

"It was the logical place to go," Holly said. "Warburton works here, though I doubt very much if he'll continue to be employed by the University, no matter what happens next. I know about the student complaints about him. I figured the same as you; I'd take a look around his usual hunting grounds and see what I could find. I wasn't expecting to see him getting wheeled off to the hospital. You really did a number on him, didn't you?"

"I used appropriate force, proportional to the situation," Erin said through gritted teeth.

"That's a press-conference answer," Holly said. "We're speaking candidly here, remember?"

"I'm telling the truth," Erin said. "It was an accident. He slipped and hit his head. Believe what you want."

"And Valerie Richards, I assume, hasn't been found?"

"Don't you think you'd know if she had?" Erin countered.

"I thought not," Holly said.

"How come you're not chasing the ambulance?" Vic asked. "That's what skeezy reporters and cheap lawyers do, isn't it?"

"Because that's not where the story is," Holly said. "Oh, there'll be reporters there, talking to cops and doctors. But it'll all be a big nothingburger. The docs never talk, thanks to HIPAA laws, and the cops just stonewall you with 'no comment.' But that's not the point."

"What is the point?" Erin asked.

"You've got the wrong guy," Holly said.

"Hold on," Erin said. "You're telling me Warburton is innocent?"

"Innocent? Hell, no. He's a total creep, a perv, and even if he doesn't belong in jail, he sure as shit doesn't belong on a college campus. The only place he'd be worse is an elementary school."

"More common ground," Vic said. "I only hate you half as much as usual."

"That's sweet of you," Holly said. "But he didn't take Valerie Richards, which I'm guessing means he didn't take Laurel Peterson either."

"How do you know that?" Erin asked.

"A good reporter never reveals her sources."

"And a good cop never takes hearsay at face value," Erin retorted. "If you can't back that up, you're just blowing smoke."

"The FBI is so wedded to their precious profile," Holly said. "But Warburton isn't violent. He's a creep, but a totally harmless one. He's also a wimp. He couldn't overpower a ten-year-old child, let alone a college athlete like Laurel."

"He could've drugged her," Vic said.

"Did Laurel's autopsy turn up any evidence of drugs?" Holly shot back.

"You know we can't tell you that," Erin said. "Besides, after almost a week, there'd be nothing left in her system."

"True," Holly admitted. "But also consider the logistics. You saw Warburton. Could he carry a girl Laurel's size? Or Valerie's?"

"He is kind of a little guy," Erin said. "And pretty uncoordinated. I don't think he works out much."

"Laurel Peterson weighed a hundred thirty pounds," Holly said. "Can you picture that wet noodle of a man carrying her?"

"He might not have drugged her," Erin said. "Laurel was taken at or near the bus stop. That means she probably left under her own power, or somebody would've remembered seeing her after the story hit the airwaves."

"That's true," Holly agreed. "So the real question is, would Laurel and Valerie both have gone willingly somewhere with a guy like him?"

"He's neat and tidy," Erin said. "Quiet. He really isn't threatening."

"Would *you* have followed a neat, tidy, quiet man twice your age that you didn't know?" Holly asked. "When you were that age?"

"Of course not," Erin said. "But I was raised by a cop. I was taught to be suspicious. Laurel was an innocent from a small town in Minnesota."

"Valerie isn't," Holly said. "She's a Brooklyn girl. You think her mom didn't warn her about guys like that? What, you think he hung around outside the ladies' room at the bowling alley, accosted her, and she went with him by choice?"

"I'm thinking he had a gun," Vic said. "A lot of people will do what you tell them when you shove a .38 in their face."

"If your precious suspect had Valerie locked away, what was he doing here tonight?" Holly asked. "There's just too many inconsistencies. My gut tells me you're looking for someone else."

"Oh yeah?" Vic asked. "Who?"

"I'm not sure yet," Holly said. "But *that's* where the story is. Believe it or not, I want to find Valerie Richards as badly as you do. Even if you don't believe I'm a human being who doesn't want a sweet girl to get strangled, it's good for my career. It's a better story if she's rescued. So why don't we work together? You get to be heroes, I get the scoop of the decade, Valerie goes home to Mom and Dad. Everybody wins."

"You're proposing some sort of partnership?" Erin asked.

"An exchange of information," Holly said. "I'm going to keep digging around no matter what. I have my own sources and methods. If I find anything juicy, I'll get it to you. In return, all I ask is that you let me be in on the arrest when you finally nail your perp. Deal?"

Erin considered the other woman. Holly seemed earnest and genuine, but everyone lied to cops. *Everyone.* She wondered what Carlyle would say, and almost immediately knew the answer. He'd tell her that people looked after their own interests. That was the only thing you could really trust them to do. If Holly's interests coincided with those of the NYPD, that meant she could be trusted within a very specific and narrow framework.

"Find out what you can," Erin said. "If it leads to an arrest, I promise we'll let you know when it goes down. And I'll do you one better. Once we've got our guy in custody, you can interview me. I'd say you could interview Vic, too, but who knows what would come out of his mouth."

Holly beamed. "Fantastic," she said.

*   *   *

"What a load of crap," Vic said. He put the Taurus in gear with a savage yank of his arm.

"I think she was on the level," Erin said. "And we need a break here. It can't hurt."

"Oh yeah? I'm pretty sure it can."

"Why do you hate her so much?"

"Besides the fact she's a skanky whore who'd strip down on live TV if it'd get her ratings?"

"Yeah, Vic. Besides that. Because we run into lots of unpleasant people on the Job, including rapists, murderers, and drug dealers. Holly may not be the most wholesome woman out there, but I've seen you respect plenty of nastier folks than her."

"That's just it," he said. "Respect."

"What do you mean?"

"I don't respect her because she doesn't respect me."

Erin was surprised. "Vic, what have you ever done to deserve her respect? You insult her every breath you take within twenty yards of her. You're surly and unpleasant. You're basically a complete asshole whenever she's around."

"Well, Erin, this may be news to you, but I *am* an asshole."

"And you think that's deserving of respect?"

"No! But I'm also a man."

"I'd noticed," Erin said. "You leave a trail of testosterone wherever you go."

"Thanks."

"That wasn't a compliment."

"Yes it was. You just didn't mean it to be. Holly Gardner's an insult to men, so she's insulting me."

"You're going to have to explain that," Erin said.

"She thinks, just because she's a good-looking babe with fantastic legs and... well, everything else, all she has to do is unbutton her blouse and bat her eyes, and I'll drool all over her. If you think I've got a low opinion of her, it's because she's got a low opinion of guys like me. She assumes I'm a horndog whose brain shuts down the moment the bloodflow goes below my belt. She treats me like I'm a cheap date, like she's doing me some sort of favor by smiling at me. That bitch thinks she's God's gift to men. If a man acted toward women like she does toward guys, would you respect him?"

"Do you want to sleep with her?"

"The hell kind of a question is that?"

"The kind you're not answering."

"For Christ's sake, Erin!" he burst out. "Are you asking if I think she's hot? Yes, she is. Of course she is! She's a blonde with a fantastic bod. Put her in a bikini and she'd cause traffic accidents, even on Miami Beach! But so what? I have a girlfriend. Hell, I have a daughter! I've never cheated on Zofia!"

"I never said you did," Erin said quietly.

"And I'm not going to!"

"Glad to hear it."

"Do you believe me?"

"I do," she said. "Do you believe yourself?"

Vic gripped the wheel so hard Erin half expected him to rip it clean off the steering column. A vein stood out on his forehead. She could've sworn she could see it pulsing in time with his heartbeat. She braced for the explosion.

It didn't come. He let out a very long breath and relaxed his fingers. "I'm trying to," he said.

Erin put a hand on his shoulder, feeling oddly touched. "You're a good guy, Vic," she said. "Better than you think you are. I trust you, and so does Zofia. Is that why Holly pisses you off? You think she's trying to lead you astray?"

"Not exactly," he said. "It's more like she assumes I'll go astray as soon as I have the chance."

"She's just using the tools she's got," Erin said. "If she was big and strong, she'd use her muscles. She's got looks, so she uses those. You know how it is on the street. You grab whatever you can, and you use every advantage."

"For some reason I'm thinking of that old song," he said. "*Love is a Battlefield.*"

"I wouldn't have taken you for a Pat Benatar fan," she said.

"You kidding? That lady kicks ass. Eighties rock is awesome. You know what the problem is?"

"What's the problem, Vic?"

"The goddamn media."

"You're still hung up on Holly?"

"No. I'm talking about messaging. You know why every teenage girl has these screwed-up ideas about beauty and how they're supposed to be sexy but not slutty, and look as good as those photoshopped models?"

"I think I know a little more about being a teenage girl than you do," she said dryly.

"Then you get my point. What matters most to girls is how they're supposed to look. At least that's what they tell you."

"True."

"Well, what do they tell boys?"

"That you can save the world with nothing but a gun and a bad attitude?"

He grinned. "Yeah, but that's not where I was going with that."

"It wasn't? Vic, how many guns do you own?"

"Just a sec. I need to count."

"No need. You've already made my point."

"Okay, okay. But I was talking about sex."

It was Erin's turn to grin. "Just like a man."

"See, that's exactly my point! Boys get told that to be a man, you gotta score with every hot girl you see. It's like earning trophies in sports. And the point isn't to have some deep, meaningful relationship, it's to get laid. That's what we're supposed to care about, and afterward, you move on to the next hot chick. And you don't respect any girl who puts out too easy. Talk about double standards! You want to know when I lost my virginity?"

Erin made a face. "Not really."

"But I'm supposed to brag about it," he said. "Because it shows what a macho, strong, bullshit guy I am. And you know what? I'm friggin' sick of it. I still notice hot girls, sure, but that's just biology. I don't have to do anything with them. Maybe from here on out, Zofia's the only girl I really want to go to bed with. What's wrong with that?"

"Not a thing."

"You won't think I'm a sap? A pussy? A wimp?"

"How much do you bench press?"

"Three hundred even."

Erin whistled. "And you're worried I'll think you're a *wimp?!*"

"I guess not," he said. "But what it comes down to is, there's this little part of me that thinks so. And that little voice is the one Holly friggin' Gardner is talking to, and I wish she'd knock it the hell off. That's why I don't like her, okay? Does that satisfy your goddamn curiosity?"

She smiled. "Vic, you just said one of the most wholesome things I've ever heard you say. Too much cursing for a Hallmark movie, but that's just you being you. I'm your partner. I'm also your friend. Do you trust me?"

"We've saved each other's lives too many times not to," he said.

"Then listen to me, not those mass-market idiots who're just trying to sell you something. Don't ever apologize for being decent. And don't screw up your life trying to fit some stupid idea of what a man ought to be. You don't have a damn thing to prove, you copy that?"

"I copy," he said with a sheepish smile.

"Good. Because we're coming up on my car and it's time to knock off the touchy-feely bullshit and get back to work. A girl's out there counting on us to find her."

Chapter 12

"My patient can't help you," Sean O'Reilly Junior said.

"Why not?" Erin demanded. "He's awake, isn't he?"

"You of all people should know that when someone takes a hit to the head, it isn't something they can just shake off," Sean said. "How are your headaches these days, since we're on the subject?"

"My brother gives them to me, just like when we were kids," Erin retorted. "And now that he's a know-it-all trauma surgeon, he can cause them with anatomical precision."

"Are you still having headaches?" Webb asked, shooting her a concerned look.

"Nothing out of the ordinary," Erin said, lying only a little. The months-old bullet wound on the side of her head only occasionally flared up.

They were in a consultation room at Bellevue Hospital. Sean had just come from Warburton's room, which was guarded by a pair of uniformed officers. Now he, Webb, Vic, Piekarski, and Erin were seated in not-very-comfortable chairs around a Formica table. Rolf was under the table.

"Forget Erin's head," Vic said. "She hardly uses it anyway. We're here about that asshole Warburton. You're telling us he can't answer questions?"

"I'm telling you the answers will be useless," Sean replied. "Even if he was in a condition to be interrogated, which he isn't, his information wouldn't be reliable. He's extremely disoriented and confused. He's lapsing in and out of consciousness. He's lucky to be alive. And he's my patient, so I have an ethical obligation to advocate for his wellbeing."

"He's a goddamn creep and he might have a girl locked in a basement," Vic said. "She's scared and pretty soon she's gonna get hungry and thirsty. What about your ethical obligation to her?"

Sean spread his hands helplessly. "I'm sorry, Detective. My honest medical assessment is that he's suffered a serious head injury resulting in a subdural hematoma. It's fortunate you got him to us as fast as you did. Another hour and he probably would have been dead."

"You hear that, Rolf?" Vic said, nudging the dog with his foot. "You were *this* close to picking up your second confirmed kill."

Rolf, unimpressed, scooted away from Vic's shoe and nestled closer to Erin's feet.

"This isn't funny, Vic," Piekarski said. "What if it was Mina out there in some basement?"

"Don't even go there," Vic said.

"Who's looking after your daughter at the moment?" Webb asked.

"My mom," Piekarski said. "Don't worry, she loves Mina. You wouldn't believe how much she's been pestering me about giving her a granddaughter."

"I might," Erin said, thinking of her own mother.

"What's Warburton's prognosis?" Webb asked.

"He should recover fairly well," Sean said. "Though it's always hard to tell with TBIs. I'm not a neurosurgeon, but my best guess is that in a couple of days he should be more or less cogent. Barring further complications, he should make an almost complete recovery. He may have some gaps in his memory. That wouldn't be uncommon."

"Great," Vic muttered. "What if he forgets where he stashed Valerie Richards? Or if he forgets taking her at all?"

"I'm not sure he did take her," Erin said.

Webb's head whipped around. "Why do you say that?"

"Holly Gardner says he didn't," Vic said, rolling his eyes.

"Since when have the two of you been talking to the press?" Webb demanded.

"It wasn't like that!" Vic said. "She came to us and offered to help."

"I fear the Greeks, even bearing gifts," Webb said under his breath.

"Greeks?" Vic echoed. "That Carver chick is Greek, isn't she? The tabloid bitch?"

"Your Lieutenant was quoting Homer," Sean said.

"Homer Simpson?" Vic was totally lost.

"No," Webb said wearily. "Dr. O'Reilly is talking about Homer the Greek poet, but I was quoting the *Aeneid*, by Virgil. Laocoon is the guy who says it in the poem. He's a Trojan priest who doesn't think they should bring the Trojan Horse inside their city."

"He got that right," Vic said. "Why don't they listen to him?"

"The goddess Athena sends a pair of giant snakes after him," Webb said. "They strangle him and both his sons, so the Trojans figure he's pissed off the gods and ignore him."

"Harsh," Vic said.

"We're getting a little off topic, aren't we?" Erin said. "Holly thinks the FBI profile is a load of crap. And she doesn't see why

Warburton would be stealing underwear from a locker room when he's got a girl locked up. I think she might be right. Laurel Peterson was still wearing her underwear, remember? And the timeline's a little weird. And Rolf couldn't get any whiff of Valerie. If Warburton had grabbed her, Rolf could've sniffed her on him, even if she wasn't anywhere nearby. But I'm sure she wasn't in the stadium."

"Damn," Webb said. He sat back in his chair and rubbed his face. "So we're back where we started."

"Except Valerie's closer to dead and we've got a brain-damaged pervert in ICU," Piekarski said.

"That pretty much sums it up," Webb agreed.

"So do we go home?" Vic asked. "Get some sleep and try again in the morning?"

"If you want," Webb said. "But I'm going back to the Eightball to see if I can think of something."

"I'll come with you," Erin said. "Where are the Feds?"

"I have no idea," Webb said. "I'm not responsible for them, thank God. I have enough to worry about right here in this room. If I had to guess, I'd say they're probably hanging around Major Crimes updating their damned profile."

"So you're giving me the choice between butting heads with the Feebies or hanging around Zofia's mom," Vic said. "Talk about a no-win situation. Ouch!"

Erin was impressed. Piekarski hadn't been sitting all that close to Vic. The blonde didn't have long arms, but she was *fast.*

"Go home," Webb told Vic and Piekarski. "Both of you. That way we'll at least have a couple of detectives who've gotten a few hours of sleep. And look on the bright side. If Warburton isn't our guy, Valerie Richards should be okay for a few more days."

"Until she gets strangled, just like poor what's-his-name in the poem," Vic said. "Except our bad guy uses a silk scarf, not a big-ass snake."

*   *   *

Agent Willard was in the Major Crimes office, but Agent Rockwell was nowhere to be seen. Willard was standing in front of the whiteboard, staring holes in it.

"What gives?" Erin asked. "I thought you government guys always went around in pairs, like Jehovah's Witnesses."

Willard had a nice smile, less showy than Rockwell's. "It's a fair comparison," he said. "We wear plain black suits, too, and people usually aren't too glad to see us. Maybe we should hand out literature when we knock on doors."

"Where's your partner?"

"On a plane down to Quantico."

"Really?" Webb was surprised. "In the middle of an investigation?"

"He didn't have a choice," Willard said. "After that thing outside Warburton's apartment, the Deputy Director called him in for a face-to-face."

"And an ass-chewing?" Erin guessed.

"Fair bet," Willard said. "What's going on?"

The detectives both looked at him without speaking.

Willard sighed. "Look, Lieutenant, I know things went sideways," he said. "What can I say? I'm sorry. None of this was my idea."

"Did you tell your partner what a bad idea it was?" Webb asked.

"I know you haven't known Rockwell long," Willard said. "But does he seem like the sort of guy who's likely to listen to that kind of advice? Mark's smarter than you think, he's ambitious, and he's been lucky so far. Take a guy who's smart and lucky, and he's likely to think he's smarter than he is. Maybe getting tripped up is what he needs. It'll bring him back down to Earth."

"That's nice," Webb said. "And if this was a self-help group, I'd be pleased at the prospect of his personal growth. But this is Major Crimes, Agent Willard. I have a murderer on the loose and a teenage girl to find. I frankly don't care whether Agent Rockwell finds humility, himself, or Jesus. But I admit I'm glad he's in Virginia and out of what's left of my hair. What can I expect from you while he's gone?"

Willard met his eyes without flinching. "You can expect the full support of the Federal government, along with every bit of assistance I can personally provide, sir," he said. "Up to and including placing myself on the front lines, if that's what it takes. Are you a father, Lieutenant?"

"Yes," Webb said. "I have two daughters about Valerie's age."

Willard nodded. "Mine are younger. A boy and a girl. If they were in danger, there isn't a single brick in this city I wouldn't turn over to find them. What can I do to help?"

"What's your opinion of the profile your people developed?" Webb asked.

"I'm not a psych guy," Willard said. "I'm a field agent. I used to work bank robberies. I'm a good shot, I don't panic under stress, and I'm good at tactics and bank security. That's about it."

"What're you doing on this detail?" Erin asked.

"Same as you, I expect," Willard said. "If I'm the man in the office when the call comes, I go. Rockwell's more of a PR guy and a talker. I take care of the dirty stuff behind the scenes."

"Have you ever gone after anyone like this?" Webb asked.

Willard shook his head. "Closest I've come was a robbery crew who liked to take a teller with them on the way out of the bank. They figured the police would be less likely to shoot at them if they had a hostage. That wasn't a sex crime, it was a tactical decision."

"How sure are we that these are sex crimes?" Erin asked suddenly.

"What else could they be?" Willard replied.

"That's an excellent question," Webb said. "Why did you say that, O'Reilly?"

"Laurel Peterson wasn't assaulted," Erin said. "As far as we can tell, she wasn't molested in any way. She wasn't starved or tortured. According to the autopsy, she wasn't harmed in any way until she was strangled. Her face wasn't hacked up until after she was dead."

"Strangulation and postmortem mutilation indicate rage," Willard said. "Of course there's a sexual component to the killing."

"Of course?" Webb repeated. "Why?"

"Because the victim's... well... look at her," Willard said.

"I see," Webb said dryly. "And the only reason to kidnap and murder a pretty young blonde is because she's pretty, young, and blonde?"

"I see what you mean," Willard said. "Are you suggesting there was a different motive?"

"It's worth looking into," Webb said. "Here's something you can do to help, Agent Willard. Take a dive into the Peterson family. I particularly want to know if her parents were into anything shady. Did they owe money to loan sharks? Did her dad screw someone over on a business deal? Are they in financial trouble?"

"Didn't we already look at this?" Erin asked.

"No," Webb said. "We didn't. Missing Persons might have, but if so, they didn't pass anything on to me. We've been so fixated on the serial-killer angle, I don't think anybody's bothered to check on the family."

"Then what about Valerie Richards?" Erin asked.

"What about her?" Webb replied. "She might be unrelated. She might've run off to Atlantic City with her boyfriend. Or there may be a connection between the families. I'll check on that."

"What should I do?" Erin asked.

"Go down to the morgue," Webb said. "Talk to Levine. If we don't find a personal connection that leads us to our perp, our best bet is forensic evidence. Find out if there's anything we might've overlooked. If we can figure out where Laurel was kept, there's an excellent chance Valerie is there right now."

"The morgue at midnight," Erin said. "Is Levine still here?"

"I think so. Last I heard, she was working on a Jane Doe that turned up in a storm drain."

"Any connection to our case?"

"Not that I know of."

"Sir?"

"Yes?"

"How sure are we that Levine isn't a vampire?"

Webb cracked a weary smile. "Eighty-seven percent."

"You just made that number up," she said.

"Ninety-two percent of statistics are made up on the spot," he said.

"Including that one?"

"As far as you know."

*　　*　　*

The nice thing about electric lighting was that the basement morgue was no creepier in the middle of the night than it was any other time. But that wasn't saying much. Erin wrinkled her nose at the chemical and biological odors that hung in the air. Rolf's nostrils twitched with interest. She'd never understand how her dog, with his incredibly keen sense of smell, could possibly enjoy such strong, foul scents.

Levine was standing over a pale, still form on the slab. The ME was taking notes.

"Can I talk to you for a minute, Doc?" Erin asked.

"Apparently," Levine said.

"I wanted to ask you some questions about the Peterson autopsy."

Levine continued writing on her clipboard. Erin took this as permission to continue.

"Those mold spores you found," she said. "How common are they?"

"*Chaetomium* spores are found worldwide," Levine said.

"How common are they in New York City?"

"Extremely. Like other mold spores, they are common in any building which is not rigorously cleaned."

Erin blinked. "Right," she said. "If somebody was obsessive about cleanliness, they'd be unlikely to have mold spores around, wouldn't they?"

"That is a logical conclusion," Levine said. "They would also have lower than normal concentrations of bacteria in bathrooms. Interestingly, research suggests that overuse of antiseptic soaps and cleaners can actually result in lower resistance to infection due to an underdeveloped immune system."

"There wouldn't be any mold in Ethan Warburton's apartment," Erin said thoughtfully. "And he wouldn't keep a girl in a place that had it. Holly was right. We went after the wrong guy, damn it. Doc, did you find anything on Laurel's body that could tell us where she was?"

"Nothing definite," Levine said. "The principle of transference postulates that she certainly left skin cells in the environment, while the environment left residue on her, but my microscopic analysis did not discover anything unusual."

"What about the food?" Erin asked. She was grasping at straws now, but it wasn't like she had anything else to reach for.

"What food?"

"The contents of her stomach. Didn't you say she'd eaten chicken and salad?"

"I performed a more rigorous analysis, which is detailed in my report," Levine said. "Have you read it?"

"I tried. Could you explain?" Levine was a brilliant medical examiner, but the readability of her prose left something to be desired. Her reports tended to be thick with technical terminology.

"The deceased's last meal was consumed less than three hours prior to death," Levine said. "It was chicken. The meat was ordinary in every respect and was likely store-bought. I lack the necessary tools or knowledge to determine which store sold it. The chicken was infused with a marinade containing lemon, yogurt, oregano, garlic, and vinegar. I suspect salt was also involved, but salt dissolves so readily that it may have come from another source."

Erin had whipped out her own notepad and was scribbling down ingredients. She didn't know whether they'd be important, but didn't want to miss anything. "What else?" she asked.

"The stomach also contained cucumber and tomato in diced fragments," Levine said. "And I found pieces of flatbread. Additionally, the victim's blood-alcohol content was slightly elevated, at point-zero-two."

That bit of information made more sense to Erin, who'd pulled over many a drunk driver. "That's way below the legal limit," she said. "A BAC that low wouldn't obviously impair her. Any idea what she was drinking?"

"White wine," Levine said at once.

"How on Earth could you tell?"

"Chemical analysis. Red wine has sulfides and complex chemicals, due to the inclusion of grape skins. White wine is much simpler in composition."

"You're telling me she had chicken, flatbread, a cucumber-tomato salad, and white wine for her last meal?"

"That is an accurate conclusion. I found no other food in her stomach."

"A body metabolizes about one drink an hour," Erin said.

"That is broadly accurate," Levine said.

"So for our girl to still have alcohol in her bloodstream, she'd either drunk a lot or had a drink within an hour or two of death. Your body doesn't keep breaking it down after death, does it?"

"No," Levine said. "Fermentation can occur in the body postmortem, however, resulting in the production of ethanol within tissues as glucose is broken down."

"Sounds like a pretty decent last meal, at least," Erin said. "Maybe the perp got her drunk so she wouldn't be able to resist."

But that was a weak hypothesis and Erin knew it. Laurel had been tied up and imprisoned for the better part of a week. The killer wouldn't have needed to get her boozed up in order to kill her. The whole thing was so strange.

"It's like our killer wanted his victim as comfortable as possible," she said. "Right up until she died. What sort of weirdo does that?"

"I'm not well-versed in abnormal psychology," Levine said. "Though I have read the DSM-5 in its entirety."

"Of course you have," Erin said under her breath. Then, louder, "What could you determine from the knife wounds?"

"According to analysis of blood-flow, they were inflicted postmortem," Levine said. "The lacerations were made by a sharp steel blade. By the kerf marks, I determined they were likely all inflicted by the same blade, which is the approximate size and shape of a butcher's knife."

"Anything unusual about the knife?"

"It was particularly sharp," Levine said. "Most kitchen knives are fairly blunt. I speculate this weapon was either new or unusually well-maintained."

Chapter 13

"They're going to rename our killer," Webb predicted gloomily. "It won't be the Central Park Strangler once the press gets ahold of this. It'll be the Gourmet Ghoul, or maybe the Culinary Killer."

"Gourmet Ghoul has a nice ring to it," Willard said.

Webb gave him a level, unamused stare. "If you breathe one syllable of that outside this office, I guarantee you'll regret it."

"There has to be some significance to the choice of weapons," Willard said. "What does a kitchen implement mean? It could stand for domesticity or home. It could be connected with the killer's feelings regarding his mother…"

He trailed off. Webb and Erin were staring at him.

"I thought you didn't have psych training," Erin said.

"I don't," Willard said. "But after you hang around the Behavioral Analysis guys long enough, some of it rubs off on you. They're really big on childhood trauma."

"I know, I know," Webb sighed. "Every murderer has daddy issues, or mommy issues, or both. He got beaten for wetting the bed, or abused by a creepy uncle. None of that helps us."

"Bed-wetting is actually one of the chief indicators for whether a child develops into a serial killer," Willard said.

"Bullshit," Erin said.

"I'm serious," the FBI agent insisted. He held up three fingers. "Bed-wetting, arson, and cruelty to animals are the red flags. Any one by itself is probably nothing, but put two or three together and you've got a big potential problem. If I had to guess, our profilers are going to modify their profile once they get this new information and come back with something about an abusive, controlling mother."

"How does that help us locate Valerie Richards?" Webb asked.

"It doesn't," Willard admitted.

"Do you really buy into this profiling crap?" Erin asked.

"Yes," Willard said. "It's not magic. It's not a hundred percent accurate. But it's not a party trick. It really does help us catch bad guys. Serial killers fit into patterns of thought and behavior. As I understand it, what you need is a psychopath who undergoes severe trauma at an early age."

"So you can *predict* when someone's going to start slashing up cheerleaders?" Erin asked, raising an eyebrow.

"Like I said, not a hundred percent," Willard said. "This isn't exactly *Minority Report*."

"Thank God," Erin said. "That movie is creepy."

"Behavioral Science is all probabilities," Willard said. "Just applied math."

"I'm liking the chef angle," Webb said.

"You mean that, sir?" Erin asked.

"Yes," Webb said. "If Laurel had been eating McDonald's, this would be a different situation. I want you to look up recipes for chicken marinade."

"Yes, sir," Erin said. It wasn't the weirdest thing she'd had to do as a Major Crimes detective.

She settled behind her computer, fortified by a fresh cup of coffee, and started looking at cooking websites. It didn't take as long as she'd feared. This sort of thing would have been a lot harder for her dad's generation, but the Internet streamlined the process tremendously.

Webb was startled out of either a thoughtful reverie or a light doze by Erin's triumphant exclamation. He lurched up and out of his chair, nearly hitting the floor. Willard came running out of the break room, sloshing hot coffee over his hand and cursing his scorched knuckles.

"I've got the recipe!" Erin announced.

"I thought maybe you'd found us a suspect," Willard said, ruefully wiping his hand with a paper napkin. Webb and Willard came to her desk and looked over her shoulder.

"Chicken gyros," Webb read aloud.

"Everything matches," Erin said. "The marinade, the spices, the yogurt. It's usually served with tomato and cucumber salad and eaten with flatbread."

"Excellent work, O'Reilly," Webb said.

"I'll update the board," Willard said, hurrying to the whiteboard and uncapping a marker.

"Not that it helps us much," Webb added. "It's just another little piece of the puzzle."

"It's ethnic food," Erin said. "Maybe it'll tell us something about the killer's background."

"We're in New York City, O'Reilly," he reminded her. "There's half a dozen ethnic restaurants within a block of us right now, not counting food carts. Just because I'm eating a Haitian... what do they eat in Haiti?"

"I think they go hungry a lot, sir."

"Okay, bad example. Just because I'm eating an Ethiopian... damn. Name a country that isn't famine-stricken."

"Um... Hungary?" Erin suggested.

"Really? The whole world to choose from and you made *that* pun? Okay, whatever. Just because I'm eating Hungarian goulash doesn't mean I'm Hungarian. It just means I felt like eating goulash. Personally, I like good Chinese food, and I'm about as Chinese as a Viking. You can't get it here like you can on the West Coast. Chinatown in LA, that's where the best stuff is."

Webb's eyes took on a faraway look.

"Are you hungry, sir?" Erin asked.

"A little, now you mention it. I could really go for some chow mein right about now. Good Lord, it's late. I'm too old for this crap. What point was I making?"

"That you can't judge someone's background by the food they eat?"

"Right. But it might give us a break. I want you to look up restaurants that serve chicken gyros. I specifically want ones within, say, an eight-block radius of Columbia University or that bowling alley in Brooklyn, but get a list of every one in the city."

"They may not all have websites," Erin said.

"Do the best you can," he said. "And cross-check the phone book. If any of them are open overnight, call them and check their menu."

"Yes, sir," Erin said. She groaned inwardly. She'd just been handed several hours of tedious work, for a very uncertain payoff.

"This is the Job, O'Reilly," Webb said. "Sometimes it moves fast, sometimes it's a grind."

"I know that, sir. I'm not complaining."

He smiled. "You're a stand-up woman, O'Reilly. I'm going to place that order now. Do you want anything from that Chinese place down the block?"

"Chow mein sounds good, sir," she said. "This looks like an all-nighter."

"Would you mind adding a double order of egg rolls?" Willard asked. "Pork or shrimp, either one."

* * *

Sometimes police work was exciting, tense, and exhilarating. Other times it felt like working some tedious municipal desk job. Over the following hours, Erin learned more than she'd ever wanted to about the New York restaurant industry. She compiled a spreadsheet of Lebanese, Greek, Turkish, and Arab restaurants, carts, and food trucks. She learned the difference between *gyros*, *shawarma*, *donair*, and *al pastor*. It was a good thing Webb had the foresight to order takeout, because her research gave Erin a terrible case of the munchies.

The trucks and carts presented a problem, because they moved around. The unhappy but inescapable conclusion she reached, at the cost of a night's sleep and a bad headache, was that pretty much everyone in New York was within reasonable walking distance of at least one place that served marinated chicken, flatbread, and cucumber salad.

Webb was trying to find any thread that linked Laurel and Valerie. But as he admitted, a college girl from Minnesota and a high schooler from Brooklyn didn't have much connection. As the media had already noted, the only common denominators were that they were young, blonde, female, and conventionally attractive.

Willard, meanwhile, had deployed his laptop at Piekarski's desk. Piekarski was much tidier than Vic, so Willard had chosen to borrow the desk that wasn't covered with empty soda cans and food wrappers. The FBI agent was digging into the Peterson family's history, looking for skeletons in the closet.

Webb called them together at five AM to compare notes. Webb didn't look any more tired than usual. That, however, wasn't saying much. All of them were a little bleary.

"You first, Agent Willard," Webb said.

Willard shook his head. "They're squeaky clean," he said. "Mr. Peterson is in the earth-moving business. He has some contact with construction unions, but outside Chicago, Midwestern unions aren't connected with any major criminal enterprise we're aware of. The Petersons are comfortably upper-middle-class, but not suspiciously wealthy. I've been over their financials as thoroughly as I can and I'm telling you, there's nothing there. Hell, my own bank records are probably more suspicious."

"Any personal problems?" Webb asked.

"Nothing that left any footprints in the courts. There was one lawsuit against Peterson's company eight years ago, but it was settled out of court. None of them have ever been arrested, or even suspected of a serious crime. Laurel herself is white as snow."

"New York snow?" Erin asked wryly.

Both men chuckled. "No," Willard said. "Fresh snow, not the gray mushy kind. But Laurel was a true innocent. No arrests, no speeding tickets, no parking tickets for God's sake! Like I said, the family's cleaner than my own, or anyone else's in this room."

"Thank you, Agent Willard," Webb said. "I can summarize my own findings in pretty much the same way. Zip, zilch, nada. There's no connection whatsoever between the Peterson family and the Richards family. As far as I've been able to check, the girls didn't know one another and neither did their parents. O'Reilly, tell me you have something more substantial."

"I have a really long list of restaurants," she said. "Mostly family joints. Anyone still hungry?"

"What kind of food?" Willard asked.

"After looking up a lot of recipes, my best guess as to Laurel's last meal is it was either Lebanese or Greek chicken gyros."

"That's not really my thing for breakfast," Willard said. "Though the Lebanese make good coffee, I hear."

"Mediterranean," Webb said thoughtfully. "Does that mean our killer is from those parts, or is it a coincidence?"

"It's a little odd," Willard said. "Most serial killers target their own ethnic group. Peterson and Richards are both northern European Caucasian. Probabilities again. Speaking of profiles, I got a text from my partner. He's on his way back on a red-eye, updated profile in hand. He's very excited about it."

"I can hardly wait," Webb said in a flat deadpan. "Okay, since you want probabilities, let's think about them."

He stood up with an audible popping of knee joints. He winced, stretched, and walked over to the whiteboard.

"Item one," he said, picking an open bit of board and starting to write. "Whoever kidnapped Laurel Peterson was able to approach her in a high-traffic area without arousing suspicion or alarm. Therefore, our perp probably doesn't look like a drooling maniac."

"But Laurel was interested in helping people in need," Erin said. "Maybe the perp posed as a beggar or one of the homeless."

"Good thought," Webb said. "Either he's innocuous enough to get close, or was wearing a convincing disguise. Which leads us to item two. Our perp does his reconnaissance. It's a safe bet he knew Laurel's schedule and routine, but also probably studied her personality and habits. He knew how to lure her close enough to strike."

"So he's patient and meticulous," Willard said. "He's definitely an organized killer, not a disorganized one. He may have an overpowering urge to kill, but he's able to keep it in check long enough to plan his attacks carefully."

"Item three," Webb continued. "There is no overtly sexual component to the killing. This suggests, if I understand serial-killer psychology correctly, that he has displaced his feelings of attraction, replacing them with violence, probably due to some sort of deep-rooted sexual inadequacy. He's probably unable to perform normal sex acts with his victims. He neither rapes nor molests them, as far as we know."

"Item four," Erin said. "No torture. Whatever gets this guy off, it isn't pain. I really think it may be something other than sex."

"Serial killing is *always* about sex," Willard objected.

"Sigmund Freud thought neuroses were always about repressed sexual urges," Webb said. "But he was wrong. Let's not oversimplify here. We'd better stick with what we know or can infer about our particular perp."

"Item five," Erin said. "He feeds his victims and keeps them healthy. The chicken gyros meal is a dead end, unless our profile has room for a cook who likes Mediterranean cuisine. But he keeps them in an unhealthy environment, probably a basement full of mold. Maybe there's a Lebanese or Greek restaurant with a flooded basement, but that's a long shot."

"Item six," Webb said. "He's not interested in ransom or negotiation. He takes his victim, keeps her for a few days, then kills her. He mutilates the body and disposes of it."

"Specifically, he dumps the body in an obvious place," Willard said. "A few yards off a major walking path in Central Park? Hardly inconspicuous."

"That's right," Erin said. "As soon as the sun came up, somebody would be bound to spot it. The killer *wanted* Laurel to be found, and found fast."

"That suggests he was sending a message," Webb said. "I think we have to consider the facial lacerations within that context. He took a beautiful young woman and marked her up so badly, there's no way she'd have an open-casket funeral. And the face is the key. She didn't have a mark anywhere else on her body."

"It's the look of the thing," Erin said suddenly.

Both men looked quizzically at her.

"That's the message," she said, thinking of Andy Carver. "Our killer is taking these innocent, beautiful girls and marking them up so they're not beautiful anymore. Think about it. The killer's not trying to kill the women. He's trying to make them ugly. He's killing their beauty. Maybe it's *because* he wants them and feels ashamed of his own desire."

Webb and Willard considered this for a moment.

"That's pretty twisted," Willard said.

"But your typical rape, torture, and murder isn't?" Erin retorted. "This killer wants attention. That's the point. If he's getting off on anything, it's the TV coverage."

"And the media is helping him," Webb said. "You might be on to something, O'Reilly. It's as close to a motive as I can think of. It's insane, of course, but we're not dealing with a normal psychological specimen."

"Where does that leave us, sir?" Erin asked.

"The bowling alley is pretty close to Brighton Beach," Webb said thoughtfully. "A lot of that area ended up underwater in Hurricane Sandy. Those basements would be likely to have mold. I really think our perp is in south Brooklyn."

"We can't just start knocking on doors," Erin said. "We're talking about thousands of houses."

"I'm going to start cross-referencing Columbia staff with Brighton Beach," Webb said. "If any of them live in buildings that suffered water damage, we can take a closer look at those. And if any of them are Lebanese or Greek or Turkish, that moves them right to the top of our list."

"Are we building our own profile now, sir?" Erin asked. "Competing with the FBI?"

"I'll be interested to see what Rockwell brings back from Quantico," Webb said. "And no, we're not competing. We all want the same thing."

"Rockwell's name on the front page of every newspaper in North America?" Erin guessed.

"Okay, not precisely the same thing," Webb said. "But as long as we catch this bastard, I don't personally care who gets the credit. Curtain calls make me tired."

"Doesn't everything?"

"What difference does that make?" Webb replied.

Chapter 14

Major Crimes was quiet for almost three hours. Willard made a quick supply run and came back with a poster-sized map of Long Island, a corkboard, and a box of pushpins. The detectives used Sharpies to map out areas which had received flood damage and began putting pins in the map with the names of Columbia employees. The map soon bristled with multicolored bits of plastic.

A little before eight, Vic arrived with a big cardboard box in his arms. The others gathered around him in the break room as he revealed row upon row of what looked like jelly donuts coated with powdered sugar.

"You're a lifesaver," Erin said, snatching one up and biting eagerly into it. "Mmm, what's in these?"

"Stewed plums," Vic said. "They're homemade. Zofia's mom went on a baking spree last night. They're some kind of traditional Polish donut. I think they're pronounced 'poonch-keys,' but don't ask me how to spell that. It uses one of those funky letters that aren't in the English alphabet, so I've got no idea what's going on there."

"Pass my compliments on to Mrs. Piekarski," Webb said, already halfway through his first pączki. "I've heard Zofia mention her mother, but never her father. Why is that?"

"He died," Vic said. "A couple years ago. Heart attack."

"Sorry to hear it," Webb said. "So Mrs. Piekarski is currently single?"

Everyone stared at him.

"What?" he said. "When a man's young he looks for beauty and sex appeal. When he gets a little more life experience, he looks for a woman who can cook. These are delicious."

"Sir, there's so much wrong here, I don't even know where to start," Erin said.

"I do," Vic said. "Suppose, for a second, you and Zofia's mom hit it off. Then, suppose Zofia and I get married someday. You never know, crazier stuff happens all the time. That'd make you my father-in-law."

"Good Lord," Webb said, shuddering. "You're right. Forget I mentioned it. Nobody's that good a cook."

"Already forgotten," Vic said, sharing the shudder. "I'm good at repression. If I had a therapist, he'd say it was one of my strengths."

"Where's Zofia?" Erin asked.

"Home with Mina," he said. "But she made me promise to call her if we're about to make an arrest. What'd I miss?"

"A lot of boring busywork," Erin said. "But I think we're zeroing in on some suspects."

Vic looked at the map. "Jesus," he said. "This looks like a dartboard for the blind."

"We're still collecting and collating data," Webb said.

"Did you catch any of the news?" Vic asked.

"Not on your life," Erin said. "We've been working here. Don't tell me you've been tuning in to listen to those bastards."

"Not deliberately," he said. "But all the talk radio people are going off about the Central Park Strangler. Sheesh. He's strangled one girl, and maybe didn't even do it in the park. Hell, I've shot more people than that, but do people call me the New York Gunman? Hey, I kinda like the way that sounds. That reminds me of a joke."

"Is this really the time?" Webb asked.

"So, a stranger comes to this little town," Vic said. "And he runs into an old man crying by the side of the road. He stops to ask the poor guy what's wrong. The old man says, 'My name's Bob. You know that bridge you crossed to get into town? I built that bridge. But do they call me Bob the Bridge Builder? No. And you see that church? Its steeple was falling down. I rebuilt it with new cement and everything, and it's just like new. But do they call me Bob the Church Fixer? No. I built half the buildings in town, and nobody cares. But you screw *one* goat—"

"And we're done here," Webb interrupted. "Neshenko! There's a lady present."

"Really?" Vic looked around with an expression of shocked surprise. "Where?!"

"Ha ha," Erin said.

"On the subject of the news," Vic said. "You might want to know there's a couple news crews camped out in the lobby. I passed them on the way in."

"Channel Six?" Erin guessed.

"No," he said. "I guess our friend Holly had bigger fish to fry. Have you heard from her?"

"No," Erin said.

"I guess that whole thing about helping one another was bullshit," Vic said. "Can't say I'm surprised."

"Are the reporters causing trouble downstairs?" Webb asked.

"Not really," Vic said. "The desk sergeant said one of them tried to bluff his way up here about an hour ago, but they're being pretty quiet. One of them stuck a mic in my face when I arrived, but I stared him down and he got out of my way."

"You didn't say anything, did you?"

"Nah, I glared at him and he just about pissed himself. He must've had a guilty conscience."

"Or it's because you're a scary-looking guy," Erin said.

Vic looked pleased. "You think so? I've been working on my death stare. Sometimes I practice it in the mirror and quote DeNiro in *Taxi Driver*."

"Vic?" Erin said. "Are you... okay?"

"You talkin' ta me?" Vic replied. "You talkin' ta me? Then who the hell else are you talkin'... you talkin' ta me? Well, I'm the only one here."

"Your impression needs work," Webb said.

The elevator dinged, announcing the arrival of Agent Rockwell. He came in, Erin thought sourly, like Christ coming to kick the money-changers out of the Temple. He strode purposefully, his face set in a stern expression. He had a computer bag on his shoulder, an expensive suit on his back, and a camera crew trailing him.

"Jesus Christ," Vic muttered, echoing Erin's unspoken thought.

Erin stood up, trying to think what to say. For once Webb was quicker than she was.

"What do you think you're doing?" the Lieutenant snapped.

Rockwell faltered. His eyes lost a little of their triumphant gleam. "I came straight from JFK," he said. "I have the new behavioral analysis. I thought you'd want to see it as soon as—"

"Get those people out of here!" Webb roared. "Right now! No pictures! No interviews! Neshenko!"

"On it, sir!" Vic replied. He was as startled as Erin. Webb almost never raised his voice. The last time Erin had seen him this mad, he'd been threatening to have her arrested as an accessory to attempted murder. And he'd meant it.

Vic sprang up and crossed the room in a few brisk strides. Before the cameramen could do more than sputter out a few halfhearted protests, he'd crowded them back into the elevator. He reached around to the control panel, pushed a button at random, and stood in the doorway with his arms crossed like the world's surliest bouncer until the doors slid shut and the elevator car departed to make trouble for cops on some other floor.

"That was out of line, Lieutenant," Rockwell said, recovering a little of his balance. His face was flushing red with anger and embarrassment.

"No!" Webb barked. He came around his desk and advanced on the FBI agent, index finger pointed at the G-man's face like the barrel of his .38 Special. "Here's what's out of line! We have sensitive materials right there on the board, in plain view! Do you *want* our perp to know how close we are to catching him? Are you *trying* to compromise this investigation? If he gets wise to us and we can't catch him, if another girl dies because of your desire for the spotlight, I swear to God, I will burn your ass if I have to torch the entire Federal Bureau of Investigation!"

"For crying out loud, Lieutenant, they just wanted a photo op!" Rockwell protested. He tried a shaky smile and a good-natured laugh, attempting to defuse the situation.

"And that's more important to you than solving this thing?" Webb demanded. He was less than a foot from Rockwell now. Webb was a few inches shorter, many years older, and many pounds heavier than Rockwell. The FBI man was Hollywood's version of a cop. Webb was the run-down, used-car-lot model. Put them side by side and you'd lay odds of fifty to one against

Webb in a fistfight, but at this moment, Erin wouldn't have bet against her commanding officer. He looked like he'd decided to pitch Rockwell through the nearest window without bothering to open it and was about to do it.

Rockwell was bright enough to see it too. He backed up a step, raising a hand placatingly. "Sheesh," he said. "We're all on the same side here. I came to help. I really think this will be useful. Can we take it down a notch?"

Webb stood there and seethed for a moment. Erin traded glances with Vic, who had an uneasy smile plastered on his face. Vic was happy enough to see one of the Feebies get put in his place, but the situation was awfully volatile. It was all very well to talk about punching a Fed in the nose, but the fallout if it actually happened would be biblical.

"We were just talking about the behavioral patterns of our perp," Erin said with brittle perkiness. "Why don't we compare notes and see where we stand?"

"That's a great idea," Vic said, copying her tone. "Don't you think, sir? I mean, we're on a tight clock here, so the sooner we get our shit together the better, right?"

"Right," Webb said in a tight, strained voice. "Agent Rockwell, thank you for your continued assistance. What did you bring from the brain boys at Quantico?"

Rockwell took out his laptop and flipped it open. "Just a second," he said. "I'll bring it up."

On his way back from the elevator, Vic passed close to Erin. "He could've just e-mailed us the thing, you know," he said in an undertone.

"Worse optics," Erin replied out of the corner of her mouth.

"Our people have taken into account the quirks of the unsub's MO," Rockwell said. "They've looked at the behavioral indicators of the various, ah, eccentricities on display. Here's the updated profile:

"The postmortem knife strokes indicate a ritualistic component to the murder, showing the unsub to be acting out of rage, but within a specific channel. This suggests a rigid upbringing, probably by a very strait-laced mother. He does not dare violate his victim sexually, due to deep repression and identification of his victim with his mother, but he harbors deep-seated rage against her. He is torn between this rage and his natural shyness. When confronted, he is likely to be quiet and polite until prodded beyond the bounds of self-control, at which point he will lash out violently. He is likely to come quietly if arrested, but if questioned he may fly into homicidal rage.

"The unsub is troubled by feelings of self-hatred and inadequacy. He may have attempted self-harm at some point in the past. Suspects' medical records should be examined for such actions. He would definitely be a suicide risk if taken into custody."

"We can't look at medical records," Webb said. "Not without a court order."

"Of course not," Rockwell said. "I'm familiar with HIPAA law."

"If I'm understanding this," Vic said, "our perp is offing teenagers because he's pissed at his mom?"

"Specifically at her strict child-rearing and discipline," Rockwell said. "She would have forbidden romantic or sexual contact with girls, so over time he has projected his frustration onto the forbidden fruit of nubile females."

"Of which now?" Vic said.

"Attractive women," Webb translated.

"Geez," Vic said. "You could've just said hot chicks. We're not studying for the SATs."

"Thank you for this," Webb said to Rockwell. "Let's combine it with what we've come up with here. Let me show you what we've been working on."

Erin and Vic retreated to the break room while Webb and Willard brought Rockwell up to speed. Vic closed the door behind them as Erin made a beeline for the espresso machine.

"Our Lieutenant really tore Rockhead a new one," Vic said. "I didn't think he had it in him."

"Yeah," Erin said. "That was a little bit of an overreaction, don't you think?"

"Oh, I dunno," Vic said. "When I was on my way to throw those news jockeys out, I saw what was on his computer. He had pictures of a couple teenage girls up."

"Our victims?"

"No. They look like his kids. His daughters, who are about the same age as our victims."

"Oh."

"So I'm thinking that's why he's pissed."

"That makes sense." Erin finished filling her cup and reached for the creamer. "I know Rockwell's annoying, but I do believe he's trying to help."

"Really? What did he bring us that's worth a damn? Nothing in that precious profile helps us catch the son of a bitch. We need something concrete and that's exactly what we don't have. Valerie's gonna die and they're gonna blame us."

"Don't say that. Don't even think it. We'll figure something out. Let's get back out there."

Webb was talking as they emerged, but was interrupted by his phone. His current ringtone, Erin noted wryly, was a snippet of the old Beth Hart hit "LA Song."

"Man, I gotta get out of this town,
Man, I gotta get out of this pain..."

"Excuse me," Webb said, hoisting the phone. "Webb. What? Copy that. I'm not quite clear on why you're calling us. Isn't this a job for the local Homicide squad? Oh, that's what you thought? No, I understand. I'll send a couple of my people down. Yes, they'll be there as soon as possible. Webb out."

He hung up and turned to Vic and Erin. "That was Captain Fink at the Six-Oh in Brighton Beach. I need you to run down to Brooklyn. Local uniforms found a body."

"Oh, no," Erin said. "Valerie Richards?"

"No," Webb said. "They don't have an ID yet, but it's an older woman."

"Then what's that got to do with us?" Vic asked.

"That's what I asked," Webb said. "He said it's a blonde who got slashed up and the press are going to be all over him. He thinks it's somehow related to our case, and even if it's not, he wants Major Crimes on it right away."

"Jesus Christ on a tinfoil cross," Vic said. "We can't go running after every dead girl in New York! Do they want us to find Valerie or not? We don't have enough bodies in this office!"

"Which is why Agents Willard and Rockwell will stay here with me," Webb said. "We'll keep working the problem. I'll see if Piekarski can come in, too. In the meantime, I'm giving you a very polite but nonnegotiable order to get your ass down to Brighton Beach and see if you can sort this shit out. You copy?"

"Yes, sir," Vic said. "Right away, sir."

* * *

"This is political bullshit is what it is," Vic said from the passenger seat of Erin's Charger.

"Captain Fink's just covering his own ass," Erin said. She was concentrating on her driving. Rolf, head poking out between the seats, was the only one in the car who seemed to be having a good time.

"That's what I said," Vic said. "Political. You know we've got a hotline set up for tips about the Strangler?"

"Of course we do," Erin said. "And I pity the poor bastards who have to answer it. They get all the false confessions, the psychics, and the crazies who come out of the woodwork every time something like this happens."

"Yeah. That's why the calls don't come straight to us. Half a dozen unis are working the phones. They filter out the crap and pass the rest on to us. Talk about your shit details."

"I haven't seen anything from them," Erin said.

"That's because so far it's been a hundred percent crap," Vic said. "But they're getting hundreds of calls. The whole damn city's obsessed. And this is what happens. Every murder, especially if it's a woman, will get laid on us. Next thing you know, we'll be dealing with UFO sightings or some shit. You know, I knew Captain Fink when I was down in Brighton Beach."

"Really? What was he like?"

"He was only a Lieutenant then. He was okay, I guess, but he was always real good at making sure somebody else was there to take the fall when something went wrong."

"The buck stops somewhere else?" she said.

"Anywhere else," he agreed. "That's probably how he made Captain. He got away with everything. He was good at managing his optics. Me? I can't get away with nothin.'"

"I think we could do with a few reporters fewer in this whole mess," Erin growled. "Why can't any of *them* get offed? It might make our job easier."

*   *   *

The crime scene was Asser Levy Park, just off West Fifth Street. Erin, Vic, and Rolf followed the directions of one of the Patrol cops on the perimeter and found themselves at the public restroom a short distance into the park. Another uniform stood guard outside. Erin flashed her shield and he got out of the way. The detectives donned their disposable gloves and went in.

"What is it with friggin' restrooms?" Vic asked. "They're a lousy damn place to die. If I'm gonna get knifed, it's gonna happen somewhere less depressing. Where's this dead girl, anyway?"

"In the stall, I guess," Erin said. She could smell the blood underlying the overpowering odors of disinfectant and stale urine. So could Rolf. His nose was twitching.

A CSU guy was standing outside the stall, taking photographs. He nodded to them.

"White female," he said. "Blonde hair. Don't have a firm cause of death yet, but I'm gonna go out on a limb and say she got stabbed."

The detectives peered past him into the stall.

"Yeah," Vic said. "That is one stabbed woman. Jesus. I see why they called us. Look at her face! She's cut to friggin' shreds!"

"I'd rather not," Erin said, but she didn't turn away. You didn't get to avert your eyes when you wore a gold shield.

"I can see why they don't have an ID yet," he said. "Her own mom wouldn't know her."

"Yeah," Erin said. "It's got to be the same killer. But that's not Valerie Richards."

"No way," Vic agreed. "Look at her hair. This woman dyed."

"You can say that again," the CSU guy said.

"Not *died*," Vic said, rolling his eyes. "I mean she dyed her hair. She did a good job, but you can see the roots. She's a natural blonde but she lightened it up. Valerie's a hundred percent *au natural.* And this lady's definitely older. Look at the clothes. And the figure. She looks almost like..."

Vic trailed off. Erin got it then, too. Maybe it was the too-tight blouse, open to show a bloodstained but still impressive cleavage. Maybe it was the underlying shape of the face, visible through its mask of blood.

"Holy shit," she said. "That's Holly Gardner."

Chapter 15

"What was that you said a minute ago?" Vic said. "You were hoping a reporter would get popped?"

Erin shook her head. She felt dizzy. "That wasn't... I mean... I didn't mean it!"

"Don't they always tell reporters not to become part of the story?" Vic said. "Like for cops, they tell us not to become part of an accident. Don't be a statistic, that's what they say. Shit, I'm babbling."

"Right," Erin murmured absently. She was staring at the dead woman. "This is part of our case."

"Of course it is," he said. "It's the same MO. She was looking into it. She found the damn killer, Erin!"

"Looks like it," Erin said, recovering herself a little. "But it isn't the same MO. Not even close."

"Hot blonde corpse?" he retorted. "Knife marks all over the face? Sound familiar?"

"Look at her," Erin said. "What do you see?"

"I see a dead woman."

"Damn it, Vic, you're a detective! Really *look* at her!"

"Fine!" Vic hadn't, in truth, been looking closely at the body. He wasn't usually this squeamish. Now he did as Erin asked and took a closer look.

"Well?" Erin asked after a moment.

"She's been stabbed," he said. "In the chest. More than once. Lots of blood on her blouse."

"Not strangled," Erin agreed. "And check out her hands and arms."

"Defensive wounds," he said. "A couple deep gashes on her forearm, plus those fingers. Looks like she damn near lost two or three digits."

"She was free and fighting for her life," Erin said. "I figure she blocked the first few attacks, taking them on the arm and hand. But the perp just kept stabbing and eventually got through."

"Not quite," Vic said. "You haven't been in many knife fights, have you?"

"I try to avoid them," Erin said.

"Look at the cut across the fingers," he said, bending closer. "Straight across. See the blood on the palm, but no cut on it? She grabbed the knife, either trying to keep it away or pulling it out of herself, and the killer yanked it free. That tells us it was a single-edged knife. If it had two edges, it would've cut her palm. That's a sharp goddamn blade. Those fingers are hanging by flaps. Talk about your manicure from hell."

"Butcher's knife," Erin guessed.

"The work on the face looks like the Peterson girl," he said. "But not the stabs to the chest. Whatever our perp is, he's no professional knife-fighter. He's just a vicious amateur, and that's scarier, if you ask me."

"How can you tell?" Erin had seen a lot more shootings than stabbings.

"This was a sewing-machine attack," he explained. "If you don't have training and you want to disable someone in a hurry, the best thing to do is just get in close and stab in and out, as fast as you can, center of mass, as many times as possible. Like a sewing-machine needle. Bam-bam-bam-bam."

He turned to face her, clenching his right fist as though holding a knife. He illustrated his words by bringing the fist in toward her abdomen several times in rapid succession.

"Yikes," Erin said.

"It's crude, but effective," he said. "Your pal Corcoran wouldn't do something like that. He's got too much fancy style. He'd go for the throat, or maybe a surgical strike to the heart or lungs. Not our boy here. He didn't give a crap about style. This was about brutal results."

"Are you a knife-fighter?" she asked.

"I've done some classes," he said.

"What would you do if someone came at you like this?"

"Run."

"Are you serious?"

He nodded. "Damn straight. It's hard to block that many strikes and it only takes one to friggin' end you. If you ever need to knife someone, it's probably your best bet. Just remember, it's kinda hard to claim self-defense after you've just stabbed some poor schmuck ten times in the guts."

"Copy that." Erin returned her attention to the body. "Take a look at her skirt."

"I was trying not to," Vic said.

"This is no time to get embarrassed looking at a woman's legs," Erin said. "See how it's hiked up? It's a little risqué, don't you think?"

"If you're asking whether I'm finding any part of this sexy, the answer is no, I'm not. I'm not a psycho."

"Vic, Laurel Peterson was posed modestly," she reminded him. "Fully clothed, jeans buttoned, zipper fastened. Holly's skirt is hiked up and her legs are spread. It's a pretty indecent pose."

"Jesus," Vic muttered. "What's your point?"

"Our killer respected Laurel," Erin said. "I don't think he respected Holly. I think he wanted her to look obscene."

"After my shift, I'm gonna need a whole lot of vodka," Vic said. "Maybe if I drink enough of it, I'll forget what this looks like."

"It could be worse," she said. "There isn't enough blood here, considering how many wounds were inflicted."

"Not nearly," Vic said, glad of the change of topic. He looked at the floor. "See that blood trail?"

"We know," the CSU photographer said. "Looks like someone dragged her in here. She wasn't stabbed in the restroom. This is just where the body was dumped."

Vic and Erin looked at one another. Then they looked down at Rolf.

The K-9 cocked his head at Erin.

She pointed to the droplets of blood on the bathroom tile. "*Such!*" she ordered.

Rolf zeroed in on the smell. Fresh blood was *easy*. This would be the simplest path to his Kong ball he could imagine. Not that he was complaining. An easy Kong ball was still a Kong ball. Nostrils flaring, tail wagging, the Shepherd was on his way.

Erin was expecting the trail to lead to the street and disappear. Holly had probably been brought to the park in the trunk of a car and discarded. But Rolf led them the opposite direction, onto a foot path into the park.

"What the hell is going on?" Vic wondered as he trotted beside them.

"This is where the blood came from," Erin said. She pointed to a few droplets that stained the asphalt. It was comforting to have visual confirmation, though she hadn't doubted Rolf's abilities.

"But why?" Vic asked. "Hauling a corpse through the park in the open? Even if it was the middle of the night, there's lamps all along this path. Why risk getting spotted when he could've ditched the bitch anywhere he wanted?"

"Laurel was left in plain view," Erin said. "She was meant to be found. Maybe Holly wasn't."

"Bullshit," he said. "People go into public restrooms, Erin. Because they need to take a piss. Somebody would've found her. Somebody *did* find her! Who do you think called the cops?"

"She wasn't found right away," Erin said. "And she wasn't found where she was killed. Stashing the body gives our killer time and distance. This wasn't planned, Vic. This was spur of the moment. I think Holly surprised the perp. She ran into him and he panicked. He killed her, but probably in or near where he lives. So he tried to shift her to throw us off. We're close!"

Rolf thought so too. He strained at the leash, panting and lunging. They followed a path that curved around the northwest corner of the park to its exit on Sea Breeze Avenue.

"Our perp's strong," Vic observed. "Holly wasn't huge, but she had to weigh at least a one-thirty. You ever try dragging over a hundred pounds of deadweight meat a couple hundred yards? It's not easy."

"Hold on," she said. "Rolf! *Fuss!*"

The Shepherd immediately pulled up, turned a tight circle, and returned to Erin. He stood at her hip, looking up at her and wagging impatiently. He was a good boy and he'd do as he was told, but they hadn't gotten to the end of the trail yet.

"What?" Vic said.

Erin pointed to another small spatter of blood. But it was just off the trail, and next to it was the distinctive imprint of a narrow wheel in the dirt.

"That's a cargo dolly," he said with reluctant admiration. "That son of a bitch loaded her up like friggin' cargo and wheeled her to the restroom. If he had her in a box, nobody would've looked twice. And it would've been a lot easier to shift her. Clever bastard."

"If he had her in a box, it was leaking," Erin said.

"Cardboard isn't watertight."

"Remember this spot. CSU will want the tire impression. If they can match it to a wheel that belongs to our guy, it might be enough hard evidence to nail him."

"Copy that. Are we going on?"

"Absolutely. Rolf, *such!*"

And they were off again. They went through the gap in the low metal fence that ringed the park and across the sidewalk and Sea Breeze Avenue. Without hesitation, Rolf angled to an apartment tower directly across from the park. He scratched at the southwest entrance and barked once.

Erin glanced at Vic and nodded. They didn't need a warrant yet; not until they needed to enter a private dwelling. The main apartment complex was fair game. Vic opened the exterior door, revealing an atrium with a pair of elevators and another door to the stairs.

"Hey, look," Vic said. "They have an indoor pool. Swanky. Remember that dead chick we found in that hotel swimming pool?"

"I try not to," Erin said. She caught a whiff of chlorine as Rolf pulled past the pool entrance. To no one's surprise, he was making for one of the elevators. The killer wouldn't have wanted to muscle a dolly down God knew how many flights of stairs. Elevators were annoying, since they didn't know which floor the perp had come from, but it was just a question of trying every floor until they got to the right one. Vic knew the drill as well as Erin did. He punched the button for Two, starting their brute-force search.

It could have been better and it could have been worse. On the eighth floor out of twenty, Rolf hauled Erin out and down the hall. The building was clean and in good repair, unlike too many New York apartments. But Erin found something sinister in its spare, angular lines and plain carpet. They hadn't seen anyone since coming inside. That was hardly unusual; it was during normal work hours on a weekday. But she felt a crawly sensation on the back of her neck. Holding Rolf's leash in her left hand, she dropped her right to the butt of her pistol.

Vic felt the same. He'd drawn his Sig-Sauer and was gripping it in both hands at waist height, ready to bring it up and into action at the first hint of trouble. Erin didn't blame him. They were closing in on someone who'd killed at least two women and might have a third tied up somewhere in this very building.

Rolf stopped at unit 814. He pawed at the door.

"*Platz!*" Erin hissed, warning him to get down and be quiet. "*Sei still!*"

The Shepherd instantly sank to his belly in utter silence, planting his chin between his front paws. But his weight still rested on his haunches, hind legs tensed to spring.

"I say we take the door," Vic said in a low voice. "Right now."

"We can't," Erin murmured. "Rolf isn't enough for probable cause."

"Jesus Christ!" he hissed. "Val could be in there!"

"I know," she said, trying to think. "You watch that door. But don't touch it!"

She tossed Rolf his ball to keep him distracted and to reward his efforts. Then she retreated to the end of the hallway and took out her phone.

"Webb," the Lieutenant said, almost before the end of the first ring. "What's the word on your victim?"

"It's Holly Gardner, sir."

"Who?"

"The reporter. Channel Six News."

"Oh, right. Wait, what? Are you telling me one of the reporters covering this story got stabbed to death last night?"

"Yes. I'll explain later. Right now I need to know whether any of the Columbia staff live at 227 Sea Breeze Avenue, Apartment 814."

She could feel Webb's confusion even over the phone, but to his credit he didn't waste time on questions. "Just a moment," he said. "227 Sea Breeze... yes. Donald Lambert. He's an electrician. We don't have much on him. No police jacket, no priors. Quiet sort. But I'm sure this isn't a lucky guess. You're there?"

"Vic's outside his door as we speak. Rolf followed Holly's trail up."

"Is he home?"

"I don't know."

"It's funny," Webb said. "But we just got a lead forwarded to us from the hotline a few minutes ago. Anonymous caller, female, said Lambert's the guy we want. No details."

"Why didn't you lead with that, sir?"

"An unsubstantiated accusation from an unvetted source? There's thin, and there's really thin, and there's that. But taken together with the FBI profile, the Columbia connection, and your dog, it adds up. I can have an ESU team there in half an hour."

Erin thought about what Vic had said about the perp's knife work: amateurish. "We don't need ESU," she said. "Vic, Rolf, and I can take him if he's here. This guy's panicking, sir. He just killed a woman he didn't intend to. We might not have half an hour. He might do something to Valerie before the doorkickers can get here."

Webb considered this for a long moment. "Fine," he said. "You're the ranking detective on scene, so it's your call. But if Valerie Richards is there, keep her alive. You understand?"

"Copy that, sir."

"And I'm sending backup. You should have uniforms on site in minutes."

"Thank you, sir. O'Reilly out."

She hung up and rejoined Vic. "Showtime," she said, drawing her Glock. "Rolf, *hier.*"

"I'll go first," he said. "On three. One... two... three!"

Vic had come to Major Crimes from ESU. Calling the Emergency Services Unit "doorkickers" was mostly metaphorical. Vic, however, took it literally. His boot hit the door like a sledgehammer, all his considerable weight behind it. The door was solid wood, double-locked with a high-quality deadbolt engaged. It didn't stand a chance.

Vic was through the doorway while the splinters were still flying. "NYPD! Hands up!" he roared, moving fast and clearing the bottleneck at the apartment's entrance.

It was a nice suite, a corner unit. A sliding glass door opened onto a balcony. The apartment was spotlessly clean. Erin caught brief glimpses of white furniture and stainless steel as she and Rolf swung to Vic's right. She saw no bloodstains on the carpet, nothing to indicate a murder had been committed. She also saw no sign of Donald Lambert.

"Clear!" Vic called from the direction of the bedroom.

Erin swung through the kitchen and connected dining area to the living room. All were neat, tidy, and deserted.

"Clear!" she called back.

She met Vic on the return loop from the bedroom and bathroom. "We missed him," he said. "I guess he's at work."

Erin started to agree, then froze. The sliding balcony door was ajar and she couldn't see the whole balcony. She cocked her head toward it.

Vic was across the room in three strides. He slid the door the rest of the way open and lunged onto the balcony, gun in hand. He disappeared to the right. Erin heard a squawk. Then Vic came back in view, holding a struggling man by the collar.

Donald Lambert wasn't really a small guy, but Vic's massive hand and arm made him look scrawny by comparison. He was flailing at Vic's arm with both hands and having no effect whatsoever.

"Where's the girl?" Vic demanded. Lambert's feet, Erin saw with shock, weren't touching the ground. Vic was holding him up with one hand and making it look easy. Adrenaline was a hell of a thing.

"You're hurting me!" Lambert croaked. Vic's fingers were twined around his shirt collar, knuckles pressing into his throat. The big Russian thrust the man against the balcony railing. Lambert's upper body was suspended in space, his center of gravity dangling over an eight-story drop onto concrete.

"Where is the girl?" Vic shouted in his face.

"Vic!" Erin yelled, running out onto the balcony. Rolf, beside her, barked excitedly. The dog had no idea what was going on, but it looked like a fight and he and his teeth were ready to pitch in.

"What girl?" Lambert whimpered.

Vic rammed the muzzle of his pistol up under Lambert's chin. "I'll blow your brains out, you sick sack of shit!" he snarled. "Start talking, dammit!"

"Vic, stop it!" Erin shouted. She wanted to grab his arm and force the gun down, but knew better than to go for his weapon. It might go off by accident, or he might let Lambert fall.

"You're a cop!" she yelled into his ear.

Vic gave Lambert a good hard shake. The man's eyes practically rattled in their sockets. Lambert made a weak mewing sound, like a sad kitten, and sagged in a dead faint. As he went limp, his body tried to tumble over the railing. Erin lunged and grabbed at the man, getting a handful of his shirtfront. The fabric held.

Vic dragged the unconscious man back over the balcony and let him fall to the floor like a sack of flour. "Damn," he said in disgust. "I hate when they do that."

Chapter 16

Lambert took his time waking up. Vic slapped cuffs on him, hauled him inside, and left him lying in the middle of the living room on the beige carpet. The Russian kept an eye on the suspect while Erin and Rolf started searching the apartment.

They quickly determined that nobody else was present. If Lambert had Valerie Richards, he was keeping her somewhere else. That came as no surprise to Erin; Lambert was too much of a neat freak to allow mold to grow on his walls. However, other evidence was waiting to be found.

"There's a dolly in the front closet," she reported. "Stains on it that look like blood. Rolf says they smell like it, too."

"You oughta taste it," Vic called back. "Just to make sure."

"No thanks, I'm full. I ate too many of Zofia's mom's donuts."

Erin didn't touch the dolly. CSU would want to dust it for prints. She moved into the kitchen. "Got something else in here," she said. "Or we're missing something, to be precise."

"What?" Vic asked.

"The knife block has an open slot. No butcher's knife."

"Well isn't that interesting," he said. "Our boy must've ditched it down a storm drain or something. Good luck finding it."

"What I'm not finding is other bloodstains," she said, returning to the living room. "If Holly was killed here, Lambert did one hell of a job cleaning up afterward."

"All that stabbing?" Vic replied. "Forget about it. There'd be spatter all over the place. Rugs, walls, windows, even the ceiling. No way could one guy get rid of all of it. Anyway, CSU will shine those whatchamacallits, their luminol lights. They'll see the traces even if he did clean up. But I think the stabbing happened somewhere else."

"Where?" Erin wondered. "And if it did, why wheel the body all the way up here?"

"He probably didn't," Vic said. "I think he brought the dolly back up after transporting the body. That's what your dog was tracking. It'd still smell like blood."

"NYPD!" a man shouted from the hallway.

"In here!" Erin answered. "The apartment's clear! We have one suspect in custody. Put your guns away!"

Two pairs of Patrolmen had arrived in answer to Webb's call for reinforcements. At Erin's direction they set up a perimeter summoned CSU. Two uniforms would stay on the door while the scene was processed. In the meantime, Erin and Vic could take their prisoner.

Lambert was finally coming around. He was visibly confused and obviously frightened. He was about five-foot ten and a little over average weight, but his natural shyness made him seem smaller. His hair was thinning and he wore wire-rimmed glasses. He certainly didn't look like a brutal murderer, but then, they often didn't.

"Where should we take him?" Vic asked. "The Lieutenant will want to take a crack at him, but the Eightball's on the wrong side of the river. I say we haul his ass to the Six-Oh."

"Excuse me," Lambert said. "Who are you, sir? What do you want from me? Is it money?"

"Is this guy for real?" Vic said. "Did he seriously just offer me a bribe?"

"Bribe?" Lambert echoed. "I'm sorry, but there's been a misunderstanding. I thought you were here to rob me."

"I'm a cop, asshole," Vic said. He held up the gold shield on its chain around his neck. "See this? It means I'm a detective with the New York Police Department. And those bracelets on your wrists mean your ass is mine. So bend over, buddy, because we can do this easy or hard, and if you choose hard, you'll be walking funny for a long, long time."

"What's he talking about?" Lambert squeaked. He shrank away from Vic and tried to scoot backwards, only succeeding in losing his balance and tipping over.

"Vic, try not to scare him any more than you have to," Erin said. "Look at the poor guy's pants. You made him piss himself."

"Oh no," Lambert moaned. "Oh no, not that!"

To the astonishment of both detectives, he began to cry. He rocked back and forth on the ground, sobbing.

"What the hell is this crap?" Vic growled. "I came here expecting Hannibal Lecter and what I got was Weeping Willie. He's gonna give serial killers a bad name."

"Bad little boys wet the bed," Lambert whimpered. "Bad little boys wet the bed. Bad, bad, bad, bad…"

He began rhythmically thumping his head against the floor.

"Hey!" Erin snapped. "Stop that!" She grabbed his shoulders and pulled him up to a sitting position. Lambert's nose was running as much as his eyes. His glasses hung askew and were splotchy with tears.

"We'd better get him out of here," Vic said. "Before we have an even worse sanitation problem. I'm glad you drove. You'll be the one who has to hose out your car."

"Donald Lambert," Erin said. "You're under arrest for the murder of Holly Gardner. You have the right to remain silent..."

She read him the rest of the Miranda warning, but wasn't sure he was even listening. She had to ask three times whether he understood his rights before receiving a whispered assent. She tried to come across as firm but kind, positioning herself to play good cop in the upcoming interrogation. Vic, of course, would be bad cop. He could play that role without trying; probably because he wasn't playing.

*   *   *

"I apologize for my disgusting behavior," Lambert said.

He had undergone an amazing transformation. After Erin had suggested he be allowed to change into dry pants, and they'd carted him off to the Precinct 60 interrogation room, Lambert had recovered his calm. Now he was polite and soft-spoken. His hands were cuffed in front of him, but he had them folded neatly on the tabletop. The only really odd thing was the way he wouldn't look directly at either Erin or Vic. His eyes kept sliding off to one side or the other, or staring down at his own hands.

"Forget about it," Erin said. "Vic sometimes has that effect on people. I'm sorry he scared you."

That was a bare-faced lie. The best way to take down a suspect was to shock and disorient him, to scare him half out of his wits. A man that frightened was a man unlikely to fight back.

Vic hunched forward and growled low in his chest. Lambert quivered slightly.

"Look, Donald," Erin said. "I know you're scared. And I want to help you. But this situation looks pretty bad. Maybe you can explain a few things."

"I would very much like to help you, ma'am," Lambert said. "What can I do?"

"Do you like to cook, Donald?" The repeated use of his first name was deliberate, to make him subconsciously think of her as a close acquaintance rather than a detective looking for any possible way to burn him.

"Cook? Yes, I'm an excellent cook. I have Julia Child's *Mastering the Art of French Cooking, Volume One.* I have *The Silver Palate Cookbook.* I have Mark Bittman's *How to Cook Everything: Simple Recipes for Great Food.* I recently acquired *The Silver Spoon.* And, of course, I also have *The Joy of Cooking,* but almost every kitchen has a copy, so it hardly bears mentioning. Those are my main books of recipes. I have several others. There's—"

"You don't need to list all of them," Erin said, holding up a hand. "I assume you keep your kitchen well stocked with food, appliances, and utensils."

"Naturally," Lambert said. "I've read that a craftsman is only as good as his tools."

"You keep your knives sharp?"

"I sharpen them daily."

"When?"

"Just before I start cooking supper."

"So you'd notice if one of them was missing?"

"Obviously."

Gotcha, Erin thought. She'd just scored a point, but Lambert's lack of reaction puzzled her. He should have been nervous or worried.

"Where is your butcher's knife?" she asked.

"In my knife block," he said. Then he hesitated. "Isn't it?"

"I don't know my way around your kitchen," she said. "Is there anywhere else you would have put it?"

"If I'd recently used it, it would be drying in the dish drainer," he said. "But I didn't."

"Where do you keep your freight dolly?" she asked.

He blinked. "I don't own one."

"So you're saying the dolly in your closet doesn't belong to you?"

"I don't know what you mean. Which closet?"

"The coat closet just inside your front door."

"All I keep in there is clothing," he said. "I have a winter parka, two windbreakers, a middleweight topcoat, three scarves, four hats, a pair of rubber galoshes, my work shoes, my black wingtip dress shoes, and three pairs of gloves."

"You have a good memory for your belongings," she said.

"Thank you," he said.

"How about faces?"

"What?"

"Do you remember faces?"

"Not... not well." Lambert faltered. "It's somewhat difficult for me to look people in the eye."

"Why is that?" she asked gently.

"I don't know," he said. "I've been like that ever since I was a boy."

"Do you have a girlfriend?"

"No."

"Boyfriend?"

"No." His inflection was exactly the same.

"Where did you grow up?"

"About two miles north of here."

"Do you visit your parents often?"

"No."

"Why not?"

 White Lady

"My father left when I was very young," Lambert said quietly. "I don't know where he is. And my mother... my mother died."

"I'm sorry," Erin said. "When did it happen?"

"Fifty-eight days ago."

Meticulous and fastidious in his personal habits, possibly obsessive-compulsive, Erin thought. *Polite and unthreatening in appearance. Lives alone. He comes from a home in which his parents were divorced or separated.* Donald Lambert was the spitting image of the FBI's first behavioral profile.

"Does this woman look familiar?" Erin asked, laying a computer printout on the table. It was a publicity shot of Holly Gardner. The reporter was flashing her megawatt smile and a lot of tanned skin.

Lambert gave the picture a sidelong, sneaky sort of look. He seemed reluctant to fully face it. "No," he said. "She's very pretty."

"You're sure?" Erin pressed. "You haven't seen her?"

"No. Who is she?"

"Her name was Holly Gardner," Vic interjected. "And we know you know her!"

"Oh!" Lambert exclaimed. His eyes went wide with recognition at the name.

"What?" Erin asked. "When did you meet her?"

"I didn't," he said. "That is, I was supposed to. She was coming to talk to me last night. At least, that's what she said. But she never arrived. I cleaned my whole place for her, top to bottom. I wasn't cooking for her, since it was after supper, but I made a pavlova."

"I love pavlova," Vic said, his bad-cop instincts momentarily suppressed by the thought of dessert.

"What's pavlova?" Erin asked and immediately regretted it.

"It's a meringue-based fruit dessert," Lambert explained. "But there are several ways to make the meringue. You have to be very careful handling meringue, because it is prone to cracking if overbaked or if it dries out. The best way..."

Erin knew it was important to listen to everything a suspect said in interrogation, but she wasn't much of a foodie and she fuzzed out as he explained, in excruciating detail, the dessert he'd prepared.

"How did Holly contact you?" she managed to ask when he finally paused for breath.

"By telephone," he said. "So you see, I didn't know her face."

"And it didn't strike you as odd? That a complete stranger would be coming to visit you at home without ever meeting you anywhere else?"

"I don't understand women very well," he said, becoming very interested in his hands. "I just wanted to make a good impression."

"Did she say what she wanted to talk about?" Erin asked.

"She said I could help her with her work."

"When was she supposed to come?"

"Eleven o'clock."

"That's a little late for dessert, isn't it?"

"That was the time she was available. I had no other plans. I often stay up late."

"What did you do when she didn't show?"

"I put the pavlova in the refrigerator. It's still there; you can check. At midnight I went to bed."

"So you never heard from her after that?"

"No."

"Did you try calling her back, to ask where she was?"

"No."

"Why not?"

"I didn't know if she'd want to hear from me. She might have changed her mind."

"We took a phone out of your pocket when we brought you in. Is that the one she used to contact you?"

"Yes."

"Donald," Erin said softly. "Where's Valerie Richards?"

"I don't know," Lambert said.

"I think you do," she said. "I think Valerie's alone and frightened. If you can help us find her and bring her in safely, it'll buy you a lot of goodwill with the judge. I don't think you want to hurt her."

"Of course I don't," he said. "I don't want to hurt anyone. But I can't help you."

"Bullshit!" Vic snapped.

Lambert flinched.

"I think you're lying," Vic said.

"No," Lambert said. "I'm telling you the truth. Please believe me."

"I want to believe you," Erin said. "This is your chance to tell me everything. Now, while there's still time."

"I've told you what I know," Lambert said. "Didn't you say I had the right to an attorney?"

Damn, Erin thought. "That's right," she said through clenched teeth. "But you don't need one if you don't have anything to hide."

That was another lie, but a very helpful one for a cop to tell.

"I don't understand what's going on," Lambert said. "I think I'd better engage a legal professional. I... I don't think I'll say anything else without one."

And that was it for the interrogation.

Chapter 17

"You decided to interrogate our prime suspect without waiting for me?"

Webb wasn't shouting anymore. This was his quiet, tired anger. Vic and Erin relaxed. They were used to this version of him.

"We thought time was of the essence, sir," Erin said.

"Whenever you talk like that, it makes me suspicious," Webb said. "I got here as fast as I could. Traffic was terrible. Not that I need to explain myself to you anyway. I outrank both of you put together."

"I don't think that's how rank works, sir," Vic said.

"Shut up, Neshenko."

"Yes, sir. Right away, sir."

"Now Lambert has clammed up and lawyered up," Webb continued. "You know the first interrogation is our best chance to break a subject, before he has the chance to construct an alibi. Now we have no confession, no murder weapon, and most importantly, no kidnapped girl."

"We have a bloodstained dolly, a missing knife, and a perp who admitted to inviting our victim over last night, sir," Vic said.

"I thought I told you to shut up," Webb said.

"Stating facts, sir," Vic said. "That doesn't count as talking."

Webb blinked. "What?" he said blankly. "That doesn't make any sense at all."

"Facts don't have to make sense, sir," Vic said, staring straight ahead.

Webb started to answer. Then he realized there was really nothing to say to that and decided to pretend he hadn't heard it.

"Did you get anything else out of him?" he asked Erin. "Other than that tidbit about him talking to Gardner on the phone? Which, by the way, we could have gotten from examining his phone."

"Nothing usable, sir," Erin said. "I just thought—"

"Go on, Detective," he sighed. "Tell me what you thought."

"We had strong physical evidence tying him to Holly's death. I was sure the person who killed her is the same one who killed Laurel and snatched Valerie. He fits the FBI profile. *Perfectly.*"

"Speaking of the FBI," Vic said. "Where are they?"

"Agents Willard and Rockwell are meeting with the Commissioner," Webb said. "He requested a status report."

"They're not going to announce they caught the Strangler, are they?" Erin said. "Because that isn't proved yet! We don't even know for sure he killed Holly, let alone Laurel! And we don't have the slightest idea where Valerie is!"

"Relax, O'Reilly," Webb said. "This was already scheduled. The PC's set to give a press statement on the investigation, but it was set before any of this happened."

"But the PC knows about Lambert's arrest by now," Erin said. Her throat was suddenly very dry. "Either Rockwell or someone in the Department would've told him. He's going to tell everyone we caught the bad guy. On camera."

Webb shook his head. "He'd never be that irresponsible," he said. "Not before we've even formally charged the guy."

"Because no politician would ever shoot his mouth off to score points with the press," Vic said, laying on the sarcasm even more heavily than usual.

"When's the conference?" Erin asked.

Webb glanced at the clock on the wall of the Precinct 60 Homicide department. "It started five minutes ago," he said dully.

Vic jumped up.

"Where are you going?" Erin asked. "It's too late to do anything about this."

"I'm going to turn on the TV," he said, going into the nearby break room.

"Do you really want to know what he's saying?" she asked.

"Of course not," he said. "But it's better than burying my head in the friggin' sand. Better to know the worst right off the bat, right?"

"*Now* he decides to start making sense," Webb said. He followed Vic. So did Erin. Rolf brought up the rear.

The Police Commissioner's broad-shouldered bulk filled the space behind his podium. He had a rolling, booming voice that could fill a room even without the assistance of the bank of microphones in front of him. Agent Rockwell was just visible at the edge of the shot. The FBI agent was beaming. That smile told Erin everything she needed to know, even before she saw the text banner scrolling across the bottom of the screen.

...ANNOUNCES CAPTURE OF SO-CALLED CENTRAL PARK STRANGLER...

"And I'd like to thank the Federal Bureau of Investigation for their tireless and expert assistance," the Commissioner was saying. "Without their insight into this individual's psychology, his capture might have been indefinitely delayed. But I'd also like to congratulate the members of the NYPD's Major Crimes Unit for their incredible efforts on behalf of the people of our city. They're a really great bunch of men and women, and I'm sure I speak for all when I thank them for a job well done."

"At least the Feds aren't hogging all the credit," Vic muttered. "And I mean, we did get the guy, right? The DA can probably get him to cough up Valerie's hidey-hole."

"They've released Lambert's *name*," Erin said, staring at the TV. "And his picture. That poor guy's life is ruined."

"Erin?" Vic said. "I don't know if you're keeping up with the news, but word on the street is, that 'poor guy' is a murderer. His life, if you want to call it that, is gonna consist of trying not to drop the soap in the prison showers."

"What if we're wrong?"

The question hung in the air. Webb and Vic turned to look at her, ignoring the Commissioner, who was still talking but saying very little.

"You arrested him, O'Reilly," Webb said at last.

"We had to! The physical evidence was too strong. And I really thought we had him. But..."

They waited.

"But...?" Vic prompted.

"Too many things are out of place," she said.

"This is a murder investigation," Webb said. "Not a jigsaw puzzle. Or, if you have to think of it like a puzzle, imagine one you got cheap at a garage sale. Pieces are missing. There might be pieces from a totally different puzzle mixed in. You don't have the picture on the front of the box to work off of. You'll probably never see the whole picture. This isn't your first investigation. I shouldn't have to tell you this."

"I know," she said. "But the pieces we do have need to fit together right, and these don't."

Vic rolled his eyes. "You goddamn Irish," he said. "You're so used to losing, you don't know when you've won. We've got the guy! You said it yourself, he's a perfect personality match. What about the bloody dolly in his closet? What about the missing knife? What about the friggin' phone call? We have all sorts of shit pointing to this asshole! It's more than we need to get him charged, and probably convicted, even without a confession!"

"Let's talk about it," Erin said. "First off, where's the crime scene? It wasn't in his apartment. Holly was stabbed at least five times, maybe more. She would've bled all over the place. There's no way he could've cleaned the apartment that fast, not without leaving traces."

"The guy's a neat freak," Vic said. "He's good at cleaning."

"But he didn't bother to wipe the blood off the dolly?" she replied.

Vic opened his mouth. Then he closed it again.

"Go on," Webb said.

"We can match a knife to the wounds it inflicted," she continued. "Dr. Levine is good at that."

"She is," Webb agreed.

"The bad guys know that too," Vic said. "That's why he got rid of the damn knife!"

"He got rid of the knife but left the dolly?"

That shut Vic up again.

"But he did admit to talking to Holly Gardner," Webb said. "Why would he?"

"Because he doesn't think it makes him look guilty," she said. "He acted like he didn't understand what was going on. He acted like he didn't even know Holly was dead."

"Why did Holly call him in the first place?" Vic asked.

"She was conducting an independent investigation," Erin said.

"Yeah," he said. "But what led her to him? Columbia University has hundreds of employees. Why him?"

"She said she had sources," Erin said. "But you're right. It's almost like she'd seen the FBI's profile."

"Gee," Vic said. "Too bad she wasn't all chummy with an FBI publicity hound who was eager to share that profile with someone."

"You think Rockwell leaked it to her?" Webb asked.

"You got a better explanation, sir?" Vic replied.

"I don't," Webb admitted. "No, that scans. But there's something I'm not clear on, and that's what you're driving at, O'Reilly. I agree, this doesn't quite add up. But that still leaves the problem of the evidence. If Lambert is innocent, and if we match the blood on the dolly to Ms. Gardner, and I expect we will, what is it doing there? Are you saying this is all some elaborate frame-up?"

"That's the only other possibility I can think of," Erin said.

"Who'd want to do something like that?" Vic asked.

They looked back at the TV. There was the Commissioner, still blathering on. And there was Agent Rockwell, smiling for the cameras.

"Holy shit," Vic said. "You don't think..."

"I don't suppose you've read Nietzsche," Webb said quietly.

"The guy who said God was dead?" Vic said. "Nah, he sounds like an asshole."

"What are you thinking of, sir?" Erin asked.

"'He who fights with monsters might take care lest he thereby become a monster,'" Webb recited. "'And if you gaze for long into an abyss, the abyss gazes also into you.'"

"Are we really talking about this?" Vic said. "We really think an FBI agent is a goddamn serial killer?"

"Let's go back to the basics," Webb said. "Motive, means, and opportunity."

"Rockwell's motive is personal advancement," Erin said.

Webb nodded. "What better way to advance in the Bureau than to be one of the guys who caught the Central Park Strangler?"

"Hold on," Vic said. "He went after that other guy first, Warburton."

"It wouldn't matter who he framed," Erin said. "He could get whoever he wanted to take the fall. For all we know, he brought evidence to Warburton's apartment to plant it there, but we moved too fast, and Warburton turned out to be a creep but not the right kind of creep."

"Yeah," Vic said, making a face. "It's a shitty alibi that he was swiping panties from the girls' locker room, but it beats being a killer. You really think he's offing girls just to get a damn promotion?"

"People kill for less," Webb said. "And it would explain why the killer doesn't want the girls to suffer unnecessarily."

"As far as means and opportunity, it's convenient that he wasn't around when Holly was killed," Erin said. "He says he was en route from Quantico. Can we verify that?"

"We can check," Webb said. "But we want to move carefully. This could make a really big stink if it gets out that the NYPD is investigating the FBI."

"Should we call somebody?" Vic asked. "Someone at the Bureau, I mean?"

"Vic Neshenko, going through proper channels?" Erin replied. "It's a miracle."

"No, it's just me not wanting the Feds to jump down my throat," he said. "Damn it, I never liked that smug, smirking bastard. Do you think Willard is in on it, too?"

"No," Webb said. "This feels like a lone wolf operation to me."

"Me, too," Erin said. "Maybe we should talk to Willard."

"Bad idea," Vic said. "Don't ask a man to turn on his partner. A guy will cheat on his wife before he betrays his partner."

"That isn't saying much," Erin said.

"Hey!" Vic said. "I'll have you know, just because some guys cheat on their wives—"

"Knock it off," Webb said. "Both of you. We're getting ahead of ourselves. You're making a very serious accusation on the basis of very thin evidence."

"Somebody leaked Lambert's name to the Gardner chick," Vic said. "And it damn sure wasn't anybody in this room. It seems pretty goddamn clear to me that whoever it was is probably our killer."

"Okay," Webb said, making up his mind. "We know where Rockwell is right now."

"Yeah," Vic said. "Standing behind the PC grinning like the Worcestershire Cat."

Webb and Erin looked at him.

"You mean the Cheshire Cat?" Erin guessed.

"Yeah. You know, that freaky-ass cat in that movie. The one who disappears except for the smile. You can't tell me that wasn't made by people on some really good drugs. I had nightmares about that damn cat when I was a kid."

"Whatever," Webb said. "You know what he drives, Neshenko?"

"Bureau car," Vic said. "You know, they don't all drive black SUVs with tinted windows, since they might actually want to blend in a little. But this asshole does. He *wants* people to know he's a Fed. Black Tahoe, extra antenna."

"You noticed his car?" Erin asked. "Before he was a suspect?"

"I notice cars and guns," Vic said. "For instance, Agent Willard, who isn't an asshole, carries a standard-issue FBI Glock 17, while Rockwell has a tricked-out .45. Nickel-plated, if you can believe it."

"Some guys get fancy guns to compensate for their manhood inadequacies," Erin said in a flat deadpan.

"Get down to One PP," Webb said. "And get eyes on that car. I want you tailing Rockwell when he leaves that press conference."

"We won't have time," Erin said. "The conference is almost over and it'll take twenty minutes to get there."

Webb shook his head. "Not if I know our target. He'll circle the TV lights like a moth at a campfire. Find out where he goes, but don't get made."

"Copy that," Vic said, already in motion. "I'll keep you posted."

"Yes, sir," Erin said. Rolf trotted beside her.

"But don't confront him!" Webb called after them. "We don't know for sure!"

"You're hoping Rockwell leads us to Valerie," Erin said.

"If he does, we'll have him," Webb said.

Chapter 18

"Tailing the FBI," Vic said cheerfully. "One more thing off my bucket list."

"You're as bad as Rolf," Erin said. "Just give you someone to chase and you're happy."

"Coming from you, that's a compliment," he said.

"At least you don't bite them," she said.

"I could, you know."

Rolf stuck his head between the seats and grinned.

Erin flicked on the radio and tuned it to the news. A couple of commentators were talking about the press conference.

"—must come as a relief to the people of New York City," the female pundit was saying. "I know I've been scared to step outside my own door without an escort."

"Sheesh," Vic said. "Hundreds of murders a year in this town and this chick is freaking out about one whack-job. If she wasn't scared before, why now?"

"It's not about the math," Erin said. "It's never really about safety."

"Come again?"

"It's like airport security," she said. "You know how they confiscate your nail clippers, but leave your ballpoint pens?"

"What've pens got to do with anything?"

"Vic, if you had the choice of killing a guy with a pen or a pair of nail scissors, which would you use?"

"The pen. It's longer, you get better penetration." Then he snickered. "That's what she said."

It was Erin's turn to roll her eyes. "My point is, all those rules about taking off your shoes and your belt, and not bringing a pair of scissors on board, aren't about actually being safe. They're about making you *feel* safe."

"Yeah," Vic said. "I call it 'security theater.'"

"Good name for it," she said. "Because it's mostly an act. You know the real reason nobody's going to take over a plane with a knife again?"

"Yeah," he said. "Because if some bozo tries it, half a dozen guys like me will jump him and beat the shit out of him. He'll stab one, maybe two people, and that'll be it. Which is probably why Al Qaeda hasn't tried it again. Nine-Eleven was only ever gonna work once."

Erin nodded. "New Yorkers aren't really any less safe with the Strangler running around than without him. Eight million people, call it four million women. Even if you're in his target age range, hair color, you name it... you're still looking at thousands and thousands of potential targets. You're more likely to get run over by a taxi on the way to lunch."

"Ain't that the truth," he said. "Taxis will friggin' kill you. Those bastards don't even look where they're going."

"Heart attacks and cancer," she said. "That's what kill Americans. But what's all over the news?"

"The Central Park Strangler," he said. "And Valerie Richards. I see what you mean. Coronaries and cancer just aren't sexy enough for prime time, I guess."

"Holly was right," Erin said. "It really is about entertainment."

"What's entertaining about the news?" he retorted. "It's practically designed to make you feel bad. If you took it all seriously, you'd be terrified to go for a walk, just like that chick on the radio said. Isn't entertainment supposed to make you happy?"

"Maybe," she said thoughtfully. "But we've only got the right to the *pursuit* of happiness, not the destination."

He snickered again. "You're a philosopher today," he said. "But you're onto something. Know what I think? It's because of capitalism."

"Oh, God," she said. "Vic, I know you're Russian, but the Cold War ended decades ago. We were kids. You're not a Communist."

"No, hear me out. Happy people don't spend as much money. Unhappy people want to buy something that'll make them happy. That's what the entire drug trade is based on, and I'm not just talking about the illegal street drugs. Big Pharma's the same way. Buy this pill and you'll lose weight. Buy that pill and you'll kick your depression. Buy this other pill and you'll get a raging stiffy whenever you want it. But if it lasts more than four hours, talk to your doc and he'll probably give you another damn pill to make it go down again. Forget the military-industrial complex. What we've got now is the anxiety-medication complex. Just pick your poison. Drugs, fast food, porn, booze, social media. It's all self-medication, right?"

"Stop it," Erin said. "The news isn't scaring me nearly as much as you are right now."

"Yeah," he said. "Let's get back on nice, safe, comfortable conversation topics. Like serial killers. Look, if Rockwell does lead us somewhere, how do we know if Valerie's there? And if she is, do we go in, or do we wait for ESU?"

"We'll have to see what the situation is," she said. "But we're not putting Valerie in danger if we can help it. If Rockwell's our guy, remember he's armed and dangerous. He has FBI training."

"Yeah," Vic said. "Do they teach you how to use knives at Quantico?"

"I have no idea," she said. "Do I look like a Feebie? Don't worry about knives, worry about guns."

"The Twenty-One-Foot Rule says I can worry about knives within seven yards," Vic said. "And if that son of a bitch wants to bring a knife to a gunfight, it's his funeral."

*   *   *

They had the make and model of Rockwell's vehicle, but One Police Plaza was crawling with government people and half of them seemed to be driving black SUVs. Manually checking all the license plates was out of the question. They knew Rockwell's cell number, but couldn't trace the phone without a court order. Erin finally decided the best thing to do was to dismount from her Charger and stake out the entrance to the building on foot. Accordingly, she parked in a nearby garage.

"One of us needs to stay with the car," she said, holding out the keys to Vic.

"I agree," he said. "You."

"You're six-foot three," she reminded him. "And you look like a thug. You're not exactly inconspicuous."

"Are you planning on dragging the mutt with you?" he retorted. "He's more obvious than I am. And you're a damn celebrity. Rockwell's gonna be where there's the biggest concentration of cameras, bet on it. If even one of those media jerks sees you, they'll be all over you. You're the face of Major Crimes."

"That's not fair," she said. "Webb's in command and you do as much as I do."

"I said you're the face," he said. "Let's compare faces. You're a woman that could be good-looking, with the right makeup and in the right light, after a guy's had two or three beers."

"Thanks," she said wryly. "You know how to sweet-talk a girl. I see why Zofia likes you."

"Whereas I've got a busted nose and some scars and Webb's... well, Webb. Zofia's your only competition and she's not here. Trust me, they won't recognize me. Besides, you have to be ready to go wheels-up as soon as Rockwell starts rolling. And you hate when I drive your car. I forget to move the seat and I screw up the rearview mirrors."

"Okay, okay," she said. "Go on, go. But I didn't ask to be a celebrity, you know. And I hate it."

Vic moved off in the direction of City Hall, leaving Erin and Rolf kicking their heels in the Charger. Rolf panted at her and nosed her ear.

"Sorry, kiddo," she said. "Vic's right. We stand out these days. Yeah, you too. How do you like being famous?"

Rolf expressed no opinion on the subject. He hadn't let fame go to his head.

"I guess this is how you feel every time I go somewhere and lock you in the back," she said. "It sucks, I know."

Rolf licked her cheek.

She rubbed his ears. "At least you've got me this time."

Then they waited.

Cops, like many others in supposedly exciting occupations, spent a surprising amount of time doing nothing. You had no business working stakeouts if you got twitchy sitting in a parked car for hours at a stretch. Ian Thompson, former Marine Scout Sniper, had once told her his secret.

"It's not about not moving. The more you think about not moving, the more you want to move. It's about stillness."

"Isn't that the same thing?"

"No. Stillness isn't absence of movement. It's a state of being. Think about a mountain lion crouched on a rock. Lion isn't moving. Rock is still. Mountain lion can stay in one place a while, but not more than a few minutes. Rock can stay still for millions of years. Don't be the lion. Be the rock."

Erin suspected Ian was a lot better at this sort of thing than she was. Vic had only been gone about five minutes when she started getting antsy. It was better when you had someone to talk to. Rolf was better than nothing, but conversations with him tended to be pretty one-sided.

"Something's still not right," she told the Shepherd, who sat back on his haunches and cocked his head attentively. "We're missing something."

Rolf listened. He usually agreed with his partner, to the extent he understood her.

"Lambert isn't our guy," she went on. "I'm sure of it. But someone wants us to think he is. The evidence is good, but it doesn't quite fit. He cleans blood off some things but not others? And he just throws away the murder weapon but keeps something else with the victim's blood on it right there in his apartment? No way."

Rolf wagged his tail encouragingly. He wanted her to know he was here to help with whatever needed doing, especially if it involved running and biting.

"We might've tumbled to Lambert eventually," she said. "We were brute-forcing the Columbia staff roster. But in the meantime, what if he'd replaced his knife and gotten rid of the dolly? Then there'd be no evidence tying him to Holly's death.

Rolf got us there, but the bad guy couldn't have known he'd succeed. How..."

She trailed into silence. Rolf waited, but nothing more was forthcoming. The dog gradually sank to the floor of his compartment, gave a deep sigh, and got ready for some serious napping.

Erin snapped her fingers. "The anonymous phone tip!" she exclaimed.

Rolf's ears popped upright, followed an instant later by the rest of the K-9. He sprang to attention, awaiting orders.

"Webb told us," she said. "Somebody called the hotline. They said Lambert was our guy. How the hell would they know? The caller has to be either working with the killer, or else..."

What had Webb said about the call? Not much; he hadn't been the one to talk to the tipster. Erin tried to think.

Then she got it. It was absurdly simple, but explosive. For a moment she just sat behind the steering wheel, staring at nothing. Then she fumbled for her phone and called her commander.

"Webb," he said. "Any word on Rockwell?"

"Forget Rockwell!" she burst out. "And forget the profile! It's totally wrong! We've been looking in all the wrong places!"

"Slow down, O'Reilly," he said. "What do you mean?"

"Profiling is about probabilities," she said. "More than half of the guys we're looking for are this thing, so that's what goes in the profile. Right?"

"I think that's how it works," he said. "We're not using crystal balls here, or even Magic Eightballs."

"There's a ninety percent chance our killer is something, so that's part of the profile," she continued.

"Ninety percent is pretty good odds," Webb agreed. "But why—"

"Ninety percent of serial killers are what, sir?" Erin interrupted.

"I don't know," he said irritably. "I'm not a profiler."

"You do know, sir," she said.

"Maybe so," he said. "But what I don't do is play games in the middle of important cases. So start speaking clearly about this guy. That's an order."

"That's just the thing, sir," she said. "We're not looking for a guy!"

If Webb was shocked, or even impressed, he gave no evidence of it. "That's an interesting hypothesis," he said. "Why do you say so?"

"The call about Lambert," she said. "It was a woman. Did she say why Lambert was our guy?"

"I'd have to check with the hotline people," he said. "They'll have it recorded. Hold on, are you saying the caller *is* the killer?"

"Yes!"

"Is this just a hunch?"

"No! Think about it. Our killer was able to get close to both girls without making them suspicious. Women are a lot less scared of other women than they are of men. And we think Valerie got snatched from the Ladies' room at the bowling alley. A guy loitering in there would be suspicious, but a woman wouldn't be. Our killer has a good set of knives, but doesn't know how to fight with them. There's no sign of sexual violence on our victims. And they're well fed, home-cooked food."

"Lots of men can cook," Webb said. "But I see your point. That's quite a theory. It's also a very inconvenient one."

"More inconvenient than our chief suspect being a damn FBI agent?"

He sighed. "No, not quite *that* inconvenient. But if you're right, what's the motive? If it's not a sex crime?"

"Some women are attracted to other women, sir," Erin said.

"I'm from LA, O'Reilly," he reminded her. "I've encountered sexual orientations you've probably never even heard of. I know what lesbians are. You think it's a woman who can't make peace with her own urges? Some sort of violent repression?"

"Maybe," she said helplessly. "Does it matter? You know more criminal psychology than I do. But we need to re-evaluate our suspects. Hell, we need a whole new list!"

"Obviously," he said. "Since every one of our current persons of interest is male. Do you have any idea how to track down this mystery woman? Any place to start?"

She'd been thinking about this. "I want to go back to Brooklyn," she said. "And check Lambert's apartment building. I think we'll find more clues there."

"CSU is already working the site," he said.

"Not Lambert's unit," she said. "The building. The grounds. I want to get Valerie's sneaker and put Rolf back on her trail."

"Hold on," Webb said. "You were sure Lambert wasn't our guy. Now you think the Richards girl was in his building?"

"Maybe," she said grimly. "Or the real killer made sure to leave something of hers lying around, just to make sure we got the message about Lambert."

"All right," Webb said. "Fine. You win. But I'm not ready to give up all our other angles. I wish we had more detectives. Okay, call Neshenko and—"

At that moment Erin's phone buzzed with an incoming call from none other than Vic Neshenko himself.

"Just a second, sir," she said. "He's calling right now. I'll conference him in. Okay... there. Vic?"

"Rockwell's on the move!" Vic announced. "I'm trailing him, but he may not be in the same garage as you. How do you want to do this?"

"O'Reilly has another assignment," Webb broke in.

"Jesus Christ!" Vic exclaimed.

"Harold Webb," Webb corrected him. "I'm on this call too."

"Thank God for that," Vic said. "For a second I thought I was going crazy."

"We'll see what your next psych evaluation says," Webb said dryly. "O'Reilly has an alternative theory she wants to follow up. She's coming back to the Eightball, then heading to Brooklyn."

"And how am I supposed to trail Numbnuts McFed here?" Vic demanded. "Hijack a bicycle messenger? Or maybe stick out my thumb and hitch a ride?"

"You're outside Police Headquarters," Webb said. "There have to be a couple hundred officers and dozens of police vehicles within a two-block radius. Some of them will be unmarked. Display adaptability, Detective. Enlist some help. But stay on Rockwell. Find out where he goes and what he does. I'll expect a full report."

Vic muttered something unintelligible and probably unprintable.

"I didn't copy that last, Neshenko," Webb said.

"I said, it's a great day to be a cop and I'm just happy to be here, sir," Vic said, venom dripping from every word. Then he hung up.

"I think he's unhappy," Erin said.

"In other news, the sun came up this morning," Webb said. "I'll get Ms. Richards's shoe out of Evidence and have it waiting for you. See you soon."

* * *

Half an hour later Erin was driving south from the Eightball with Valerie's shoe in a paper bag, an enthusiastic German Shepherd in the Charger's back compartment, and a petite blonde in the passenger seat.

"The Lieutenant insisted on you having some backup," Piekarski explained. "I think he would've rather come himself, but he needs to mind the shop."

"Really?" Erin said. "Webb doesn't usually love field work."

"He's afraid Rockwell's going to make Vic. If he does, and Rockwell complains, the Captain's going to chew somebody's ass, and it'll probably be whoever's standing closest to his office."

"I didn't even know you'd come in today," Erin said.

"Mom's watching Mina again," Piekarski said. "Vic seems to think you're pretty close to nailing the Strangler, so I wanted to be in on it and do whatever I could."

"I appreciate it," Erin said. "But I'm not sure we're as close as all that."

"This is my first chance at an honest-to-God serial killer," Piekarski said. "Geez, if we catch this one, we'll be famous!"

"You say that like it's a good thing," Erin said darkly.

"Isn't it?"

Erin didn't answer.

"Look," Piekarski said. "My grandparents were dirt farmers in Poland. My dad worked in a damn steel mill. I used to think the only way I'd get noticed was if I joined the cheerleading squad in high school."

"Did you?"

"Hell no. I had enough trouble with jock douchebags trying to get me in the back seat without wearing one of those little skirts."

"But you still wanted to be noticed?"

"Of course! But not because of my ass! I did a lifeguard gig in high school to bring in a little cash, and the swimsuit got me too much attention. I thought being a cop would get me some respect. But you know how hard it is to get other cops to take a female officer seriously. Sometimes I wish I wasn't pretty, you know?"

Erin thought of another woman whose high-school story she'd heard not long ago. "Zofia," she said quietly. "Did anything... happen to you? When you were young?"

"Nothing ever happened to me," Piekarski said. "That's what I mean. I had the most boring, blue-collar childhood... oh. *That.*"

"Yeah," Erin said. "That."

"No. I mean, not exactly." Piekarski was staring out the windshield, avoiding looking at Erin. "There were always some guys. You know how boys are. You just gotta deal with it. Don't let them get too frisky. Make them respect you. Boys are such assholes. Don't get me wrong, I like boys. I mean, I like them a *lot.* But Vic's the closest thing to a grownup I've ever gone with, and that ought to tell you something."

"Vic's okay," Erin said, smiling.

"He's more than okay," Piekarski said. "He's a lot better than he pretends to be. He's really sweet. And kind. He really sees me as more than a pair of tits. And he's great in the sack."

"I didn't need to hear that," Erin said. "And I didn't want to."

Piekarski giggled. It was an oddly girlish sound from the tough street cop. "He's manning up," she said. "He's real sweet with Mina. He goes all soft and gooshy whenever he's with her. And he'd kill me if he knew I told you that."

"He won't hear it from me," Erin promised.

"I didn't really mean it," Piekarski said. "About not wanting to be pretty. I guess it comes down to attention. We all want it, but we want it for the right reasons. And if we can't get it for the right ones, we try for the wrong ones. If I want people to remember me, maybe I ought to put a sex tape online."

Erin made a face. "Don't even joke about that. And I'm serious about fame. It's not all it's cracked up to be. People make all these assumptions. They think they know you, just because of what they saw on the news or read in the paper. I didn't know any of that crap would come with the O'Malley case. If I had, maybe I wouldn't have done it."

"Seriously? Erin, guys tried to kill you! One of them put a bullet in your head! You're saying making the front page of the *Times* was worse than *getting shot?!*"

"It's different, is all," Erin said. "Look, if we do catch the Strangler, I promise we'll all get front-page credit. You can do all the talk shows you want. But if you do, Vic's going to be punching a lot of jerks on your behalf."

"He already does," Piekarski said. "It's sweet, in a Neanderthal way. What are we looking for at this apartment?"

"Planted evidence," Erin said.

"And that helps us how?"

"It might point us toward real evidence."

"That seems like kind of a long shot."

"Maybe," Erin said. "It's like when you're interrogating a suspect. They'll lie to you. Everybody does. But the lies tell you things too. You can figure out the shape of the truth from them. It's like a photo negative. I hope if we figure out what the killer wants us to think, it'll tell us how she's thinking."

"You're sure it's a woman?"

"No," Erin admitted. "I'm not sure of anything."

"I kinda hope you're wrong," Piekarski said. "I'm a fan of gender equality in most fields, but I'm okay with leaving serial murder to the men. And I don't care what you say. I still wouldn't mind getting my picture in the paper."

Chapter 19

Lambert's apartment tower looked the same as before. Nobody had put up a plaque advertising that the Central Park Strangler had lived there—yet. Erin didn't even see any TV vans around. Probably, she thought sourly, they were all still clustered around One PP for the fallout from the press conference.

"Did Vic really threaten to throw the guy off the balcony?" Piekarski asked, looking up.

"If Internal Affairs asks, I'll say no," Erin said.

"Are we going up to the apartment?"

"That depends on Rolf."

Erin opened the bag and held it in front of the dog. *"Such!"* she said.

Rolf hardly needed the order. He knew the drill and he recognized Valerie's smell. His ears perked and his nostrils flared. He raised his snout and tested the air, seeking any trace of the girl.

"How good is his nose, exactly?" Piekarski asked, watching him with interest.

"You wouldn't believe it," Erin said. "If she's here, or if she was, he'll find her."

"But she isn't," Piekarski said. "That's the point, right? Anyway, CSU has been all over the place. They would've found anything that was there."

"CSU are human," Erin said. "We're all a bunch of short-noses who can't smell a thing. How often do you pay attention to your nose on the Job? I mean, *really* pay attention?"

Piekarski wrinkled hers. "I try not to."

"Exactly," Erin said.

Rolf paused, head cocked. Then he lunged forward, tail lashing eagerly. Erin jogged after him.

"See what I mean?" she called over her shoulder. Excitement surged up in her. She'd thought they might get something from Rolf, but this was a stronger reaction than she'd hoped for.

Piekarski hurried after them. "Does that mean she's here?" she asked.

Rolf scratched at the front door. Erin opened it for him.

"Probably not," she admitted. "But he's smelling her, so either she was here not too long ago, or something that belonged to her was."

She expected the Shepherd to lead them to the elevators, but he stopped at the door next to the elevator bank. He scratched again and barked.

"I'll call it in," Piekarski said.

"Not yet," Erin said. "We don't even know what we're looking at here. And think about it. If we call Dispatch and tell them we've found Valerie Richards, it's going to get out. Someone will be listening to the police band, or someone will leak it, and next thing you know we'll have two dozen damn reporters breathing down our necks. If we find her, the poor girl will be getting microphones shoved in her face and questions shouted at her, and she'll be all over the news. And if we don't find her, it'll be a shitstorm."

"Copy that," Piekarski said. "But what if she really is here? That'd be huge. We'd be friggin' heroes!"

"What'd they tell you at the Academy about trying to be a hero?" Erin retorted.

"They said 'don't,'" Piekarski said sheepishly. "They said that's how we end up on a memorial wall."

Rolf barked again. The humans weren't paying attention. It was a good thing he was there to remind them what was important.

"Stop chasing the glory," Erin said, opening the door to reveal a concrete stairwell. "It'll come, don't worry. And when it does, you'll wish it hadn't."

"Says the famous girl."

"Then I ought to know what I'm talking about. Where are you going, kiddo?"

Her last words were directed at Rolf, who was nosing at the metal gate that stretched across the basement stairs. Most high-rises had these gates at the ground floor. Their purpose was to keep people from accidentally going down to the basement if they were evacuating the building. Otherwise, if the place was on fire, victims might just keep going in the smoke and confusion and end up trapped underground.

"What's down there?" Piekarski asked.

"The basement," Erin said, pulling open the gate. Rolf scrabbled impatiently at the stairs. He was really sure the smell led down.

"I guess that makes sense," Piekarski said as the three of them started down. "Lambert wouldn't have kept her in his apartment, right? And didn't the last victim have that mold in her lungs?"

"Yeah," Erin said. "Maybe she really is down here."

"Didn't our people check the basement?"

"I don't know. It's a big building, and if Lambert didn't have access, they might not have thought to do it." Erin clenched her fist. "Damn it, I don't think anyone told them about the mold spores."

She shortened Rolf's leash, looping it around her left wrist, and drew her Glock with her right hand. There was no reason to expect violence, but her street instincts were whispering warnings and it was a good idea to listen to them.

The tower had two basement levels. Rolf went straight past the first one, all the way to the bottom. He pawed at the door, which made sense. It was the only possible way forward. Erin paused and glanced back. Piekarski was four steps from the bottom. The other woman had also drawn her gun and was holding it in both hands. Piekarski nodded to her.

Erin got a good grip on the doorknob with her leash hand. She could feel her pulse pounding in her ears. The moment before making entry was always intense. You never knew what was waiting for you. Blood, bodies, guns, pain, death, horror.

She twisted the knob and shouldered the door open. "NYPD!" she snapped, bringing up the Glock and moving fast. Rolf was already inside, nose forward, paws in motion.

Sometimes you got all keyed up for a dynamic entry and nothing happened. You busted into an empty room and found yourself with a whole lot of adrenaline and nothing to do with it.

Erin found herself in a plain concrete hallway, insufficiently illuminated by a handful of weak overhead lights. She saw a fire extinguisher and alarm box, some overhead pipes, ventilation ducts, and a light switch. The walls were pierced by a pair of steel doors on either side and one more at the end.

Rolf didn't hesitate. He was already on his way to the first door on the left. Erin laid her hand on that door. A key was already inserted in the lock. That was unusual. She tried the knob. It turned easily.

Piekarski was at her back. The blonde smiled at Erin. There was a little nervousness in the grin, but mostly excitement. Piekarski was an action junkie at heart. That was why she'd fallen for Vic, and vice versa.

"One," Erin murmured. "Two... three!"

The door swung inward and banged against the wall with a hollow clang. "NYPD!" Erin shouted again. She took two quick steps in, swinging to the right to check that corner. Piekarski was on her heels, moving left, covering Erin's blind side. Erin saw a small room, made smaller by a cluster of pipes and valves. It was lit only by the light from the hallway. A chair sat in the middle of the room; a plain metal folding one. There was a bucket on the floor, a few other scattered objects, and...

"About time you got here," a woman said. She was standing next to the door, a camera hanging from a strap around her neck, her face twisted into a sardonic half-smile by the puckered scar on her lip.

Erin's heart tried to bang its way straight out of her rib cage. "Show me your hands!" she yelled, leveling the Glock.

Andy Carver raised both hands to shoulder height, empty palms toward Erin.

"Take it easy, Detective," she said. "I'm glad you're here. That's some amazing response time. I was expecting the boys in blue, not a couple of gold shield girls."

"What're you talking about?" Erin demanded. She kept her gun trained on the reporter. "What're you doing here?"

"Same as you," Andy replied. "And the same as poor Holly Gardner, I expect. I'm following a lead."

"Clear," Piekarski said behind Erin. "What the hell's going on?"

Rolf barked at Andy. It was loud and echoing in that small space.

"This is a crime scene," Erin said.

"No shit," Andy said. "That's why I called it in. Wait a second. You're not responding to my call?"

"What call?" Erin demanded.

"The one I placed to 911 a few minutes ago. Your dispatcher didn't tell you?"

"No," Erin said. "They didn't. Zofia? Want to double-check that?"

"Gladly," Piekarski said. Without holstering her gun, she took out her phone with her off hand.

"In the meantime, I'm going to ask you to step outside," Erin said. "Like I said, this is an active crime scene. We're going to need you to stay close, though. Where did this lead of yours come from?"

Andy moved toward the door, keeping her hands in plain view. "I can't reveal my sources," she said. "You know that. But I'm pretty sure you're going to find something belonging to Valerie Richards in here."

"Me too," Erin said. "Because someone wants us to think Valerie was in this basement."

"I don't follow," Andy said. "You mean somebody other than Donald Lambert? He's the guy you want. It's just bad luck he moved Valerie before you got him."

Erin was standing close to Andy. She caught a faint whiff of something out of place. It was a kitchen smell: garlic.

"Ms. Carver," Erin said slowly. "Turn around and place your hands on the wall."

She was angry, mostly at herself. How could she have missed it before? It wasn't one particular thing. It was a dozen little ones, all fitting together. Andy Carver, who always seemed to know where to be. Andy Carver, with her awful facial scar and tragic history. Andy Carver, hiding in plain view. Andy had been a victim, but Erin knew better than that. Life wasn't clean and tidy, and sometimes victims and perps turned out to be the very same people.

But some part of her wasn't completely convinced and still saw Andy as just a victim. And that part hesitated, so when Andy turned obediently toward the wall, then darted to one side and through the door, Erin didn't shoot her in the back.

But the momentary paralysis was only in her hands. *"Fass!"* she shouted.

Rolf sprang at the fleeing woman, but Andy had grabbed the edge of the door as she ran past and it was already swinging shut. It slammed with an earsplitting clang less than half a second before Rolf's claws scrabbled helplessly at it. The light was blotted out, leaving them in pitch darkness.

Erin was two steps behind her dog. She fumbled for the doorknob. As she grabbed it, she heard a click. The knob wouldn't turn. Andy had locked them in.

Erin banged her fist on the door, as much out of frustration as anything. "Open up!" she shouted.

A faint light came from Piekarski's phone, lighting the side of the woman's face. "I've got no signal," she said. "Must be all that concrete and metal."

Erin dropped Rolf's leash, reached for her pocket flashlight, and turned it on. The bright LED beam sprang to life. She panned it around the room. Rolf's eyes reflected it in a brilliant flash of greenish-white. The Shepherd was leaping at the door, clawing at it and snarling. He'd been ordered to bite. He *wanted* to bite. And he was determined to get his teeth in even if he had to dig through a couple inches of steel to do it.

"Platz!" she ordered, not wanting him to hurt himself. The K-9 sank to his belly but kept growling low in his chest.

Erin saw a light switch and flicked it, but nothing happened. Either the bulb was burned out or it had been removed altogether. She holstered her Glock and took out her phone without much hope. Sure enough, she had no bars of service either.

She banged on the door again, making a lot of noise but accomplishing nothing. "Damn it, Carver, open this door!" she shouted. There wouldn't be an answer. Andy was already gone, making the most of whatever head start she had.

"No," a female voice said from the other side of the door. "I don't think so. You stay right there. I'll be back in a few minutes."

"Carver!" Erin yelled as loudly as she could. But this time she was met with silence.

A second flashlight beam came on. Piekarski was holding her own light. She smiled ruefully.

"How long have we been doing this job?" she said.

"Long enough not to get caught like this," Erin said. She was studying the door, particularly the hinges.

"At least the unis should be here soon," Piekarski said.

"What makes you say that?"

"The call to Dispatch."

"You don't seriously think she made that call."

There was a pause. Then Piekarski said, in embarrassed tones, "I guess not. Why didn't you shoot her?"

"I should have. I guess..." Erin sighed. "I guess it was because she's a girl."

"I hate to be the one to break it to you, Erin, but we're girls, too," Piekarski said.

"I'm aware of that."

"Bad guys shoot at us sometimes."

"Yeah, I know."

"We shoot back. We're dangerous people."

"I know that too."

"Evil is equal-opportunity."

"So I've heard."

"Safe to say she's our guy?"

"Yeah."

"How did you know?"

"I was already a little suspicious. But it was the garlic that decided me."

"The which?"

"She smelled like garlic. The spice. She's been feeding her victims with it. She's got Greek family. That's why she's named Andromeda. God *damn* it."

Erin took out her Swiss Army knife, opened the flat screwdriver attachment, and tried to insert it into the hinge pin. It didn't work. The hinge was too tightly put together. There was room to slide a sheet of paper in, maybe, but nothing wider.

"There's blood on the floor back here," Piekarski said.

"That's probably Holly Gardner's," Erin said.

"So this is where she was killed?"

"Looks that way."

"And I found a hairclip. Blue plastic."

"I'm guessing it belongs to Valerie Richards," Erin said. She tested the doorknob. The plate didn't have any visible screws. She rattled it and found it was solidly affixed to the door.

Rolf watched her intently. He understood the general principle of how to open a door, but wasn't very good at it. His partner didn't usually have this much trouble. That was a problem. The woman he was supposed to bite, and by extension, his rubber Kong ball, lay on the far side of the door. But he had full faith in his partner's doorknob ability. He waited with the patience of a good dog.

"Why did Carver kill Gardner?" Piekarski asked.

"You can ask her when she comes back," Erin said. She stuck the screwdriver attachment into the lock and jiggled it. The tumblers didn't budge. Lock-picking was easy in the movies, but in real life you needed the right skills and the right tools. Erin had neither.

"You really think she's coming back?" Piekarski asked.

"She said she would."

"If she does, is she going to try to kill us?"

"Probably."

"What a bitch."

"That's the tabloids for you. I can't believe you read those things."

"They're entertaining. I know they're all bullshit. They're the magazine version of junk food. Don't judge. Vic reads a bunch of those stupid techno-thriller paperbacks and they're not much better."

"Vic reads?" Erin replied. "For fun?" She stooped and peered at the slit at the bottom of the door. It was maybe an eighth of an inch wide; much too narrow to do anything with.

"There's an air vent here," Piekarski said. "I think it joins up with the hallway."

Erin sprang to her feet and quickly panned her light in the direction of the other woman. But her excitement immediately faded. Whoever had designed this building clearly hadn't watched enough action movies. The vent was way too small for a person to fit through. It looked to be about twelve by eight inches.

"I could pop the cover," Piekarski suggested. "Then, maybe..." She trailed off.

"Stick your hand out and wave?" Erin said. "Flip off Carver when she comes back? And that's assuming there isn't another cover on the outside. We wouldn't be able to reach those screws. I could shove Rolf through, but he doesn't have thumbs.

He can't open a door for us. Hell, he can't even get out of the basement."

"What's she going to do to us?" Piekarski asked. "Does she have a gun?"

"I don't know. We haven't seen any sign of one. But even if she does, she'll have to open the door to take a shot at us."

"If she does, I'll get her," Piekarski said grimly.

"You'll have to get in line," Erin replied. "Don't worry, she's probably on the run. And Webb knows where we went. When we don't check in, and he can't get in touch with us, he'll send a Patrol unit. We shouldn't be down here more than a couple of hours, tops."

"And in the meantime, that bitch runs off with a nice comfy head start."

"Yeah," Erin sighed. Her hand curled into a fist around the flashlight. "After she kills Valerie."

"Shit," Piekarski said. "You really think she will?"

"Why wouldn't she?"

"Damn it!" Piekarski started pacing around the room. "There has to be a way out of here. We could shoot out the lock."

"That's a last-ditch option," Erin said. "This door's steel. The bullets would ricochet. I don't want to explain to Vic how I accidentally shot his girlfriend in the face. Maybe Webb will try to call us sooner and get suspicious. Keep checking your phone."

She took a moment to type out a text message to Vic and Webb, telling where they were and briefly explaining the situation. Her phone couldn't send it, but it ought to go out as soon as she got back where she had service.

"I can't believe I was that careless," she muttered. "You're right, I should've shot her. You know all that flap about minorities getting shot by cops, but you know what the number-one thing the people we shoot have in common is?"

"They're men?" Piekarski guessed.

"Exactly. Cops shoot when we see a threat and we're not as scared of women. I've shot one, but she was unusual."

"There's always that one exception," Piekarski said. "If it's any consolation, I'll be glad to shoot Carver the next chance I get. Why's she knocking off teenagers?"

"Does it matter? I think it has something to do with her getting raped as a girl."

"God," Piekarski said. "Is that how she got that scar on her face?"

"She told me she gave it to herself afterward."

"So the boys wouldn't come after her anymore?"

"That's part of it. I think maybe she was punishing herself, too."

"That's messed up," Piekarski said. "It wasn't her fault. She should've taken the knife to the rapist and cut his friggin' balls off."

"Victims aren't always thinking about revenge," Erin said. "Sometimes they blame themselves. But I think Andy Carver was carrying around a lot of bottled-up anger. She doesn't hate the girls, at least not exactly. They're not the ones she's trying to punish."

"I don't understand," Piekarski said.

"Neither do I," Erin said. "Not completely. But if I had to guess, I think she wants to punish society itself. Pop culture, rape culture, something like that. I hope we'll get an explanation from Carver."

"Are you sure we can't shoot out the lock?"

"I'm sure we don't want to try unless we absolutely have to. If I fire at that door, the bullet could end up almost anywhere."

"Do you have any other ideas?"

"No. You?"

"Hey, I'm just a rookie Detective Third Grade. I don't know what the hell I'm doing. You're supposed to be my mentor. Aren't you this big, gushing fountain of police knowledge?"

"I don't know how to pick locks, I don't have a hacksaw or an acetylene torch, I'm a little short of high explosives, and I can't squeeze into a midget-sized air vent," Erin said sharply. "So right now I've got nothing."

"Me neither," Piekarski said. "They didn't cover this at the Academy, and in Street Narcotics it never came up. Same with lifeguard training."

"Yeah, you mentioned you were a lifeguard. Does any of your lifesaving training apply to our current situation?"

"Only if you swallow water or get a really bad sunburn. Or I can do CPR, but the whole NYPD knows how to do that. Can we do anything but wait?"

"We can try to think of something else."

So that was what they did.

Chapter 20

Time crawled. Rolf lay beside Erin, but the K-9 wasn't relaxed. He could feel her tension and knew they were waiting for something. He planned to be ready when it happened. Dogs were champions at waiting. He watched her every movement, chin resting between his paws, ears pivoting toward every little noise, nostrils flaring to catch every molecule that drifted past.

Piekarski was working on the door. Erin had lent her Swiss Army knife to the other woman, who was grimly hacking and prying at the hinges with a complete lack of success. Erin herself, as she'd told Piekarski, was trying to think.

"Andy was a pretty girl," she said. "She was a cheerleader and caught the attention of one of the boys at her school. She was a little flirty and he figured she was offering more than she wanted to give. It'd be hard to make a legal case for rape, but that's what it was. Afterward, she was ashamed of herself for leading him on and asking for it."

"Nobody asks to be raped," Piekarski snapped.

"I know that," Erin said. "But how many times does a girl get told it wouldn't have happened if she hadn't worn that short skirt or that low-cut blouse? Or if she hadn't drunk so much at the sorority house? Or if she hadn't smiled at the wrong boy? So Andy did the one thing that would push boys away from her. She cut herself up so they wouldn't even want to look at her."

"Unwanted male attention is a bitch," Piekarski said. "I get that. But you just gotta deal with it. You did. So did I. That didn't turn her into a goddamn serial killer!"

"No," Erin said thoughtfully. "I think the tabloids did that."

"Erin, if those rags turned people into murderers, we'd have half the population of New York getting whacked."

"I'm not talking about everybody else. Just her. She ended up in a job where she roots through the seedy personal lives of celebrities. The whole point of her career is digging up dirt on the beautiful people. That's going to twist you, sooner or later. You end up believing everybody's ugly on the inside, or maybe that the better someone looks, the worse they behave."

"Wait a second," Piekarski said. "You think she killed Laurel Peterson *because* she was beautiful? That she thought that girl was all rotten on the inside?"

Erin shrugged. "It's a theory. But I think it's more complicated than that. I think Andy wanted attention. Think about it. She got hurt when she reached out to another person as a girl, and that left her with a messed-up idea about relationships. So she didn't want a normal courtship, marriage, any of that. But she still felt the need to be noticed and wanted. And now she gets what she wants. She's all over the front page, all across America."

"What a load of crap," Piekarski said. "She isn't in any of the papers! Nobody knows who she is!"

"We do," Erin said quietly. "So maybe she won't try to kill us after all. Maybe she *wants* her secret to come out. But that's not really the point. What matters most to her is that people are taking notice of what she's doing. She's got respect."

"She's got fear," Piekarski corrected. "That's not the same thing."

"It is with the guys I used to hang out with. The O'Malleys and the Lucarellis."

"That's because they're violent criminals."

"True."

"You think she's milking this thing for attention?"

"Yeah. That's why she doesn't kill her victims right away. She stretches it out as long as she can. But if she holds onto them longer than a week or so, people get bored. She's timing her murders to maximize the media coverage. As soon as attention starts wandering off poor missing Laurel, Andy kills her and dumps the body. Suddenly it's front-page news again. And then she grabs another, quicker than we expect, to spark even more attention."

"Sheesh," Piekarski said. "There's attention whores and then there's *this*. What a sick, twisted bitch."

"She's a victim," Erin said.

"And a murderer! Are you making excuses for her?"

"I'm trying to understand her."

"Good God, why would you want to?"

"So maybe the next one like her who comes along, we don't get sidetracked by the wrong profile."

"Oh." Piekarski sounded a little chastened. "We'll catch her, even with a head start. With that scar, she stands out. She won't get far."

"Yeah," Erin said with as much conviction as she could muster. "You know what's really screwed up?"

"You mean there's something in this whole mess that *isn't*?"

"Even if we catch her, she wins. She wants attention, we'll be giving it to her. She can't lose."

"Unless we blow her crazy brains out."

"Even then," Erin said. "She'll be notorious. Half the reason people remember Bonnie and Clyde is because they got shot to pieces. A dramatic death might be exactly what she's looking for."

That shut both of them up for a little while. Piekarski morosely studied the door, trying to plan a new attack on it.

Metal clanked and scraped outside, like someone dragging it across concrete. Erin froze and hissed sharply through her teeth. She and Piekarski listened. They heard the faint but unmistakable sounds of a screw being rotated.

Erin pointed toward the vent. Piekarski nodded. Andy was unscrewing the outside cover of the vent. But what could she do then? She couldn't open the inner vent; those screws were on the detectives' side of the wall. Even if she had something like a hand grenade, which Erin doubted, it wouldn't fit through the slits.

"We know what you did, Andy," she said, talking to the door. "And we know why."

"Is that so?" Andy sounded almost amused. "I don't think that'll make much difference. The truth doesn't matter much, these days."

"You set up Lambert," Erin said, wanting to keep the other woman talking. Every moment that passed was a moment the murderer couldn't use to run or to kill Valerie.

"Why would I do something like that?" A screw fell and tinkled on the floor. Andy started on the next one.

"To keep the news rolling in," Erin said. "You needed to keep things interesting for the public. What better than an IV drip of shocking revelations to keep the case alive?"

"That's a good line," Andy said. "Do you mind if I use it in my next article?"

The absurdity of the question nearly took Erin's breath away. "What if I say you can't?" she asked.

"Then I won't," Andy said, finishing the second screw and beginning on the third. "I have my journalistic integrity, after all. If you want this to be off the record, that's where it'll stay. I try to be ethical."

The woman was utterly insane, Erin thought. That wasn't comforting, given the circumstances. "Why Lambert?" she asked.

"The same reason you came after him," Andy said. "He's a pervert, just like Ethan Warburton. Neither one will probably be convicted, but so what? They're already guilty in the court of public opinion. They might as well be in prison. Look how easy it is these days. You don't even have to shoot a man to end his life. The right words at the right moment are all you need."

The cover plate on the air vent scraped against its mountings as Andy lifted it off. Erin briefly considered firing a few shots through the wall below the vent. That would have worked on a normal interior wall; nine-millimeter bullets would punch clean through lath and plaster with plenty of stopping power left over, and she knew exactly where Andy must be standing, probably perched on a chair. But the basement walls were cinder block. Her rounds wouldn't penetrate.

"Decided to do a little pest control while you were killing teenagers?" Erin asked. "Does that make you feel like the good guy?"

"There's no such thing as good guys," Andy retorted. "Everybody has dirt on them. You think you're clean? You fucked a mob boss! You're as dirty as the rest of us!"

Andy pushed something into the vent. Erin heard it clink against the inner cover.

"What are you doing?" she asked sharply.

"Pest control," Andy said calmly. "Just like you said. I'm sorry about this, Detective. I really do admire you, in spite of your extracurriculars. If it's any consolation, you'll be remembered as a hero. They might even put up a statue in one of the parks."

From the sound of it, Andy was screwing the outside cover back onto the vent. Erin felt a chill. What was in there? A bomb? A gasoline can? Was the killer planning on burning them alive?

"Why did you kill Holly?" she asked, stalling for time, her mind racing.

"Oh, that wasn't part of the plan," Andy said. "She must have been tipped off by one of your buddies, because she came poking around down here just as I was setting things up. It really screwed my timetable, too. I had to take care of her. And I panicked, I admit it. I should've just left her here. But when I saw her lying there, I... I had to move her. Get rid of her. That took time. But I figured a way it would lead back to Lambert, so it all worked out. After I did all that, I needed to check on my houseguest, and by the time I was able to get back here, cops were all over the place. So I had to wait to put the finishing touches on the scene. Too bad you showed up before I could slip out. Too bad for you, I mean. And a little for me.

"So long, Detectives," Andy said. "Cheer up. You'll be on the ten o'clock news. I guarantee it."

Erin heard a thump as Andy hopped down from her perch, followed by her retreating footsteps.

"Jesus," Piekarski murmured. "She's nuts!"

"I know," Erin said. "And she's gone. Bring the chair over here, and hand me the knife."

"What're you doing?" Piekarski asked, obeying.

"Finding out what she left for us," Erin said, climbing onto the chair and fitting the knife's screwdriver blade into one of the screws, holding the flashlight in her other hand.

"Are *you* crazy?! That could be a bomb!"

"It wouldn't be my first," Erin said. "And it might be on a timer, so we'd better work fast."

She was about halfway through opening the vent when her nose wrinkled at an unusual odor.

"Do you smell that?" she asked.

"Yeah," Piekarski said. "It smells like a swimming pool."

"And it's coming from here," Erin said. "It's strong!"

Her eyes were watering. A burning sensation crawled up her nose and down her throat. She ignored it and kept working on the screws.

"Oh shit!" Piekarski said. "That's chlorine gas! It's poisonous!"

"No kidding," Erin growled. She finally got the plate off and shone the light inside the vent. It was a tiny space, smaller than a microwave oven, and contained a metal bowl from which the caustic stench emanated.

"Erin, get away from there!" Piekarski shouted. "That shit can kill you!"

Erin jumped down. She could hardly see through the tears streaming down her face. She coughed and doubled over from the sudden, tearing pain in her throat.

"Have to block it," she gasped. She wiped her eyes on her sleeve and tried to get her breath back, looking around for anything they could use.

The room they were in, unfortunately, lacked anything remotely useful for blocking airflow. The pipes were securely emplaced, the folding chair wasn't the right shape, and they didn't have any other furniture. A couple of strips of duct tape were attached to the chair, but they weren't nearly enough to cover the gap. The gas was seeping through the hole in the wall. It was actually visible in the flashlight beams; greenish-yellow, evil-looking wisps. They seemed to be reaching down into the room, groping for the occupants.

"What do we do?" Piekarski asked. Her voice held a slight tremor, but she was holding onto a ragged edge of self-control. "We're trapped!"

"Clothes," Erin said hoarsely. "Need to use clothes."

This was no time for modesty. She quickly unbuttoned her blouse and held it up to the vent. The fabric weave wasn't airtight, of course, but it would be better than nothing.

"Wait," Piekarski said. "It works better if it's wet. Chlorine... I had to put the tablets in the pool when I was working there, growing up. Chlorine dissolves in water."

"Great," Erin said. "We don't have any."

"Yeah, we do," the other woman said. "Piss on it."

"What?!" In spite of their predicament, the suggestion was so ridiculous that Erin barked out a raspy laugh, then coughed again. "You're shitting me!"

Piekarski shook her head. "No! There's something in urine... ammonia, I think? It counters the gas. Hurry!"

This was, without a doubt, the most embarrassing thing Erin had ever been called on to do in the line of duty. To piss on her own clothes in a dirty basement? If this got back to the Eightball, she'd never ever live it down. But Piekarski was dead serious and Erin couldn't think of a better option, so she took care of business. The fear and tension made it all too easy.

The smell wasn't even all that bad, overpowered as it was by the thick reek of chlorine. She held the dripping garment over the vent and tried not to think too hard about what she was doing. But it seemed to help. The gas wasn't getting in anymore, at least not in large amounts.

"Now what?" she asked. "All this does is buys us time."

"And not much of it," Piekarski agreed, suppressing a cough. "A lot of gas is already in here with us."

"I don't know shit about chlorine," Erin said. "What else did they teach you? Think!"

"The tablets dissolve in water," Piekarski said. "But when they're just damp, they give off the gas. That's why you need to put them all the way underwater. And there's this shit called trichlor. Damp tablets aren't just poisonous. They're super dangerous."

"So we fill the bowl with water," Erin said with grim humor. "Your turn to make a contribution. I'm running on empty here."

"No!"

"Why not? Don't tell me you're getting embarrassed."

"It's not that," Piekarski said. "Trichlor isn't just poisonous. It's also explosive."

"Great," Erin snorted. "Just great. So we can die by poison or we can die in a fire."

"Or we can blow the door open!" Piekarski said, her eyes lighting up. "And you're right, we need ammonia, and there's only one way to get it."

"You're telling me we're going to make a homemade bomb and set it off in the room we're in?"

Piekarski smiled. "Unless you've got a better plan."

"If we let this into the room, it could kill us. You said that yourself."

"We'll need masks," Piekarski said. "All two... no, all three of us. Rolf, too."

"This is going to end with me ripping up my shirt, isn't it," Erin said.

They worked fast, because the moment Erin took the garment away from the vent, the gas poured in heavier than ever. Erin used her knife to quickly cut three strips of the blouse, which they tied around their faces. It was unpleasant, but cops were used to coming in contact with body fluids. Rolf wrinkled his mouth in protest, but he trusted her and let her tie the cloth around his muzzle.

Then Piekarski stood on the chair and carefully took down the bowl. Sure enough, it was full of wet chlorine tablets that gave off clouds of nasty vapor. Piekarski made her deposit into the bowl. Then she stripped the duct tape off the chair. Finally, she pushed the bowl gently up against the door, covering the knob, and taped it in place.

"How do we set it off?" Erin asked. The makeshift mask was covering her nose and mouth, but her eyes were suffering.

"Impact," Piekarski said.

"So we shoot it?"

"Yeah."

"So instead of a chance of a ricochet, we have a chance of a ricochet and an explosion?"

"Pretty much."

"How big is this going to blow?"

"I have no idea. The bowl should focus the blast on the doorknob. Not too big, I think."

"Well, we can't stay here," Erin said. "You want to take the shot?"

"You're a better shot than I am," Piekarski said. "But give it as much time as you can."

"Why?"

"To let the reaction finish."

"So I should wait until we're about to choke to death and *then* set off an explosion?"

"I don't know! I've never done this before!"

"Okay." Erin drew her Glock and held it with her wrists crossed, aiming the flashlight with the other hand. She blinked away tears and steadied herself. "We're out of time. Rolf, *platz!* Get down!"

Rolf hunkered next to her. Piekarski curled into a ball on the floor, shielding her head. Erin knelt, drew in a breath, wished she hadn't as the chlorine burned in her lungs, and squeezed the trigger.

Hollywood had conditioned her to expect a gigantic fireball. It didn't happen. What she got was an almost invisible blast, accompanied by a hollow bang, very loud in the enclosed space. Half of the metal bowl whipped past her ear, missing by a little less than two inches. The bullet went somewhere, but it didn't hit anybody so she didn't care. She felt the pressure wave roll over and through her, rattling her teeth. She closed her eyes reflexively, but the blast was already past her.

Hot shrapnel stung her cheek. A beam of light filtered toward her, wavery and greenish as it passed through the chlorine vapor. The doorknob was missing, the plate blown clean out of the door, leaving a rectangular hole.

Erin lunged for the door, thrusting her hand into the hole. The door swung easily inward, admitting light and blessed fresh air. *"Hier!"* she rasped, stumbling as far down the hall as she could force her feet.

Rolf came to her call, claws scrabbling on the concrete. The dog's eyes were streaming and he gave a racking cough as he skidded to a halt beside her, but his ears and tail were up.

Piekarski followed. She stripped off the nasty piece of Erin's shirt and swiped at her eyes with her own sleeve. Then she went down on her hands and knees and started coughing. She hacked up a glob of thick mucus and groaned.

Erin walked unsteadily over to her and laid a hand on her shoulder. "Lifeguard training, huh?" she said.

"And Mr. Schwartz's Chemistry class," Piekarski said with a shaky smile. "Tenth Grade. Great guy. Loved to blow shit up. He told us nitrogen trichloride was one of the nastiest chemicals on Earth. I guess it stuck in my head. We're just lucky we didn't blow ourselves up."

"Yeah," Erin said. "But we're not done. We need to move. You good?"

"What we need is a hospital," Piekarski said. "But yeah, I'm good."

She took Erin's hand and clambered to her feet. They made their way to the elevator, not trusting their legs on the stairs. Erin hit the button for the lobby. She sagged against the back wall as the elevator car started up.

"Get the word out," Erin said. "Then we find out where Carver lives."

"You think she's keeping the Richards chick at home?" Piekarski asked.

"Depends where she's living. But yeah, I think so."

The elevator dinged, announcing their arrival on the main floor. The doors slid open to reveal a mild-looking, balding man in a tweed sport coat carrying a bag of groceries in each hand. He was starting in before he realized the car was occupied.

"Excuse me," he said. "I'm sorry, I—oh my goodness!"

His eyes swept up and down Erin, who belatedly remembered that she was clad only in her bra above the waist. She, Piekarski, and Rolf were dirty, unkempt, and stank of urine and chlorine. She was grateful her taste in underwear tended toward functionality above sensuality. It was still probably a lot more female flesh than this guy was used to seeing in his apartment lobby. His eyes were enormous as he stared at her.

She stepped out of the elevator and unclipped her gold shield, putting it right in his face. "Sir, I'm Detective O'Reilly, NYPD Major Crimes," she said. "And I'm officially requisitioning your jacket."

"I beg your pardon?" he stammered, taking a step back.

"Take off your coat and give it to me," she said. "Now. Here's one of my cards. Call me tomorrow and I'll see you get it back."

Chapter 21

"You stole that man's jacket," Piekarski said.

"Requisitioned," Erin corrected. She checked the computer map as she steered the Charger through the Brooklyn streets.

"You look like an absent-minded professor," Piekarski said. "Or the nerdiest stripper in the world."

"Are you okay?" Erin asked.

"I'm a little giddy," the other woman admitted. "Nearly getting poisoned and blown up will do that to a girl. Now I'm not choking to death, I'm feeling pretty good. Don't you get jazzed on the action?"

"Not the way you do," Erin said. "But there's still time. Carver's house is just a couple minutes away."

"You really think she's keeping Valerie in her own basement?"

"You heard what she said about checking on her houseguest. She wouldn't have used that word otherwise."

"Good point. Patrol units should get there about the same time we do."

Erin nodded. The very first things they'd done when they gotten outside were to call Dispatch for an address check on one

Andromeda Carver and to request backup. ESU had also been notified, but they were at least fifteen minutes out and Erin didn't think they had that kind of time to spare. Andy had a few minutes' head start and that was bad enough.

Piekarski had called Webb immediately after that, while they were in transit, but the Lieutenant and Vic were all the way up in Manhattan. Even if they hopped in a helicopter, they wouldn't arrive in time to help.

"Vic's gonna be pissed," Piekarski said. "He really wanted to be in on this."

"We don't always get what we want," Erin said. She was driving fast, but not using the lights or siren. She didn't want Andy to know they were coming.

"How do you want to play it?" Piekarski asked.

"Valerie will be in the basement," Erin said. "Carver will probably be there too, but our main goal is to rescue the girl. Carver lives in a brick house. It's sturdy, but there ought to be a basement window. One of us goes to the front door and rings the bell as a distraction. The other breaks into the basement. If Carver's down there, that one takes her down. If she's not, that one finds Valerie and digs in with her until the cavalry arrives."

"You're going in, aren't you," Piekarski said. "And I'm ringing the bell."

"I've got Rolf," Erin said. "There'll be two of us."

"Okay," Piekarski sighed. "You get to be the white knight, as usual."

"For the last time, stop thinking about heroics," Erin said. "We just survived by pissing ourselves in a goddamn basement! And no, I'm not going to explain that little gem to the reporters. Don't forget what we're trying to do. There's a family who wants their little girl back."

"Damn right," Piekarski said. "Sorry for bitching. I'm ready. Let's kick some ass."

*　　*　　*

Andy's house was a two-story brick home, similar to the house Erin had grown up in. The yard was well-kept. A Toyota Camry was parked in the driveway. Nothing was out of place or indicated anything suspicious.

Erin risked a drive-by without slowing down. Then she parked the Charger around the corner. She and Piekarski got out quickly, not wasting any time. They both knew what the car in the driveway meant; Andy had beaten them here. They might already be too late. There was no sign of their backup.

"We can't wait," Erin said, strapping Rolf's Kevlar around him. She'd put on her own vest under her borrowed coat. "Give me thirty seconds. Then hit the doorbell. Another fifteen and kick it in."

"Without a warrant?" Piekarski asked as they jogged down the sidewalk.

"Hot pursuit," Erin said. "I'm ranking detective. I'll take responsibility."

"Screw that," Piekarski retorted. "I'm a big girl and I can stand up for myself. Catch you on the flip-side."

Erin took Rolf through the neighbor's yard. A fence slowed them down, but only for a few seconds. Erin vaulted it and Rolf scrambled up and over. They came down in Andy's side yard, trying to keep out of view.

The basement had a window a couple inches above ground level; three panes of glass, each about a foot square. As she got close, Erin saw the windows were blacked out, either with curtains or painted on the inside. She pulled her Glock and got ready. Piekarski was walking up to the front door, her own gun in hand.

The chime of the doorbell was faint, but to Erin's adrenaline-charged senses it was like a church bell. She gave it a few seconds, hoping the sound would draw Andy toward the front door. Then she smashed the window with the butt of her pistol.

Glass tinkled in a sparkling shower. Erin spent two more precious seconds raking the broken shards out of the frame with her gun barrel. Fresh-broken plate glass was one of the sharpest things on Earth. You could cut an artery in your wrist and bleed to death if you just tried to shove through.

"*Such!*" she snapped and pointed.

Rolf dropped low and snaked through the opening, landing almost soundlessly on his paws. He immediately began his search drill, snuffling for human scent. Erin grabbed the window-frame and went through feet-first after him, hoping she wouldn't land on something bad and twist an ankle.

She came down on bare concrete, feeling the jarring shock in her knees. She ignored the sharp pain and straightened, whipping out her flashlight and bringing up her gun.

Rolf barked excitedly from somewhere ahead. Erin sent the flashlight beam after the dog and saw him leaping and scratching at a closed door. It was an old, solid-looking door with a brand-new steel hasp and padlock securing it.

From somewhere upstairs came a splintering crash, followed by Piekarski's voice shouting "NYPD! Freeze!" Erin ignored her, running toward the locked door.

Rolf paused mid-jump and turned his head. He was looking toward a wooden staircase that led up. He barked again, loud and shrill.

The K-9's reaction probably saved Erin's life. Andy Carver sprang at her from halfway up the stairs. A butcher's knife was in her hand, the steel flashing bright in the flashlight's LED beam. Erin twisted to one side. Andy's knife slashed through the tweed jacket just below Erin's neck like it wasn't even there. The razor edge of the blade glanced off the Kevlar underneath, the knife turning in Andy's hand.

Erin tried to bring the gun around, but Andy was already too close. The reporter's scarred face was twisted in a grimace of desperation. Andy pulled back her arm and drove it forward again. Erin reflexively batted it aside, getting lucky and deflecting the stroke. Andy brought her hand back again.

Sewing-machine attack, Erin thought in the distant, analytical part of her brain. Vic had warned her about this. Unskilled but deadly. Andy intended to just deliver one rapid stab after another into her body until she went down. A lot of people thought Kevlar would protect you against knives as well as bullets. They were wrong. The weave was hard to cut, but the point of a sharp knife could stab through it. The front plate of Erin's vest was stab-resistant, which she was distinctly aware was not the same thing as being stab-proof. And the plate didn't cover everything important.

Erin backpedaled, trying to put some distance between her and the knife-wielding killer. "Drop it!" she managed to say, but Andy had no intention of doing so. The knife blurred toward Erin once, twice, three times.

The first stab was foiled by the vest's plate. The second caught nothing but air as Erin retreated. The third came in low, aiming for her stomach. Erin's left hand got in the way. She felt a slick pain, paper-thin but deep, slice across the heel of her hand. She jammed her Glock between the two of them and fired twice, as fast as she could pull the trigger. There was no aiming, no choosing of targets, just blind reflex and training.

Andy staggered back, the rhythm of her attack faltering. She made a sound somewhere between a gasp and a grunt, but she didn't go down. Erin wrapped her left hand around the right and raised the Glock, sighting at her opponent at a range of about four feet. Her left hand was wet and slippery, but that didn't seem important at the moment.

"Drop it!" she shouted again.

Andy smiled that twisted, sardonic smile that was all her misshapen mouth could manage. She raised the knife toward her own throat.

Rolf hit her from the side with ninety pounds of furry ferocity, leading with his jaws. He caught Andy's forearm just above the wrist with such force that he yanked her clean off her feet and spun her around, dragging her several yards across the floor. The knife flew from her hand and skittered into the shadows. Andy didn't make a sound. She couldn't; the breath had been knocked clean out of her.

Erin kept her gun trained on the fallen woman, but Rolf had the situation well in hand—or maybe in mouth, she thought dazedly. She choked back a laugh that might have been just a little hysterical.

"Erin?" Piekarski called. "I'm coming! Hold your fire!"

"Come on!" Erin yelled back. "Carver's down!"

A moment later Piekarski came down the stairs, flashlight and gun at the ready. But the action was over. Andy was definitely out of the fight. Rolf's jaws had punctured her arm and blood was blossoming on the side of her abdomen where one of Erin's bullets had hit her. It didn't look like an immediately life-threatening injury, but you could never tell with gunshot wounds.

"Call a bus," Erin said. "Make it two."

"In a minute," Piekarski said grimly, kneeling and handcuffing Andy. "She's not getting away again."

Andy offered no resistance. She was stunned or in shock, lying limp on the basement floor. Piekarski left her there and found a chain hanging from a bare bulb in the ceiling. She pulled it and the room was suddenly flooded with warm, yellow light.

"Erin, you're bleeding," Piekarski said.

"Yeah," Erin said absently. Blood was dripping from her left hand; a lot of blood. It didn't hurt as much as she would have expected. The sharper the knife, the less you felt it. That was a problem for later. She quickly frisked Andy while Piekarski got on the phone with Dispatch. The woman's keys were in her hip pocket, including one that looked like it would fit a padlock.

Erin tried it. The lock opened easily. She shoved the door open, keeping her Glock drawn just in case. She saw a small room containing a mattress, a bucket, and a blonde teenager tied hand and foot with strips of red silk. The girl was gagged, but she was staring at Erin over the scarf with huge, terrified eyes.

"Valerie Richards?" Erin guessed.

The girl nodded. Frantic noises came through the gag.

"It's okay," Erin said. "I'm a police detective. We're here to help. You're safe now."

Valerie's eyes filled with tears. A muffled sob burst out of her. Erin shoved her pistol back in its holster, knelt down, and went to work on the knots. It was easier to cut them with her trusty Swiss Army knife than to fiddle with them.

The moment her hands were free, Valerie wrapped her arms around Erin in a desperate embrace. She clutched her with astonishing force.

"I want my mom," Valerie whimpered. She might be sixteen, a bright, confident young woman, but here and now she was a scared little girl.

"We'll get you to her as soon as we can," Erin promised. "Everything's going to be okay. Are you hurt?"

"No," Valerie managed to say. "I'm sorry. I'm so sorry!"

"Sorry?" Erin echoed. "For what?"

But Valerie just kept saying it, over and over, alternating with sobs. Erin gave up and just held her. She was getting blood all over Valerie from her lacerated hand, but neither of them cared.

Andy Carver's basement was reasonably soundproofed. However, the broken window had made the subsequent gunshots very noticeable. When the first Patrol unit arrived less than two minutes later, they came heavy and expecting trouble. It was a bit of a letdown for them to find the suspect already in custody and the victim rescued, but they went to work with their medical kit. By the time the first ambulance showed up, Erin had a pressure bandage on her hand and they'd managed to slow Andy's bleeding.

It was a small blessing that they were on the way to the hospital, Erin and Valerie in one ambulance, Piekarski and another officer guarding Andy in the other, before any reporters got wind of what had happened.

But the reporters got to the hospital soon enough.

Chapter 22

Andy Carver had been right about one thing: they'd be all over the ten o'clock news. In fact, they were making *all* the news. Less than half an hour after Andy was handcuffed to a stretcher at Mount Sinai Hospital, before a doctor had even finished putting stitches in Erin's hand, the Internet knew about it. The old-school readers of paper newspapers wouldn't hear about it until the next morning, but the *Times* had the story on their website as fast as it could be uploaded. The news went out on radio waves, fiber-optic cables, Wi-Fi, and every other information format known to man, except maybe telegraph or bicycle messenger.

Nobody had the complete story, of course, but the twenty-four-hour news cycle couldn't afford to wait. The writers just added a notation that it was "breaking news" and would be updated, so people ought to keep clicking the headlines in their browsers. That kept the advertisers happy and the all-important viewer engagement numbers climbing.

Vic and Lieutenant Webb were unimpressed by the breathless histrionics. They pushed impatiently through the clustered reporters and bystanders outside the hospital, finally breaking through to the main building. They found Erin and Piekarski waiting on hard-cushioned chairs in a side hallway.

"You two look like creamed shit on toast," Vic said by way of greeting.

"I love you too, sweetie," Piekarski said.

"I swung by our place and brought you a change of clothes like you asked," he added. "I can see why."

"I love you," she said again, with more conviction.

"Why are you sitting here?" Webb asked. "There's better furniture in the lobby."

"And cameras," Erin pointed out.

"Good point," Webb said. "What on Earth are you wearing?"

Erin fingered the lapel of the battered tweed jacket. "I had to make a tactical wardrobe adjustment," she said. "And I didn't have a personal concierge to bring me fresh clothes."

Vic wrinkled his nose. "And what's that smell? Where'd you find our perp, the sewer?"

"It's complicated," Erin said.

"No, it's not," Piekarski said. "It's just gross."

"Where's Carver?" Webb asked.

"Operating room," Erin said. "She has a perforated small intestine and a bite on the forearm. As long as they pump her full of antibiotics, she should be okay."

"You shot her?" Webb asked.

"Just the once. In my defense, she was trying to stab me at the time."

Webb knew better than to ask for details. When a police officer shot a suspect, no matter how guilty the target was, Internal Affairs was going to get involved. It was better for everyone if they didn't have to remember any additional conversations.

"The twenty-one-foot rule exists for a reason," Vic said, looking at her hand. "Looks like she tagged you."

"I'm fine," Erin lied. Her hand had really started hurting and she was looking forward to those pills the doc had prescribed.

"Of course you are," Webb said. "I guess we can't interrogate our perp until she's out of surgery. But we've finally got the right person?"

"We found Valerie locked in Carver's basement," Erin said. "She ID'd Carver. We have the silk scarves Carver used to tie up the girls and strangle Laurel Peterson. And we have the butcher's knife. I'm betting we'll get trace blood samples off the blade, no matter how hard she tried to clean it."

"Not to mention the bitch tried to kill us," Piekarski added. "Twice, in Erin's case."

"That's pretty ironclad," Webb said. "But it's always better with a recorded confession."

"We might have to wait for her tell-all memoir," Erin said bitterly. "Published from prison. It'll make the *New York Times* Bestseller list. Book clubs, behind-bars exclusive interviews, you name it. We'll be hearing about this until we're sick of it."

"I'm already there," Vic growled. "I can't believe you guys were arresting serial killers, getting in knife fights, blowing shit up, and rescuing kidnap victims, all without me! All I got to do was follow an asshole Feebie around. You know where he went? The goddamn tanning salon! And he got his hair done. Who the hell gets his hair done *after* going on national TV?! And you can bet he did it before, too. That's twice in one day!"

"Who does your hair, Vic?" Erin asked.

"I do it myself," he said proudly. "With an electric razor, in front of a mirror."

"I never would've guessed," Erin deadpanned.

"I like it," Piekarski said, putting a hand on Vic's arm. "It makes you look tough and manly."

"See?" Vic said. "Tough and manly!"

"I still have a lot of questions," Webb said. "For starters, I'm not completely clear on what caused the explosion in that apartment basement."

"Nitrogen trichloride," Piekarski said.

"I don't care what chemical was used," he said. "I want to know exactly why two of my detectives found it necessary to set off a homemade bomb in a residential building."

"Erin's the ranking detective," Piekarski said, standing up. "I could really use a quick shower before I change. There has to be one I can use somewhere around here."

"I know this hospital," Vic said. "Here, I'll show you."

The two of them disappeared down the hall. Erin had a sneaky suspicion that once Piekarski was clean, they might not be coming back for a while. Vic and Zofia had originally bonded over the excitement of taking down perps, and Erin figured Piekarski might be planning a little something to take the sting out of Vic missing the arrest.

"Excuse me?"

A man in a suit had just come around the corner behind Erin and Webb. He practically had "bureaucrat" stamped on his forehead. He was holding a phone in one hand and a stylus in the other.

"Yes?" Webb said.

"You'd be Detective O'Reilly?" He wasn't looking at the Lieutenant.

"That's me," Erin said cautiously.

"Yes, of course. I'm an aide to the Commissioner. He's asked me to invite you to a press conference in an hour."

"I'm sorry, what?" Erin said.

"At One PP."

"Didn't you just do one of those?"

He looked embarrassed. "Well, yes. But the situation has changed. It's... ah... fluid."

"Yeah, some fluids were involved," Erin said with a grimace. She looked at Webb. "Do I have to do this, sir?"

"An invitation from the PC isn't an order," Webb said. "It's a request. So no, you don't have to."

"In that case—" Erin began.

"You only have to if you want to keep working for the NYPD," Webb interjected.

"—I'd be happy to," Erin finished through gritted teeth. "But I probably shouldn't be wearing this."

"I have a car outside," the aide said. "We can take you home on the way. You'll want your dress blues."

"What about Zofia?" Erin asked.

"Who?" the aide asked.

"Detective Piekarski. The other detective who made the bust with me."

He blinked. "I don't have any instructions about any Detective... what was the name?"

"Piekarski," Erin repeated.

"My orders are to bring you," he said. "And your dog."

"But not the rest of my squad?"

"I'm sorry, no. Look, I don't want to be pushy, but we are on a schedule here. So if we could...?"

"I don't believe this crap," Erin said, giving Webb a look of helpless disgust.

"You'll do fine," Webb said. "Just keep to the facts, speak slowly and clearly, and keep mentioning solid police work and interagency cooperation. They eat that stuff up. I'll explain to the others."

Erin hoped Vic and Piekarski were having a good enough time to make up for this. Because otherwise they were both going to be royally pissed off.

*   *   *

The last time Erin had shaken hands with the Commissioner, she'd been turning down a job offer. If he resented it, he gave no indication. His smile was as warm, his grip as firm as ever. He was a big man in New York City and a big man in general; almost as tall as Vic and a lot broader in the stomach. His laugh filled the room when it rolled out of him.

"Detective O'Reilly," he said. "I guess all of us are glad you didn't want that desk job, huh?"

"Things worked out okay, sir," she said.

He glanced at her bandaged hand. "I hope you're not badly injured."

"All in a day's work, sir."

"Excellent! Well, let's not keep the good people waiting. Remember, you're not just talking to New York; you're talking to the world."

Erin swallowed and followed him. She looked down at Rolf, who paced calmly at her side. He wasn't worried, though he was still wet from a very hurried bath to take the worst of the stink out of his fur. They'd walked into, and out of, much more dangerous situations than this. She tried to channel some of his confidence. The dress uniform helped a little. It reminded her that she wasn't on her own; she was part of the Department. Thirty-five thousand men and women had her back.

But none of them were standing between her and the TV cameras and flashbulbs of the press room. The lights dazzled her. The hubbub of excited voices was overwhelming. Residual adrenaline was still humming through her body, pushing her towards fight or flight. She tried to think of it like a training exercise. The main thing was to keep her cool and not to say or do anything stupid. Millions of people would be watching her and dissecting her every word. She tried not to think about that.

The Commissioner talked first. He led off by saying that the Central Park Strangler had been arrested by the brave detectives of the NYPD's Major Crimes unit, led by Detective First Grade Erin O'Reilly. Valerie Richards was alive, unscathed, and currently being reunited with her overjoyed parents at Mount Sinai Hospital. Detective O'Reilly had been injured in a desperate struggle with the murderer, but thankfully not severely. The alleged Strangler was a tabloid reporter named Andromeda Carver. Detective O'Reilly would now take a few questions from members of the press.

He stepped back from the podium and extended an arm to Erin, giving her another handshake and a big grin for the benefit of the cameras. She tried to match his smile but felt fake.

Every hand in the audience was raised. She picked one more or less at random and pointed.

"Dirk Cole, *New York Post*," the reporter said. "Ms. O'Reilly, how did you determine Ms. Carver was the Strangler?"

"Through steady, solid police work," Erin said, remembering what Webb had told her. "We had realized our suspect profile had assumed the killer was male. Once we theorized we might be looking for a woman, Ms. Carver was an obvious person of interest."

That was mostly true. Erin didn't think anybody wanted to know just how lucky they'd gotten. The luck of the Irish was a great thing to have, but failed to instill confidence in law enforcement. She picked out another reporter, a woman this time.

"Meredith Bly, *Daily Mirror*," the woman said. "Why did she do it?"

"I'm a detective, not a psychologist, ma'am," Erin said, earning an easy laugh from the crowd. "We hope to determine a specific motive by interviewing Ms. Carver, but at present she is recovering from injuries sustained resisting arrest."

More questions followed. Erin answered them as briefly as she could, but there were a couple of things she wanted to be sure to say. When the predictable question came about her "single-handed" arrest, Erin spoke up.

"Hold on a minute," she said. "Let me be clear about this. Our investigation, and subsequent arrest, was a team effort every step of the way. I was only one of the people involved. My colleague, Detective Zofia Piekarski, was with me. She was brave, smart, and quick-thinking, and if not for her, I wouldn't be standing here talking to you. Not only would Andy Carver have gotten away, but I'd probably be dead. I also want to thank my other squadmate, Detective Viktor Neshenko, for his solid support. He did everything that was asked of him and more. And my commanding officer, Lieutenant Harold Webb. All of them are rock solid. I don't deserve to be singled out here."

She got a round of applause for that, but she could see she wasn't getting through to them. All they heard was a hero cop being modest, like an Oscar winner at the Academy Awards thanking the friends and family who'd gotten her there. Erin felt frustrated, angry, out of control. Did nobody understand what had really happened in Brooklyn? Two detectives, a police K-9, and an innocent teenage girl had narrowly escaped death. Only luck, quick thinking, and half-remembered high school chemistry had saved them. The reporters ought to be talking to Piekarski, Webb, Captain Holliday, Dr. Levine, and everyone else who'd made success possible. But she'd tried to say it and nobody was listening. They already had the narrative they wanted in their heads and there was no getting around it.

"All right," the Commissioner said. "Let's hear it for Detective O'Reilly and, of course, her brave squad. Now, that's all the time we have—"

"Excuse me, sir," Erin said loudly, stepping forward beside him. "I have something else I need to say."

Startled, the Commissioner moved aside. Nobody had dared pull something like this on him before and he was slow to react.

Erin didn't give him the chance. "During the course of our investigation, we made two other arrests," she said. "Those names were released, even though they had not yet been charged, and will not be. I'd like to state, loud and clear for the record, that Ethan Warburton and Donald Lambert are completely innocent of the kidnapping and murder of Laurel Peterson, and of any complicity in the abduction of Valerie Richards or the murder of Holly Gardner. We were operating on the best information available to us, but those arrests were in error and do not reflect in any way on those two New York citizens."

"Thank you, Detective," the Commissioner said, recovering. He thrust a big hand up, screening her from the television cameras. "No more questions at this time. We'll be putting out a release with more information just as soon as we have it. Thank you for coming, ladies and gentlemen."

As he steered her away from the press room, the Commissioner leaned in and said quietly, "Detective, what were you thinking? You admitted culpability for two errors on the record in front of the entire country!"

"I was telling the truth, sir," Erin said, undaunted. "Those men have suffered enough damage to their reputations already. And Warburton was nearly killed! He may have some unpleasant personal habits, but he didn't touch Laurel Peterson. Even with what I said, there'll still be people who think those guys are murderers and psychos. It was the least I could do to speak up. It probably won't do any good, but I had to try."

"You practically handed them a wrongful-arrest lawsuit on a platter," the Commissioner shot back. "This isn't how you play politics!"

"I'm not a politician, sir," Erin said coldly. "And I'm not playing anything. I'm a detective. If you want someone to lie to the press, maybe I shouldn't have been the woman standing up there beside you."

He blinked. Then his smile came back, so real-looking it almost fooled her. "You're a straight shooter, Ms. O'Reilly," he said. "I can respect that. But you may want to consider your own future a little more carefully."

"I'll keep that in mind, sir," she said. The door closed behind them, leaving her and Rolf alone with the Commissioner and two of his aides.

"And you didn't thank our Federal associates for their invaluable assistance," he added.

"Assistance?" Erin retorted. "They gave us a profile that pointed us in the wrong direction and then Agent Rockwell leaked case information to a reporter. Holly Gardner died because Agent Rockwell told her about Lambert! Agent Willard was helpful, but Rockwell nearly sabotaged our whole case and he got an innocent woman killed. I'm not going to thank him for that!"

"You're right," the Commissioner said through his warm, false smile. "You're no politician. I'll have a car take you wherever you need to go, Detective. Thank you again for your assistance."

"Just doing my job, sir," she said. And she couldn't wait to get the hell out of there and get back to doing it.

Chapter 23

"Well, look at you," Vic said. "All dressed up. You getting married, or what?"

"Something like that," Erin said. "Did I miss anything important while I was doing PR bullshit?"

"Zofia's talking to Valerie and her folks," he said. "Webb's hanging around the recovery room waiting for Carver to come round. They had you on TV."

"That's kind of the point of a press conference."

"The PC's an asshole."

"We already knew that."

"I didn't know you were Captain friggin' America," he said. "Saving the city, all by your lonesome."

"Isn't Captain America a team player?" she replied. "That's his whole schtick. I think maybe you're thinking of Superman."

"I didn't have you pegged as a comic-book fan," he said. "Were you really that kind of kid?"

"I wasn't," she said. "But my brother Sean was. Look, Vic, I'm sorry, okay? None of this was my idea."

"You should've seen the Lieutenant when the PC said you were running the Major Crimes unit," he said. "I was glad we were in a hospital. I thought the poor old bastard was gonna have a heart attack on the spot."

"I tried to tell him," she said angrily. "I tried to tell all of them!"

"I know," he said more gently. "And so does Zofia. She's not gonna forget it, either. We liked the way you tried to set him straight."

"It didn't work."

"Of course it didn't. Shit like that just bounces off those sons of bitches. They tell lies like you and I drink. Hey, let's go see how Zofia's getting on with our damsel in distress. Her parents wanted to know when you got back. They want to talk to you."

In the normal course of events, Valerie wouldn't have rated a private room. She wasn't a VIP and she wasn't badly hurt. But in the current media environment, the hospital had wisely put her as far out of the way as possible. Two hospital security guys were guarding her door and they were taking their job seriously. Vic and Erin both had to show their shields, in spite of Erin's uniform.

Valerie Richards was sitting up in bed. Her mom was on the bed next to her, clutching her daughter's hand in a grip that would take a crowbar and a strong man to break. Mr. Richards stood at the bedside, arms crossed in a pose of artificial casualness. All three had streaks on their cheeks from fresh tears. Piekarski was sitting in a chair opposite them, a notepad on her knee and her phone recording the conversation.

Erin knocked quietly. "Excuse me," she said. "If this is a bad time, we can come back."

Mrs. Richards looked at her daughter. Valerie cleared her throat and straightened her shoulders.

"It's okay, Mom," she said hoarsely. "Really."

"You might remember me," Erin said. "I'm Erin O'Reilly."

"Vic Neshenko," Vic said. "We met earlier."

"How are you doing?" Erin asked. The girl looked okay. Valerie was a strikingly pretty blonde with astonishing blue eyes; the sort of girl who'd be voted homecoming queen in a landslide. She didn't have a mark on her. She was clean. Her hair was neatly brushed. Except for the haunted look hiding at the back of her eyes, you'd never guess she'd spent the last couple of days locked in a serial killer's basement.

"I think I'm all right," Valerie said. "She didn't do anything to me. I mean, she didn't hurt me. She fed me. It was scary, that's all."

"You're a very brave girl, Valerie," Erin said.

"Ms. O'Reilly," Mrs. Richards said. "We can't thank you enough for what you've done for us. You and Ms. Piekarski. If it weren't for you..."

Her voice cut off in a sudden, choking sob. Valerie looked awkward and a little embarrassed.

"It's okay, Mom," she said again. "I'm right here."

The sight of a sixteen-year-old kidnapping victim comforting her own mother put a lump in Erin's throat. Piekarski gulped and looked away. Even Vic coughed and wiped his eyes gruffly.

Mr. Richards stepped forward and put out his hand. When Erin took it, he held on harder and longer than usual for a handshake.

"Anything you need," he said. He looked at Piekarski. "You, too. Just name it. We owe you everything."

"You don't owe us a thing," Erin said. "This is our job. We're just glad we were able to bring your daughter back."

"How'd she grab you?" Vic asked. "At the bowling alley?"

"I have her statement," Piekarski said. "She doesn't have to—"

"I want to," Valerie interrupted. "I think—I think I need to talk about this. It's inside me anyway. Maybe if I get it out it'll be better. For me."

"That's probably true," Erin said. "Talking about trauma helps process it."

"I was with Ashley, Courtney, Kayla, and Jill," Valerie said. "I'd seen this lady at the alley. I noticed the scar on her face. She was at the bar. I tried not to stare at her. I didn't... I didn't realize she was watching us. Watching me."

"Why didn't the witnesses tell us?" Vic wondered. "We asked if there were any suspicious guys in the place. Nobody mentioned her!"

"You said it yourself," Erin said. "We were looking for *guys*. Men."

"Dammit," Vic muttered.

"When I went to the bathroom, she must have followed me. She was waiting when I came out of the stall. She said she was in trouble. That she'd run away from a man who'd hurt her. She said he'd done... that to her face. And her leg. She was limping. She asked for my help.

"I told her to call the cops, but she said..." Valerie trailed off.

"What?" Erin asked gently.

"She said her husband was a cop," Valerie said, looking down. "She said he had friends on the Force. She said I had a kind face and since... since I was a woman, I'd understand. I asked what she needed. She said she just needed someone to lean on out the back door to her car."

"Carver didn't drug her," Vic said, shaking his head. "She walked her right out under her own power."

"It was silly and stupid," Valerie said. "But I wanted to help her. I thought... I thought I was doing the right thing. As soon as we were outside, she put a knife against my neck. She said she'd... she'd cut my throat if I didn't do what she said. A car was right there. Before I knew what was going on, she put a bag over my head and snapped handcuffs on my wrists and put me in the trunk and drove away. Then I screamed and banged on the trunk, but nobody heard it.

"After a little while, the car stopped. She said if I screamed again she'd... she'd do things to me. She said she didn't want to hurt me, but she would if I made her. Then she took me out of the car. I couldn't see anything because of the bag. She took me into some kind of building and down some stairs. Then she changed the handcuffs for something softer and apologized if she'd hurt me."

"She apologized?" Erin asked.

Valerie nodded. "She was... nice to me. That's what was so weird. She made food for me. I could smell it cooking. It was Greek, I think. It was actually pretty good. She talked to me and asked me a bunch of questions."

"About what?"

"My life. What I liked to do, whether I had a boyfriend, all that sort of thing. When I told her I'd never had a boyfriend, she seemed sad. She said she was sorry to hear it. She was kind of weird. I asked why she'd picked me."

"What did she say?" Erin asked.

"She said she'd had water damage in her basement a while back and my dad's company had fixed it. She'd talked to him and he'd been so proud of his daughter."

Mr. Richards's mouth compressed into a tight, angry line.

"Sir," Erin said. "This wasn't your fault. You didn't do a thing wrong."

"They... they say she's the person who killed that other girl," Valerie said. "The one in Central Park."

"Looks that way," Vic said.

"Would she have done... that to me?" Valerie asked. She touched her neck with the hand her mother wasn't holding.

"Forget about it," Erin said. "There's no reason to ask yourself that. It doesn't matter. We caught her and you're safe. That's the important thing."

"She said I should be happy," Valerie said quietly. "Because she was going to make me famous."

*　*　*

"What a creep," Vic said. The three detectives were on their way down to the recovery room, leaving Valerie in the care of her parents and hospital security.

"I think it's sad," Piekarski said.

"Faking being a victim to get close to the real victim?" Vic replied. "That's some sick, twisted, Ted Bundy shit right there. I hope that girl knows how lucky she is."

"Lucky?" Piekarski repeated. "*Lucky?!* That poor kid's screwed up for life! She's gonna be in therapy for friggin' *years!*"

"She wasn't hurt," Vic said. "She could've been dead!"

"And whatever doesn't kill you makes you stronger?" Erin asked, dripping with sarcasm.

"I'm just saying it could've been a hell of a lot worse," he said. "And that nutjob was right. She's gonna be famous. Just like Harry Potter."

"Huh?" Erin didn't read fantasy literature.

"She'll be the girl who lived," Piekarski said, getting it. "She'll have someone offer her a book deal, she'll get on talk shows if she wants it."

"What if all she wants is to go back to being a normal sixteen-year-old?" Erin asked.

"Tough shit," Vic said. "That ship has sailed."

"Detectives!"

"Oh, God," Vic said under his breath.

Agent Rockwell was coming down the hallway. He beamed at them.

"What a great outcome!" he said. "I was hoping to catch you here. We need to discuss messaging."

"A great outcome?" Erin echoed. "For Holly Gardner?"

Rockwell's smile flickered. "That's very sad, obviously, but we need to focus on the positive. I saw your press conference and it was great, really great. But there's just a few details I'd like to—"

"You showed Holly your profile," Erin interrupted. "You showed her our suspect list."

"Hold on a second." Rockwell wasn't smiling anymore. "You're accusing me of leaking sensitive case information to a member of the press. Unless you have some very convincing proof—"

"Can it, pretty boy," Vic growled. "You're right. We can't do a goddamn thing to you officially. Even if you were shooting your mouth off to a hot reporter in the hope she'd bang you in the back of her news van."

"That is way out of line," Rockwell said.

"No, it wasn't," Vic said. "You want to see out of line?"

Vic was faster than he looked, and Rockwell wasn't expecting it. Vic's fist crossed the line at high speed, straight into Rockwell's face. The agent landed on his ass and slid several feet across the floor. He started to get up, sat down again, and fell flat on his back.

"Jesus," Piekarski murmured.

Vic massaged his knuckles. "You know what the worst part is?" he told the prone FBI agent. "I *hated* Holly Gardner. There were times I wanted to slap her silly, and I've never slapped a woman in my life. But she was just trying to do her job. Maybe you broke the law and maybe you didn't, but you broke a code of human goddamn decency. You were so stuck on looking good, you forgot to *be* good. You've got a hard, thick skull, but get this through it. We're not helping you with messaging, or PR, or any other greasy shit you crap out of your tight little FBI ass. And if I ever see your face again, I swear to God, the next camera lens that points your way will shatter when it sees what you look like afterward."

Rockwell managed to sit up. Blood was trickling from the corner of his mouth and the left side of his face was already swelling. "You hit me," he said, sounding dazed. "You assaulted a Federal agent."

"No he didn't," Piekarski said. "You slipped and hit your head on the floor. I saw the whole thing. Are you okay? That was a good knock you took. I'm not surprised you're a little confused. We should maybe get you checked out."

"What?" Rockwell said. He turned toward Erin. "You saw him!"

Once upon a time Erin might have agreed with Rockwell. The blue wall of silence didn't really serve the public good. Turning a blind eye to police misbehavior led to departmental corruption. But Erin had spent too much time in the gray areas on the fringes. She'd known too many basically good guys who'd done bad things, and too many of the nominal good guys who'd turned out to be bad. She knew the law, but she also knew right from wrong, and Vic was right and Rockwell was wrong.

"These hospital floors can be tricky," she said. "Especially with those smooth-soled shoes you're wearing. It's easy to slip and hurt yourself. That cheek looks bad. You should get some ice on it. Here, let me give you a hand."

Rockwell reluctantly let her pull him to his feet. He stared at the three of them for a long moment and met three blank stares, radiating false concern. Then he turned and walked away, a little unsteadily.

"Damn, Vic," Erin said. "That could've been your career."

"It would've been worth it," Vic said. "I just wish I'd hit him twice."

*　　*　　*

Webb was sitting outside the recovery room, reading a six-month-old issue of *Better Homes & Gardens*. He closed the magazine and stood up when he saw them.

"How's our perp, sir?" Erin asked.

"Resting comfortably," Webb said.

"She tried to cut her own throat," Erin said. "What if—"

"Cool your jets, O'Reilly," Webb said. "She's in restraints and we have a uniform in the room. Nothing's going to happen to her."

"Did you question her yet?"

"No. The doctor said to give the anesthetic time to wear off. She should be good now."

"She'll lawyer up," Vic predicted.

Erin wasn't so sure. "I think we should try," she said.

"Me too," Webb agreed. "Neshenko, you wait outside."

"Why?" Vic demanded. "I've had to sit this whole damn case out! Who's gonna be bad cop if I'm not there?"

"Let's consider that question," Webb said. "Maybe, this is just a shot in the dark, but one of the detectives Ms. Carver tried to murder earlier today? Someone who might be reasonably expected to be a little irritated with her?"

"What'd I do to get sidelined?" Vic asked.

"You whined," Webb said.

"I didn't whine until after you said I couldn't come!" Vic said.

"Funny world, isn't it?" Webb said with a thin smile. "Maybe I'm psychic. Mostly I don't want you in there because, according to O'Reilly, our suspect was victimized by a big, muscular, athletic man when she was young. I don't think she'd respond well to you."

He patted Vic's shoulder with one hand and passed him the magazine with the other.

Vic pouted. Piekarski kissed him on the cheek.

"This isn't the fun part," she said.

"Rolf can keep you company," Erin said. "Rolf, *sitz. Bleib.*"

Rolf mournfully hunkered down beside the sulking Vic, wearing an identical expression. Vic sourly sat and opened the magazine to an article about azaleas.

* * *

Andy Carver was pale. Heavy dark bags lay under her eyes. She looked small, pathetic, and defenseless in the hospital bed, wrists locked in leather restraints. But Erin wasn't fooled. This woman had murdered two people and come within a whisker of killing Erin herself, not once but twice. You could never afford to let your guard down around violent criminals.

Her eyes were closed, but they snapped open as the detectives approached. She smiled, or tried to. Her facial injury, as always, made it a mocking sneer.

"Look who's here," she said. Her voice was hoarse, her throat dry. "The celebrity, the burnout, and the wannabe."

"How are you feeling, Ms. Carver?" Webb asked.

"Like someone shot me, a dog bit me, and some random guy was up to his knuckles in my guts," Andy said. "But I'm on pretty good medication. How do you think I'm feeling?"

"I apologize for my detective's use of force," Webb said. "She was defending herself."

"She should have had better aim," Andy said. "I've read your service record, Detective O'Reilly. You're a better shot than that.

I was practically touching you and the best you could do was poke a hole in my side? No vital organs down there, Detective."

"You were trying to stab me at the time," Erin reminded her. "And I didn't want to kill you."

"You didn't? Why not?" Andy asked the question lightly, but Erin saw sincere curiosity in her eyes.

"I don't kill people if I have a choice," Erin said. "I'm a cop, not an executioner."

"Then you should've let me take care of it myself," Andy replied. "It was pretty stupid of you to stop me. What's the point? We all know how it's going to go. Weeks of preparation and screwing around, then a trial that could drag on for months, and it's not like I'll have much of a life to look forward to afterward. They're never going to let me out."

"There doesn't have to be a trial," Webb said.

"Of course there does!" Andy shot back. "What, you think I'm going to plead out? Why would I ever do that? Now that I think about it, I should thank you, Erin O'Reilly. I panicked with the knife. I wasn't thinking clearly. I want to hang around for this. The trial's going to be great. It'll be the lead story all over the country for *weeks!* This face isn't pretty, but it'll be on more magazines than any supermodel. And everyone's going to ask why, why, why."

"Then I'll be the first," Erin said. "Why did you do it?"

"You think I'll tell you?" Andy replied. "You'll have to wait and buy the book, just like everyone else. Though I'd be glad for any insights you can contribute. It'd be a good angle. You could go in with me and get coauthor credit. You could even earn royalties on it. I can't, thanks to that silly Son of Sam Law that prohibits felons from profiting from their memoirs. Think about it: the Central Park Strangler, told by the woman herself and the hard-driving detective who captured her! It'd be a bestseller, guaranteed."

"Very funny," Erin said.

"You think I'm joking? You could make hundreds of thousands of dollars."

"Jesus Christ," Piekarski said. "I think she means it."

"Chance of a lifetime," Andy said.

"I already have a job," Erin said.

"How did you get Laurel Peterson?" Webb asked abruptly. "She was taken from a bus stop in the middle of Manhattan in the middle of the day. Nobody saw anything."

"Of course nobody saw anything," Andy said contemptuously. "You'd think this face would be memorable, but it's the opposite. People don't really see me. They look right past me. They notice me, then they block me out. You wouldn't believe how good people are at ignoring things that make them uncomfortable. When's the last time you really looked at a homeless bum panhandling on a street corner? Could you describe them?"

"You posed as a street person," Erin said. "You'd been studying Laurel. You knew she was an activist, someone who was interested in helping the homeless. So you put on a costume and planted yourself at the bus stop where she'd see you. Then you did the same thing you did with Valerie. You lured her in close and pulled a knife. After that you just walked her to your car through the crowd and nobody looked twice. Laurel was a small-town girl. She was scared and overwhelmed and she didn't dare make a scene."

"It really would have been a waste if you'd died in that basement," Andy said. "You're clever. I'm not admitting to anything, of course. That would spoil all the fun."

"This isn't a game!" Piekarski burst out. "People are *dead!* And you think it's funny? What the hell were you trying to prove? What sort of goddamn message were you sending?"

"Pay attention to Erin O'Reilly here," Andy said. "Maybe you'll learn from her. Maybe someday, if you're very good and very lucky, you'll be half the detective she is. Then maybe people will remember your name and you won't just be the cute little blonde side piece."

Piekarski's cheeks flushed. She balled her hands into fists. "You *bitch*," she said, so quietly it was almost a hiss. "You tried to poison us! You goddamn coward! I've had people try to kill me before, but they always had the balls to do it to my face!"

"How did you get out of that room?" Andy asked.

"Where did you get the chlorine?" Erin countered.

"The swimming pool in the apartment," Andy said. "It was chlorinated. If someone had a set of keys that, say, a careless janitor didn't keep track of, it'd be pretty easy to get into the supply closet next to the pool. I'll bet they have a lot of chlorine tablets in there. Bags and bags of them. Now, how did you get out so fast?"

"Nitrogen trichloride," Piekarski said. "Add ammonia and water to chlorine and you can make homemade explosives. We blew the friggin' lock off. Not bad for a cute blonde side piece, huh?"

"But where did you get ammonia and water?" Andy asked. Then her eyes widened. So did her sardonic smile. "Oh! Well done, Detective! Very well done! That's a good one! You're right, I underestimated you."

"You're not the first," Piekarski said.

"I'm kind of tired," Andy said. "All this running around Brooklyn, trying to stab a home invader, getting shot, and having surgery has left me pretty worn. I think I'm done talking with you."

"That's what you think," Erin said. "I still have questions."

"And I have a magic word," Andy replied. "It starts with 'L.' Would you like to guess what it is?"

"I think we're done here," Webb said. "Thank you for your cooperation, Ms. Carver. Rest and recover. I wouldn't want to deprive the people of New York of any of the life sentence you so richly deserve."

Chapter 24

"So that's what really happened," Erin said, leaning on the bar at the Barley Corner that evening. "Not the bullshit on the news."

"I see," Carlyle said. "And yourself?"

She wiggled the fingers on her bandaged hand. "I'll mend."

"That's our indestructible lass," Corky Corcoran said cheerfully, raising his glass. "Bullets and blades can't stop her, bombs and poison gas only slow her down. Here's to you, love."

Erin squinted at the glass in his hand. "Corky, what in God's name are you drinking? That's not *milk*, is it?"

"Gin, mostly," he said. "With a bit of orange liqueur and lemon juice. Then you mix in an egg white. That's why it's milky. Good Lord, you thought I'd be drinking milk in a pub? What do you take me for?"

"Still working your way down the Corner's cocktail list?" she asked.

"Nearly done," he said. "I'm partway through the W's. They call this a White Lady. It's not bad, but a mite sour. Too much lemon, I'm thinking. Care for a taste?"

"I'll stick with whiskey, thanks," she said.

"I'd rather like to meet this murderous lass," Corky said.

"You're spoken for," Erin reminded him.

"To talk to!" he retorted. "I don't want to sleep with *every* lass I meet!"

"She certainly sounds fascinating," Carlyle said. "And it's a pity she devoted her energies to so bad a cause. That lad who took advantage of her in her youth has a great deal to answer for."

"And he got away with it," Erin said. "The bastard probably never even felt bad. It's everyone else who ended up suffering."

"Particularly that pair of innocent lasses," Carlyle said.

"And Holly," Erin added. "We never liked her, but she didn't deserve that. She wasn't so bad, really. Just desperate for attention, and she's hardly alone in that. We owe her, too. We might not have tumbled to the right answer without her, at least not in time to save Valerie."

"I'll drink to dear Holly," Corky said, and did so. "And to you. Now you're a bloody great hero again."

"Knock it off," she growled. "Not you, too. Everybody's acting like I'm some sort of supercop. Why is everyone pretending this is all about me?"

"It's the price of fame, darling," Carlyle said.

"I didn't sign up for it," she said. "All I did was my job, and I can't even convince anybody otherwise. Maybe I ought to just hide under a rock for the next year or so and let everyone forget."

"You'd miss the wedding," Carlyle said.

"What wedding?" she blurted. Her mind wasn't really on what she was saying.

"Ours."

"Oh!" she exclaimed. "Right. Sorry. I wasn't thinking. It's been a hard couple of days."

"What about the gas?" he asked. "Any lingering effects?"

"The doc says I should be fine," she said. "I might have some eye irritation and respiratory crap, but that's uncommon. I didn't inhale too much of it. Neither did Zofia."

"Grand scheme of hers," Corky said. "I'd never have thought to soak rags in unmentionable fluids."

"She's not the first to think of it," Carlyle said. "Back in the Great War, some Canadian lads did it when the Germans sent chlorine their way. It worked, but it wasn't pleasant."

"You don't have to tell me," Erin said. "Thanks, by the way."

"For what?"

She pointed to the big-screen TV on the wall. "That's the only television in Manhattan that isn't playing that goddamn serial killer crap."

"Lads don't come to the Corner to watch the news," he said, smiling. "This is a sports pub. If I put *Sixty Minutes* on, I'd have a riot on my hands."

"I'm glad anyway," she said. "Now I think I'll head up to bed."

"I'll be along shortly," he said.

"I can come now, if you'd like company," Corky said with a wink.

Erin shook her head. "You're incorrigible," she said. "But Teresa would kill me after she got done killing you."

"If I thought you'd say yes, I'd never have offered," he replied, leaning in and giving her an impudent peck on the cheek. "Pleasant dreams, love."

*　*　*

Erin had already showered after getting home, washing most of the chlorine traces out of her hair. She could still smell a faint hint of swimming pool, but tried to push it out of her thoughts. She changed into a baggy old T-shirt that came down almost to her knees and got into bed. Rolf clambered up between her feet and curled into a furry ball.

She was just reaching for the bedside lamp when her phone buzzed. The word PARENTS shone up at her from the screen.

Erin didn't really want to talk to her mom or dad. She was tired, wrung out, and a little depressed. But when your parents called after ten at night, you'd better take the call. Maybe Mom had broken her hip, or Dad was having heart trouble. She scooped up the phone.

"Everything okay?" she asked.

"We're fine, kiddo," Sean O'Reilly said. "We didn't mean to worry you. Your mom's on the other line."

"Hello, dear," Mary said. "We just watched you on the evening news."

"Oh, God," Erin said, putting a hand over her face.

"You looked wonderful in your uniform," Mary said. "But you didn't seem very happy. You should be so proud, rescuing that poor girl!"

"Please, just stop," Erin said. "I've been getting that from everywhere. It's not that big a deal."

"It was to her," Mary said. "And to her mother."

"Something wrong, kiddo?" Sean asked.

"Nothing," Erin said. "Everything."

"You're not having... *personal* problems, are you?" Mary asked, a little too eagerly.

"No! I'm fine. The wedding's still on. I'm not pregnant. Nothing's happening in my life right now. Relax, Mom!"

"Why don't you say goodnight, Mary?" Sean suggested. "It sounds like Erin's had a rough day."

"Fine," Erin's mom said, pouting a little. "But we're both very proud of you, dear. And we love you."

"Love you too, Mom," Erin said. "Sorry I'm grumpy."

After the click as Mary disconnected, Sean gave it a couple of seconds. Then he said, "What's wrong with the case?"

"You should've been a detective, Dad," she said. "You've got the eye and the ear for it."

"No thanks," he said. "I was a lot happier dealing with noise complaints and busted windows. You gold shields have to handle murderers and terrorists. I preferred making a difference in my neighborhood, talking with ordinary people. But even if I'm not a detective, I can still tell when someone's dodging my question."

"The case is solid," she said. "We caught her in the act and she basically confessed."

"And you got to the second girl in time," he said. "So what's the problem?"

"It's Carver," Erin said. "She's getting what she wants."

"And what's that?"

"Attention. She's got this really messed-up idea about fame and celebrity. Now she's going to be famous. She offered me a book deal, can you believe that?"

He chuckled. "That's a first," he said. "I bet that doesn't happen to many detectives during an interrogation."

"It's not funny, Dad! She's going to get to parade around on stage in front of the whole country for as long as the trial lasts. This is why kids shoot up their schools. It's why terrorists blow up buildings. When we give them attention, we give them what they're looking for. She wins!"

"Is that what this was?" Sean asked. "A game? A reality TV show?"

"Of course not!"

"Then why does it matter what she thinks?"

"It matters!"

"No!" he said sharply. "It doesn't!"

"Why not?" Erin asked. It sounded sulky as she said it.

"Because what really matters is the girl who's back with her parents tonight," he said. "Not to mention all the other girls that woman would've killed. What matters is that Laurel Peterson's parents can at least have the consolation that you caught the woman who killed their daughter. The killer? She'll be forgotten soon enough. Sure, right now she's all over the airwaves, getting her fifteen minutes of fame. But that'll be over. Fast-forward a year. You'll be on to other things, chasing down other bad guys. The media will find something else to fill their broadcasts with, don't worry about that. This whole thing will churn and burn into the future, and you know where she'll be?"

"Sitting in jail," Erin said. "Or maybe a psych ward."

"Exactly," he said. "Does that really look like winning to you?"

"But she is getting what she wants," Erin repeated. "It's not fair."

"Oh, sorry," Sean said. "I guess you became a cop with the idea the world would be fair, or maybe you could make it that way. I hate to be the one to break it to you, but I've got some really bad news."

"Okay, okay," she said. "You're right. I guess this one just got under my skin a little."

"Forget about it," he said. "That just means you're still human. You haven't let fame go to your head."

"I don't *want* to be famous! I don't want to be like that FBI bastard, Rockwell. All he cares about is image."

"That's why you're okay," he said. "If you wanted fame, you'd be an airhead. What's going to happen to the FBI guy?"

"I don't know. Probably nothing. He'll keep climbing the career ladder. He's a goddamn politician."

"You can't refuse to play politics and then get mad because the politicians do it," he said gently. "But you're my girl, kiddo.

You know what's important, and it isn't who they put on the cover of a magazine."

"I was on *Time* magazine," Erin said.

He laughed. "And your mother has a framed copy," he said. "But that's because she's your mother. How many people do you think kept copies and framed them?"

"I've heard some of the inmates at Riker's Island tape my picture over their bunks," she said wryly.

"Don't tell me that!" Sean exclaimed. "You're my daughter! And those scumbags—"

He almost choked on his indignation. Erin suppressed a giggle.

"It's okay, Dad," she said. "I know who I am. My head's just the right size for my hat, don't worry."

"That's my girl," he said. "You just keep doing your job. The rest will take care of itself."

"Thanks, Dad," she said. "I feel a little better."

"That's why we're Catholic," he said. "Confession is good for the soul."

"I think a slug of whiskey is better for mine," Erin said.

"*Irish* Catholic," he amended, with a laugh. "You have a good night, kiddo, and get some rest. There'll be another crime tomorrow."

"I know," she said. "Maybe if I'm lucky, my fifteen minutes will be over by then and I can get on with the Job."

"It never ends," he said. "They say glory lasts forever, but I think duty lasts longer. And that's the way it ought to be. I love you, kiddo."

"I love you too, Dad," Erin said. And maybe, she thought as she hung up the phone, he was right. Love and duty outlived fame and fortune. She hoped so.

Rolf groaned quietly and wriggled, unspooling out of his curl. His heavy head came to rest on her thigh. She'd have to be careful or he'd put her leg to sleep. That was okay, too. She laid a hand on the K-9's head and turned off the light.

London, Whitechapel, March 1871

The gaslights glowed in the fog like will-o-the-wisps, ghostly and eerie. The fog was a thick, tangible thing. Even in the most crowded streets, it gave the illusion of solitude. And London's streets were very crowded. One was rarely alone, even now, near midnight. The muffled clop of horse-hooves echoed constantly on the cobbles and the hushed murmur of voices came from the doors and windows of a hundred public-houses.

Coventry sniffed the air. She smelled coal smoke, unwashed bodies, cheap scent, litter, and horse dung. She wondered how many horses lived and worked in London. Too many, toiling in the filthy, stony streets. Would any of them wish to remain, given the choice, when open pastures beckoned?

A rib of whalebone pinched her just below the ribs. She winced and shifted in her corset, trying to find a more comfortable position. She was fortunate she was such a slender girl; hardly any waist to speak of. Some of her heavier colleagues had a terrible time with the tight garments. She took as deep a breath as she could, glancing down at herself to judge the effect. She hadn't much chest either, not compared to some of the lasses, but what there was had been pushed up and out in a way she knew to be enticing.

This dress was the most expensive thing she owned. Red satin, bright as fresh blood, underlay a web of fine black lace. The cut was scandalously low and the skirt just high enough to hint at her well-turned ankles. Her hair, long and wavy, was carefully and deliberately disheveled, leaving loose auburn curls wandering down her round, girlish cheeks. Those cheeks were rouged, her lips colored a shocking crimson.

She looked, in short, precisely the sort of girl any respectable lady would avoid... and any respectable gentleman would avoid during daylight hours. But after nightfall it was a different song and the gentlemen danced to a darker tune. Now Coventry prowled the pavement, watching and waiting.

She had to be careful. Whitechapel was no place to forget oneself. She knew, better than most, what sort of men lurked thereabouts. And she had no stout fellow to look after her interests, as most of the girls did. Coventry Adams worked only for herself, so she had learned to keep her wits about her.

A pair of horses clop-clopped along the lane to her front. Her keen ear caught the difference at once. These were no plodding cart-horses. This was a carriage team, perfectly matched in size and stride, stepping high and proud. She heard the creak of springs just behind them and knew they were pulling a gentleman's coach. Not only that, it was moving slowly. That could mean only one thing. Toffs would scarcely linger in such a neighborhood, not unless they were looking for something. This gentleman was either engaged in some other sort of unsavory business, or he was looking for a girl like her.

Coventry eased forward, not stepping in front of the horses, careful to keep her feet up on the curb, but making herself noticeable. She took two paces to her right, so the light of the nearest lamp shone down on her face and décolletage. And she waited.

The coach emerged from the fog scant seconds later, a fine double brougham, drawn by two beautiful coal-black Friesians. The carriage itself was finely ornamented, sporting a coat of arms on the door, though it was hard to make out in the misty night.

Coventry waited until the carriage was in the act of passing her by. Then she gave a coy glance over her shoulder. She could not see into the darkened interior, of course, but that was not the point. The point was to display herself to the best possible effect, mingling false modesty with the promise of dark delights.

The carriage went only a few paces further. Then it came to a halt as the driver, in answer to some signal from within, pulled the horses up short. The animals stood, champing their bits, the mist of their breath mingling with the fog.

The coachman stood, a towering, shadowy figure in a heavy overcoat and wide-brimmed hat. He jumped down to the cobblestones, but even then, he overtopped Coventry by nearly a foot. She had learned to watch a man's hands. His held a riding whip. That might hurt, but it was hardly a proper weapon. Still, Coventry was tensed to run. She knew the alley at her back, every twist and turn of it. Give her half a breath's start and she could be gone.

The coachman opened the brougham's door and stood back, respectful.

"My dear young girl, whatever are you doing out so late, in such a dreadful place?"

The voice that came out of the darkened coach was a round, deep, jovial sort of voice. That voice could only come from a fat, well-fed belly. It was a voice a girl could run to for comfort. Coventry did not trust it one bit.

"Please, guv'nor," she said. "It is so terrible late, and here's myself, all out on my own. I don't suppose you'd know where I might find a place to stay, maybe to lay down for a bit?"

"Oh, you poor dear thing," the man said. "And just look at you, dreadfully exposed to the cold. You must be simply shivering! Why don't you climb up here and get warm, out of the night air?"

It was the usual dance. Some of the girls laughed at such preliminaries, considering them a waste of valuable time. But Coventry knew better. Rituals were important. They put men at ease. And men at their ease were men off their guard.

"Oh, thanks ever so much, guv," she said. "If you could just give me a hand?" She raised one hand, clad in a black, elbow-length glove. Her other hand stayed at her side, near a hidden pocket she had sewn into her dress. Inside that pocket lay a long, slim blade of forged steel, about the size of a knitting needle but much sharper. One never could tell with gentleman callers, especially the ones who liked their girls young.

A large, beefy hand enclosed her slender fingers. She put her foot on the step and hoisted herself up into the carriage. The coachman immediately closed the door behind her. Coventry felt a momentary thrill of fear. She embraced it, letting the fear strip years off her voice and demeanor. She was nineteen, but she could pass for fifteen or twenty-five, as circumstances required. She had the feeling this man would like her to be very young indeed.

"This is awful kind of you, guv," she said.

"Not at all, dear girl, not at all," he said cheerfully. In the shadows, his face was still hard to make out, but Coventry had a sudden, dizzy feeling of familiarity. She was glad of the darkness. She knew this man, or had known him, years ago. Would he remember?

Not bloody likely, she thought. That had been a very different time and place. She buried memories of long ago; a big house in the country, dinner parties, fashionable events, hunts and picnics. But his name came to her. Bartleby Horrocks, Minister of Parliament. What had he been worth? Seventy thousand pounds a year?

Coventry smothered a smile. This was a real toff, a man with wealth and position, stooping to demean himself with a sweet young night flower. She was going to enjoy this.

"My darling girl," he said, still dancing the familiar steps, though they both knew the inevitable outcome. "I shall be only too delighted to place myself at your service. I am merely a visitor in London, but if I might prevail upon you to accompany me to my hotel, you might find such... ah... repose and refreshment as the hour allows."

This was better than she had allowed herself to hope. Her fear had been he might just want a quick tumble in the carriage. That would force her hand and would require speed and risky action. But to go to his room was far preferable. It should afford her plenty of more leisurely opportunities.

"Cor, guv, that's lovely," she said, placing a hand on his knee and nestling in close beside him. "I just knew some kind gentleman such as yourself would find me."

He put an arm around her shoulder in a gesture that should have been paternal and comforting but was neither. Coventry felt the trembling hunger in his touch. She cared not a toss. Her close proximity had already told her he had a gold pocketwatch in his silk waistcoat, and she was fair certain in which pocket his pocketbook resided.

This looked to be a very profitable night.

*   *   *

Keeping Mr. Horrocks's advances at bay during the carriage ride presented no great difficulty. Coventry was an old hand at promising without delivering. She remembered her early classical education. The myth of Tantalus, in particular, was useful in her trade. The trick was to offer just enough to set the hook. Then a girl could play a man like a fish on a line, letting him wriggle and exhaust himself. The difficulty was, in the end one had to either land the fish or cut the line, and it was sometimes hard to know which.

Bartleby Horrocks, however, was an amateur in such matters. Coventry's touch set him all aflutter while holding him off. Men were all the same, aiming for the destination with no thought of the journey. Coventry took a certain pride in convincing them to stop and take in the sights along the way.

By the time the carriage stopped outside the hotel, Mr. Horrocks was so much quivering putty in her skillful hands. Now was the time to conclude negotiations. A few whispered words, delivered alongside the delicate application of the tip of her tongue to his earlobe, convinced Mr. Horrocks she was worth half a crown at least. Some of the girls were content to settle for a hay-penny knee-trembler in a back alley. Coventry aimed higher. She had learned that a higher price actually commanded respect, even admiration.

With the bargain amicably struck, Coventry and Mr. Horrocks alighted from the carriage. The driver assisted Mr. Horrocks with his considerable bulk, while Mr. Horrocks gallantly offered a hand to Coventry. The doorman at the hotel looked askance at them as they approached.

"Your pardon, sir," he said. "Who is this young... lady?"

"My niece," Mr. Horrocks said blandly.

"Your niece," the doorman repeated, raising a very skeptical eyebrow and letting his eyes travel over Coventry's face and décolletage.

"Indeed," Mr. Horrocks said, passing his hand close to the footman's. There was a clink of coin as money changed hands.

"Yes, quite," the doorman said. "Welcome, sir. Madam."

So Coventry passed into a rather nice hotel on the arm of a respectable gentleman. Everyone knew what she was; her clothing and cosmetics trumpeted it. But no one raised an outcry. She idly wondered, as they walked up a carpeted stairway, whether the doorman's bribe was more than the agreed amount to purchase what remained of her virtue. A shilling would probably suffice for such a man, but perhaps the rates had gone up of late.

Mr. Horrocks unlocked his door and ushered her in with a slight bow. Coventry replied with a half-curtsy.

"You, my dear, are quite remarkable," Mr. Horrocks said. "Truly a flower among the thorns of Whitechapel."

"It's right kind of you to say, guv," she said, taking in the room at a glance. It was impressive, if not quite palatial. Bartleby Horrocks was living in somewhat understated style at present. Did that signify he had fallen on hard times? It was so difficult to tell with gentlemen. They were very skilled at keeping up appearances.

"Your speech marks you as a resident of London's, ah, lower quarter," Mr. Horrocks continued. "Yet your fresh and dewy complexion, the paleness of your skin, suggest otherwise. Might I inquire your name?"

"They calls me Coventry, sir," she said. "Like the city."

"What a peculiar name for a lovely girl. Would you care for a drop of brandy, Miss Coventry?"

"That'd be lovely, guv. What ought I call you?"

"Mr. Hanover."

A lie, of course, but Coventry could hardly complain. After all, she was being no more honest than he. None of this was true, none of it was real.

"It's a pleasure, Mr. Hanover," she said, taking his hand. He lowered his lips and kissed her hand. Even through her glove, she could feel the hunger in his lips. She suppressed a shudder, turning it to an eager quiver of her own, knowing it was effective. Men saw what they wished to see.

Mr. Horrocks reluctantly released her hand and turned to a table on which stood a decanter and several glasses. As he filled two cups, Coventry slid a hand into another hidden pocket in her dress and extracted a little packet of powder. She held it neatly between her second and third fingers, hidden from view.

Mr. Horrocks turned, glasses in hand. Coventry started to reach for one, then feigned a stumble and caught at his arm with her left hand. He made a startled noise and nearly spilled the brandy. While he was thus distracted, she passed her opposite hand over the other glass, letting the powder spill from the little packet into the beverage.

"Sorry, guv," she gasped. "It's these wee shoes I'm wearing. They do squeeze my ankles so. I don't suppose you'd mind if I removed them?"

Mr. Horrocks was poleaxed by the thought of Coventry's feet and ankles clad in naught but stockings. In that distracted state, he certainly did not notice the powder dissolving into his brandy. One of the most important tricks in sleight-of-hand was drawing the mark's attention away at the perfect moment.

"Quite all right," he said.

"Thanks ever so, guv," she said, plucking the other glass from his hand. She wanted to savor it. After all, good brandy was hard to come by on the street. But the main thing was to make sure he drank, so she tossed back her glass in one gulp. It burned pleasantly on the way down, warming her insides marvelously. Mr. Horrocks, naturally, could not allow a young woman to outdo him in the imbibing of drink, so he followed suit. An odd expression crossed his face and he looked down at the glass.

"Rather bitter, that," he said thoughtfully. "I say, Miss Coventry, did yours taste a trifle off?"

"Don't know what you mean, guv," she said. "But if you're wanting another taste on your lips..."

She stepped in close, tilted her head up, and kissed him, letting him feel the whole length of her. She laid one hand on his cheek, the other against his chest, and nibbled lightly on his lower lip.

He groaned and closed his eyes. "Oh, my dear," he said. "You really are too much."

"You've no idea," she whispered, tugging him across the room toward the bedroom. He came willingly enough. She helped him out of his jacket, hanging it on the back of a nearby chair. Then she turned him about so his back was to the bed and gave him a playful push. He stumbled backward. Then the mattress took him just behind the knees and he fell across a pillow with a soft whoosh.

"Fell over," he said, his words slurring together. "Most... curious..."

"Not to worry, guv," Coventry said. "You just need a wee lie-down is all. Just lie quiet and close your eyes."

Mr. Horrocks obediently did so. Soon he was dreaming, a smile spread across his pudgy face.

Coventry gave the drug another minute to work, counting the seconds by the beat of her own pulse. Then she said quietly, "Mr. Hanover? Sir?"

He made no response.

She leaned in quite close and nipped his ear between her teeth, something sure to make any man jump. He lay perfectly still.

Nodding in satisfaction, Coventry got to work. The tincture of opium had been prepared by a Chinese fellow she knew, a man who ran a den by the docks that catered to sailors. She had used it before, and while its effects were somewhat unpredictable, she could count on at least thirty minutes before Mr. Horrocks returned to wakefulness. Undressing the unconscious man was the work of a few distasteful moments. In the process, she divested him of the gold wedding ring he really did not deserve to wear. She rifled his clothing, acquiring thereby his gold pocketwatch, his pocketbook, three crowns, two shillings, and thruppence in loose coin, and a pair of handsome diamond-stud cufflinks. Those were distinctive, and dangerous to sell, but too valuable to leave behind. The pocketbook was the real prize. A quick glance showed her it held banknotes, rather a lot of them.

Before leaving Mr. Horrocks to his opium-fueled dreams, she thoughtfully draped a sheet over him. It wouldn't do to have him catching cold, after all. His clothes were of fine make, but selling fabric was not really in Coventry's line, so she left them in a pile on the floor and turned her attention to the hotel room.

She knew better than to steal anything belonging to the hotel. Mr. Horrocks would be unlikely to report a theft, given the nature of the young woman who had come to his room. It would create awkward questions he would have no wish to answer. But if the hotel noticed anything of theirs missing, they might report it. That was a risk not worth the taking.

She settled for pillaging Mr. Horrocks's personal baggage. The results were a fine silver shaving kit, another two pairs of cufflinks, a second pocketwatch—this one of silver—and a few interesting bits and bobs whose value she could not guess. But Fergie, the fellow who ran the rag and bottle shop, would give her a fair price for them. They went into the deep pockets in her skirt's lining, together with the rest of the loot.

Before leaving, she went to the washbasin and looked at herself in the mirror. Small details were important. One needed to show others what they expected to see. She tousled her hair and smeared her lipstick. She adjusted her dress to look as if it had been hastily rearranged. She splashed water in her eyes, making sure to leave trails on her cheeks. Then she let herself out of the room.

She knew the trick of working locks with a pair of hairpins, but there seemed little point in locking the door. She let it be and went down the stairs, trailing one hand along the wall as if she was having trouble standing. It was all too easy to put the look on her face of a young girl who had just had something dreadful done to her.

The doorman looked at her coldly. He did not open the door for her.

"P-please, sir," she whimpered. "May I... may I go?"

His face softened slightly. Then his jaw tightened and his eyes went icy, but his anger was directed elsewhere.

"Bloody bastard," he muttered under his breath. "If he wasn't a blooming minister, I'd knock his teeth down his bloody throat." He held the door for her. "Sorry for your troubles, madam."

"Th-thank you, sir," Coventry stammered, even managing to fill her eyes with artificial tears. She felt a very slight twinge of guilt. He seemed a decent chap and it was a shame to play him that way. But she held to the act all the way to the end of the street. Only once she had turned the corner and was safely enveloped in the fog did she stand upright again. Then, as she considered the long walk back to Whitechapel, a hansom cab appeared in front of her, an answer to her unspoken prayer.

It was an extravagance, surely, but one she could now afford. Coventry raised a hand and waved to the driver. Some nights, one truly was blessed by fortune.

Get a reminder when the new series is out

Join Steven's list at
clickworkspress.com/join/steven

Here's a sneak peek from Book 29: Blackjack

Coming 9/29/2025

"We've got ourselves a misdemeanor homicide," Vic Neshenko said.

Erin O'Reilly wanted to tell him to shut up, but she couldn't disagree. Cops had plenty of darkly funny names for what had happened outside the tattoo parlor: "misdemeanor homicide," "public-service homicide," "pest control," and "street cleanup" were just a few. That was what cops did with bloody violence, in order to cope with it. They made jokes. All of them came to the same punchline in this case: the body at their feet didn't represent a great loss to society.

"I heard that, Neshenko," Lieutenant Webb said. "Don't let me hear it again."

Webb had a sense of humor. But you had to dig for it, and you had to know what it looked like if you hoped to recognize it.

"Copy that, sir," Vic said. "What I mean to say is, this is a heinous crime that deserves and demands the full resources of the Department. Justice must be served, swiftly and impartially."

Vic was a lot of things, but he wasn't subtle. When he laid on the sarcasm, he used a big shovel.

"We don't dispense justice," Webb said, choosing to give a straight answer. "That's up to the courts. What do we do, Detective Piekarski?"

"Serve the public trust, protect the innocent, and uphold the law, sir," Zofia Piekarski said without hesitation.

"Good answer," Webb said.

"Where have I heard that?" Erin wondered aloud.

"*Robocop*," Vic said, grinning. "The original. That's his primary directives. We watched it last night."

"I knew it sounded familiar," Erin said. "Do you really think you should be learning policing from '80s action movies?"

"If we could return to the matter of our murder victim?" Webb said. "What do we know about him?"

"Gangland tats," Vic said. "And prison ink. He's a tough guy who's done hard time. Check out those scars. There's only one way you get marks like that on your knuckles."

"Fist-fighting," Erin agreed. "Bare-knuckled. Mickey Connor had scars like that."

"Oh yeah," Vic said, grinning again. "You got a real close look at Connor's knuckles, once upon a time."

"Yeah." Erin rubbed the side of her head, remembering. "But he was a lot bigger than our guy here."

"How's the body coming along, Doctor?" Webb asked the woman kneeling beside the corpse.

"Rigor mortis has fully set in," Dr. Levine said without removing her attention from the dead man. "Algor mortis suggests four hours since death, indicated by a five-degree drop in body temperature. Lividity confirms this, further determining that the body has not been moved postmortem. I estimate time of death was approximately eight o'clock in the evening. Decomposition has not become noticeable at the present time."

"Yuck," Zofia said.

"I'm not actually asking about the body's rate of decomp," Webb said. "I was wondering whether you'd isolated a cause of death."

"Your question was nonspecific," Levine said, irritated. "Preliminary cause of death is blunt-force trauma to the base of the skull. The crush pattern suggests a single blow with a semi-rigid implement."

"Semi-rigid?" Erin prompted.

"I hypothesize the impact was made by a bag or sack containing a number of small, hard objects," Levine said. "These objects appear to be round and of a uniform diameter of approximately eight millimeters."

"Translation," Vic said. "Somebody slapped this bozo upside the head with a bag full of ball bearings."

"That hypothesis aligns with available data," Levine said.

"A blackjack," Webb said.

"Those aren't supposed to be lethal," Zofia said.

"A half pound of metal to the back of the head can be plenty lethal," Vic replied.

"I know," she said. "I meant this might not have been a deliberate murder. Maybe it was a botched mugging."

"Yeah," Vic said. "Because we're dealing with an epidemic of muggings of young, tough, tattooed Black men. Our most brilliant mind, Zofia, just solved the case."

Zofia scowled at him. "You're sleeping on the couch," she growled. "Forever."

"What else can you tell me about the victim?" Webb asked Levine, ignoring the lovers' quarrel behind him.

"He was struck from the rear," Levine said. "He probably was unaware of his assailant, since his pistol is tucked into his waistband instead of in hand or on the ground."

"Oh, I'm sorry," Vic said. "Young, tough, tattooed, *armed* Black men."

"What kind of pistol?" Erin asked.

The body had fallen awkwardly, twisting as it struck the curb. The man's legs were on the sidewalk, his torso contorted in the gutter. The handgrip of a pistol was indeed visible. The gun was crammed down the front of the dead man's trousers.

"Ruger American," Vic said. "You can see the brand name on the bottom of the grip. It's the compact version, so looks like a ten-round magazine. Nine-millimeter. Pretty decent handgun. They just introduced them a year or two ago."

Nobody doubted him. Vic pretended to be a dumb thug, but he was an encyclopedia of firearms knowledge.

"An armed convict gets his skull crushed outside a tattoo parlor," Webb said. "I think we may end up kicking this one over to the Homicide boys, or maybe the Gang Task Force."

"Do we know anything about the tattoo place?" Erin asked. The sign on the door advertised it as The Needle X-Change. "Looks like a high-class establishment."

"Good place to pick up hepatitis," Zofia said. "Or HIV."

"You have a tattoo, don't you, Erin?" Vic said. "Didn't you get one right before that power outage a while back?"

"Yeah."

"What is it, again?"

"None of your business."

"It's a tramp stamp, isn't it?"

"No."

"Prove it."

"In your lonely, pathetic dreams. If Zofia isn't going to show you any skin, I'm sure as hell not going to."

"The victim was struck at least three additional times," Levine said. "Possibly more. The weapon does not have a specific shape, so it is difficult to determine exactly how many blows. All of these were delivered to the left temple."

"Our perp kept hitting him after he was already down," Vic said. "He was an unmoving target. Otherwise all those hits wouldn't have been in the same spot on the side of his head. And it's the side that's up. I figure the killer was in that doorway next to the tattoo shop. Our boy comes walking down the sidewalk, the killer comes out behind him and bam! Then bam, bam, bam to make sure and he's on his way."

"That doesn't seem like a mugging to me," Erin said. "It looks more like he was deliberately beaten to death."

"The additional blows were superfluous," Levine said. "The impact to the base of the cranium crushed at least two vertebrae and the skull itself. It was not a survivable injury."

"He was coming out of the tattoo parlor," Erin added.

"How do you know?" Webb asked.

She pointed to the back of the dead man's arm. "See that bandage? I'll bet that's covering a fresh tat."

Webb nodded. "You think this was an ambush?"

"Yeah," Erin said. "I think the perp followed him here, or knew he'd be here. Then he waited outside until our victim came out. Then it went down like Vic says."

"Gang hit," Vic said. "I'd bet twenty bucks on it."

"You might be right," Webb said. He was staring at the dead man's hand. "He's got something there."

"What is it?" Zofia asked. "Some sort of calling card?"

Levine carefully lifted the arm. The hand was clenched, the muscles stiff in death. In it was a single playing card.

"Jack of spades," Webb said. "You're right. It's a literal calling card. O'Reilly?"

"Sir?"

"You may want your partner to get a whiff of this."

Erin looked down. Rolf stood as close to her hip as he could get, his whiskers actually in contact with her leg. The German Shepherd stared back at her with his serious brown eyes.

"You think the killer left it?" she asked.

"Probably," Webb said.

"Gang symbol?" she guessed.

"Or maybe he's part of some freaky cult," Vic said. "Or he's named Jack."

"That'd be convenient," Webb said. "In my experience, murderers don't usually leave their names with their victims."

"Ooh! I know!" Vic said. "We're dealing with a hardcore psycho who's going to kill fifty-two people and leave a card with each one. No, wait... fifty-four people. I forgot the jokers."

"Fifty-four homicides?" Webb said, raising his eyebrows. "That seems like a lot of trouble to go to for a gimmick. Before we go jumping to ludicrous conclusions, why don't we at least get an ID on our victim and try to zero in on potential motives?"

"We shouldn't have any trouble finding out who the poor schmuck was," Vic said, jutting his chin in the direction of the body. "I guarantee we'll have his prints on file."

"It's awfully late," Webb said. He rubbed his eyes. "I'm too old to be up past midnight."

"Real cops work the dog watch," Vic said. "Isn't that right, Erin?"

"Absolutely," she said. "But the Lieutenant's right, too. We've been on the clock a really long time, counting the earlier shift."

"And we'll be a little longer," Webb said. "Don't worry, your overtime is approved. The PC still likes you for catching that pattern killer last month and it helped the whole squad. We got that extra budget allotment."

"Not quite enough for another detective, I can't help but notice," Vic said.

"Something wrong with the current batch?" Zofia asked.

"Of course not. If you ask for more of something, that's usually a sign that you like it."

"So you'd like a few more blondes on the squad?"

Vic considered this. "Hmm. Maybe."

"I want all of us back at the Eightball," Webb said. "I want an ID on our victim. And I'd love to know why he was killed. If it was a gang hit, or a mugging, or something else. Then, once we decide whether it's our case or not, we can get some sleep. Maybe."

Erin was still considering the playing card. "A black jack," she said. "On a guy who got blackjacked. That's a pretty sick joke."

"It's a dad joke," Vic said. "I've been working on some of mine, for when Mina's old enough. Why did the coffee cup call the cops?"

"Oh dear Lord," Erin muttered.

"Because it got mugged," he said. "Why doesn't the DA like to prosecute lamps?"

"Don't encourage him," Zofia said.

"Because they always get a light sentence."

"You're a dad all right," Erin said. "But if I'm going to pull overtime after midnight, it's going to be for actual police work, not to listen to dad jokes."

"We can do both," Vic said. "Let's go find out who our mystery man was."

Ready for more?

Join the Clickworks Press email list
for the latest on new releases, upcoming books and
series, behind-the-scenes details, events, and more.

Be the first to know about
new releases from Steven Henry
by signing up at
clickworkspress.com/join/steven

About the Author

Steven Henry learned how to read almost before he learned how to walk. Ever since he began reading stories, he wanted to put his own on the page. He lives a very quiet and ordinary life in Minnesota with his wife and dog.

Also by Steven Henry

Fathers

A Modern Christmas Story

When you strip away everything else, what's left is the truth

Life taught Joe Davidson not to believe in miracles. A blue-collar woodworker, Joe is trying to build a future. His father drank himself to death and his mother succumbed to cancer, leaving a broken, struggling family. He and his brother and sisters are faced with failed marriages, growing pains, and lingering trauma.

Then a chance meeting at his local diner brings Mary Elizabeth Reynolds

into his life. Suddenly, Joe finds himself reaching for something more, a dream of happiness. The wood-worker and the poor girl from a trailer park connect and fall in love, and for a little while, everything is right with their world.

But suddenly Joe is confronted with a situation he never imagined. What do you do if your fiancée is expecting a child you know isn't yours? Torn between betrayal and love, trying to do the right thing when nothing seems right anymore, Joe has to strip life down to its truth and learn that, in spite of the pain, love can be the greatest miracle of all.

Learn more at clickworkspress.com/fathers.

Ember of Dreams

The Clarion Chronicles, Book One

When magic awakens a long-forgotten folk, a noble lady, a young apprentice, and a solitary blacksmith band together to prevent war and seek understanding between humans and elves.

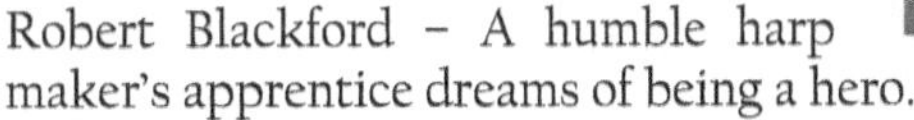
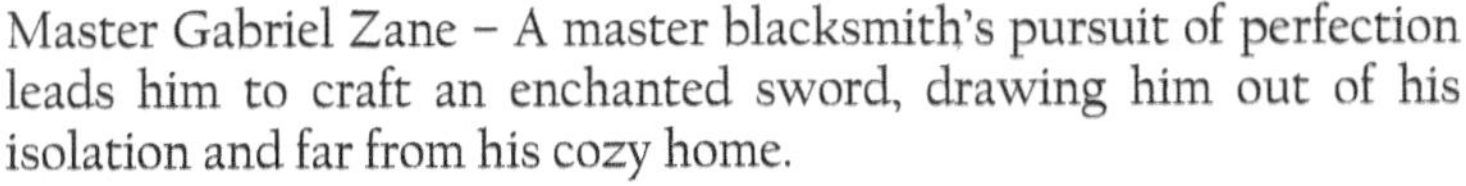

Lady Kristyn Tremayne – An otherwise unremarkable young lady's open heart and inquisitive mind reveal a hidden world of magic.

Robert Blackford – A humble harp maker's apprentice dreams of being a hero.

Master Gabriel Zane – A master blacksmith's pursuit of perfection leads him to craft an enchanted sword, drawing him out of his isolation and far from his cozy home.

Lord Luthor Carnarvon – A lonely nobleman with a dark past has won the heart of Kristyn's mother, but at what cost?

Readers love *Ember of Dreams*

"The more I got to know the characters, the more I liked them. The female lead in particular is a treat to accompany on her journey from ordinary to extraordinary."

"The author's deep understanding of his protagonists' motivations and keen eye for psychological detail make Robert and his companions a likable and memorable cast."

Learn more at tinyurl.com/emberofdreams.

More great titles from Clickworks Press

www.clickworkspress.com

The Altered Wake
Megan Morgan

Amid growing unrest, a family secret and an ancient laboratory unleash long-hidden superhuman abilities. Now newly-promoted Sentinel Cameron Kardell must chase down a rogue superhuman who holds the key to the powers' origin: the greatest threat Cotarion has seen in centuries – and Cam's best friend.

"Incredible. Starts out gripping and keeps getting better."

Learn more at clickworkspress.com/sentinel1.

Hubris Towers: The Complete First Season
Ben Y. Faroe & Bill Hoard

Comedy of manners meets comedy of errors in a new series for fans of Fawlty Towers and P. G. Wodehouse.

"So funny and endearing"

"Had me laughing so hard that I had to put it down to catch my breath"

"Astoundingly, outrageously funny!"

Learn more at clickworkspress.com/hts01.

Death's Dream Kingdom
Gabriel Blanchard

A young woman of Victorian London has been transformed into a vampire. Can she survive the world of the immortal dead— or perhaps, escape it?

"The wit and humor are as Victorian as the setting... a winsomely vulnerable and tremendously crafted work of art."

"A dramatic, engaging novel which explores themes of death, love, damnation, and redemption."

Learn more at clickworkspress.com/ddk.

Share the love!

Join our microlending team at
kiva.org/team/clickworkspress.

Keep in touch!

Join the Clickworks Press email list
and get freebies, production updates, special deals,
behind-the-scenes sneak peeks, and more.

Sign up today at clickworkspress.com/join.